D1363650

YEAR OF FIRE

STORIES

David H. Lynn

A HARVEST ORIGINAL
HARCOURT, INC.

Orlando   Austin   New York   San Diego   Toronto   London

The author wishes to thank André Bernard, friend and collaborator.

Copyright © 2006 by David Lynn

All rights reserved. No part of this publication may be reproduced or transmitted in any form or by any means, electronic or mechanical, including photocopy, recording, or any information storage and retrieval system, without permission in writing from the publisher.

Requests for permission to make copies of any part of the work should be mailed to the following address: Permissions Department, Harcourt, Inc., 6277 Sea Harbor Drive, Orlando, Florida 32887-6777.

www.HarcourtBooks.com

Library of Congress Cataloging-in-Publication Data
Lynn, David H.
Year of fire: stories/David H. Lynn.—1st ed.
p. cm.
"A Harvest Original."
I. Title.
PS3612.Y545Y43   2006
813'.6—dc22   2005002399
ISBN-13: 978-0156-03077-9   ISBN-10: 0-15-603077-2

Text set in Garamond MT
Designed by Cathy Riggs

Printed in the United States of America

First edition
A C E G I K J H F D B

This is a work of fiction. Names, characters, places, organizations, and events are the products of the author's imagination or are used fictitiously, and any resemblance to actual persons, living or dead, events, or locales is entirely coincidental.

R0405968930

For WFS, now and always.

CONTENTS

YEAR OF FIRE

MISTAKEN IDENTITY

The sleepy sack of a man was waggling a strip of cardboard with her name on it as passengers wearily surged through the arrivals gate at Gandhi International Airport. Only now did Vera Kahn first suspect that perhaps, after all, she'd made a mistake by accepting this invitation. Next to the driver, a USIS bureaucrat—he could be nothing else—was craning his neck and failing entirely to see her as she approached. Ludicrously, he was still trying to spy something, someone else, over her shoulder, even as she dropped a heavy bag nearly on his toes.

"I'm Vera Kahn," she said with hardly any smile at all.

His pale eyes registered the problem in a series of stages he did his best to mask despite the very late hour. "I'm sorry?" he managed first, belatedly.

"Kahn. Vera Kahn. I'm your poet."

The poor man, straw-haired and tie-limp—Vera was glad he made sympathy so difficult—struggled not to say the obvious: that there must be some mistake. There *had* been a mistake. She was very well aware of it. She wasn't about to let him off the hook.

"Are we waiting for someone else," she asked, "or can we go? I'm pretty well shot."

"Right—okay. But can I see some ID first? You know, security's sake. It's standard procedure over here." Although he looked miserable and confused, struggling to maintain his official good cheer, not to mention his authority, Vera was impressed that he'd managed to improvise the lie at this hour. She handed him her passport.

He studied her photo. "Right. Okay!" he shouted more cheerfully to conceal his greater dismay. "Shankar, let's get a move on." With a nod, the driver shooed away a scatter of boys eager to help and, reaching for the bag himself, let her name drop to the floor, where it joined a ragged swirl of scraps even now being swept away as travelers and greeters, officials and porters and pickpockets dispersed into the Delhi night.

The air felt less tropical, less exotic than she'd expected as they emerged from the airport. It was plenty warm—laden with a muggy haze and wood smoke and the less acrid stink of burning cow dung. Vera felt a stab of disappointment. The irritability and disaffection she'd hoped would somehow magically lift on arrival in the East was instead merely chafing into a raw, weary restlessness.

"I'm Walter Tyson," said the American official more genially as he directed her toward a small red car parked in a reserved space. "I've read your work." Then he stopped lamely once more, doubting his own truthfulness.

"That's so thoughtful of you," said Vera Kahn, and left it at that as she climbed into the back of the Maruti. She knew he hadn't read her poetry, either the one book from a good press or the couple of smaller chapbooks she'd all but paid for herself. Not that the lie was intentional this time. No doubt he'd read, more or less out of a sense of duty—whose idea had it been to extend this invitation? She'd probably find out in the next day or so—some selection from the poetry of Veera Kahn, a black woman of almost precisely her own age who taught not at the small Catholic college in Southern California and not with the glorious view overlooking the ocean (this one of the few satisfactions of the common misunderstanding), but a few miles inland at the much larger school by the same name, but with a UC in front. It used to be that Vera would imagine the two of them getting together and giggling over drinks about their ongoing entanglements. But Veera had made it clear on the occasions when they did meet, usually by accident or confusion or someone else's sense of jolly fun, that she wasn't interested in playing pals. Never did she let on how *she* came saddled with such a name, Kahn. Being confused with a now middle-aged white woman of little fame could have done Veera's own career no particular good.

For twelve years, on the other hand, Vera had felt shadowed by the other woman's celebrity. Every professional charm coming her way—engagements to read, solicitations for new work, even the occasional call for a date by some friend of a friend—increasingly seemed tainted by this confusion of identity. She knew it wasn't true. Not entirely. But she'd grown used to spying similar symptoms of mistrust, disappointment, resignation that had flitted across Walter Tyson's brow. It hadn't grown easier. It had grown harder, especially of late.

So what should arrive on her desk in mid-August but an invitation from the United States Information Service to spend two weeks on a reading tour in India? Only eight weeks' warning. Someone even more prominent than Vera's near namesake must have canceled on them, not quite at the last minute. USIS Delhi scrambled. Hence, no doubt, the sloppy research, the mistake. She'd had to scramble too, bargaining with colleagues to cover her classes, with students to water her plants and feed her cats.

That look had been in the dean's eyes too when she requested permission—he'd grown used to such confusions between Vera and Veera. Not that he'd complain or admonish her: he was perfectly thrilled for the sake of the college reputation. Still, that knowing smile on his face. She ignored it; she loathed it—any doubt about the wisdom of taking the United States Information Service up on its offer, honest mistake or not, eased itself from her thoughts.

FIVE HOURS' sleep was all she could manage that first night, and Vera rose, woozy and disoriented. She was sniffling too. Apparently, a cold had stowed away for the journey. Most of the hotel's other guests had already breakfasted by the time she appeared in the dining room. Its tightly sealed windows overlooked the bright bustle of Connaught Circus—and shielded her from it. She'd been so eager, yet now she lacked the courage to venture immediately into the mayhem. Cranky, annoyed with herself, she sipped at a second cup of tepid coffee. Perhaps she'd been expecting too much of India, or of herself. She didn't want to be disappointed.

Oh, bullshit, she thought, pushing the cup away and staring out at a street of swarming scooter taxis, of buses spewing swathes of dark smoke, of pedestrians and peddlers and darting children with shoe-shine kits, all wrestling for advantage. Only a faint but constant bray of horns seeped through the windows.

A little past one in the afternoon, Walter Tyson appeared, freshly shaven and shirted, his face lacking any trace of the suspicion and discouragement it had betrayed a few hours earlier. No doubt he and the USIS staff had already made some calls. They'd discovered their own mistake. Like it or not, intended or not, it was Vera Kahn they'd invited, not Veera. And Vera had taken them up on it. Here she was, and at least she was a poet too. Perhaps some careful political calibration about race or fame, or both, had been vexed. No solving it now. A later program could be altered. Crossing the lobby, he smiled at her with an enthusiasm that went with the job. His face was pinkly tanned and round, faintly boyish. Vera smiled back.

But it wasn't so easy as that, of course. Tyson drove her to the American Center to meet the staff and check out the room where she'd be giving a first reading that same evening. With each of the senior officers, even with the librarian who'd already hidden away the copies of Veera's books specially ordered for the occasion and who, without question, had spent the morning trying to discover whether a single copy of Vera's book existed on the subcontinent, she spied or imagined spying in their eyes the smoke of disappointment that she was only she. They probably also suspected her complicity in the matter. Her anger flared. One young cultural liaison, lips glossy with color, hair in a careful bun, nearly got herself slapped.

What right, Vera forced herself to acknowledge, sagging a bit, had she to claim any innocence at all?

"Can I sneak away from here for a while?" she whispered to Tyson, tugging at his sleeve in a hallway.

"No problem," he said, apparently relieved to be asked so little.

She hadn't really intended that he escort her, but, on the other hand, she had no clue where to go or how to get there. He seemed well accustomed to the task. "Let's swing you through some of the national monuments," he offered as they climbed into the Maruti, "mostly built by the Brits. Then we can try the Old City—you'll like that."

She wanted to be filled with wonder and exhilaration. Yet the broad avenues and Edwardian monuments of New Delhi only soured Vera's mood still further. India Gate, the Parliament buildings, cracking pavement and peeling paint, waves of stench and billowing heat, a welt of mosquito bites just behind her knee, Tyson's enthusiasm—all nagged and niggled her into a raging petulance she hadn't felt since adolescence. She was aware of it and ashamed and unable to govern her own mood. Gritting her teeth, she nodded at each banality the man offered with a wave of his hand.

Slowly the car began tacking toward the north. They passed a railway station, teeming with solitary men wearing only strips of cotton wrapped around their waists, families besieged by bundles, and young Americans weighed down by enormous backpacks. The streets narrowed, traffic slowed, boys tapped on the car's fenders as they slid past. Vera's nerves were taut with exasperation. She struggled not to shriek at Tyson, demanding that he return her to the hotel, where at least it would be cooler and she could take a shower.

Around another corner they finally made out the cause of this particular tie-up—a dozen tree trunks had slipped their chains and tumbled from a long flatbed truck. How could such a huge truck be allowed in this part of the city, on streets as narrow as these? Scooter taxis and cars were inching up one by one onto the ragged sidewalk and crawling around the blockade. And suddenly Vera realized what she was seeing, as if until this moment she'd been unable to recognize or make sense of it: an elephant heaving one of the logs off the ground and back onto the lorry. A scrawny boy perched just behind its ears tapped the animal's attention toward another piece of lumber straddling the road. It wrapped its trunk around the near end of the log, hoisting it at an angle and leaning it against the bed of the truck. Then, using the edge of the truck as fulcrum, the elephant deftly grasped the bottom end of the log and swung it up and over with a last delicate thump. Dust and exertion were smudging the elaborate pink flowers chalked across the elephant's flanks.

"Probably on its way to a wedding," Tyson said. "The mahout figures he can pick up a few rupees from the truck driver."

Vera nodded. That's what blindsided her—the apparent ordinariness of such a sight. Her heart thumped hard in her chest. Her throat swelled. Joy—there was no better word for what swept over her, so glad was she to be right here, right now, watching this elephant at its task. How long had it been since she'd experienced such joy? Tears welling in her eyes, she felt amazement as much at her own reaction as at the scene before her. Such violent swings were entirely unlike her. In an instant she'd been wrenched from raw misery to this wonder, this elation. Joy, yes, but harsh too. She sniffed and blew into a tissue, hoping to disguise her emotions. Again Tyson glanced at her. She wouldn't face him.

By the time they reached Old Delhi's web of narrow streets, she'd regained her composure. They parked the car and made their way by foot through thick crowds. As they penetrated deeper, buildings were leaning toward each other above their heads like trees in an ancient forest. Yet this strange world all seemed distant, as if she were still peering through a window. It was the woolly congestion in her head and a haze of fatigue and jet lag—everything seemed pushed beyond arm's reach.

Old men in pajamas and skullcaps gathered in stalls and tea shops. Women, mostly wearing scarves over their heads or with full chadors hiding their faces and limbs, scurried by with infants in tow or picked at plastic shoes or soap trays or children's T-shirts hanging from a wire frame. Young men hovered about Vera and Walter Tyson, shoving packs of hand-kerchiefs and small chess sets at their faces. Jeeringly persistent, the pack of boys flitted along through the winding lanes, darting forward, trying again and again. Tyson flicked his hand, shooing them, and pressed forward. "This is the best walk to the Red Fort," he cried over his shoulder.

The boys circled and swooped, calling out to her in a singsong chant. "Buy this, sweet lady. It's good for you! I make it nothing for you, no money at all. A gift from my heart. Buy, sweet lady." She couldn't quite make out all the words. The boys were pressing closer. The singsong danced about her head, mocking, crude, taunting, obscene. The boys were laughing, leering.

Suddenly a hand groped hard at her buttock and she jerked in pain. From another direction fingers jabbed one of her breasts, pinching for its nipple. Other hands snatched at her shoulder bag.

"Stop," she shouted. Was there any sound? Did anyone hear? The grabbing, pawing, clutching spun her around.

"Help!" she shrieked, flailing out, her hands balled in tight childlike fists.

The boys scattered in a single gleeful instant as Tyson waded toward her, and he was hurrying her back the other way, back toward the car, and he was saying something or asking something, but she couldn't really hear in the clotted silence all about them now. Tyson was apologetic and courteous, yet he couldn't quite mask his impatience too, as if she were making a lot out of nothing. She was furious with him, furious at those boys. Yet, curiously, the anger seemed distant too, almost beyond reach, and she wasn't weeping in the car: she was sniffling and blowing into her tissue, that was all.

"IT'S A terrific turnout," whispered the woman with her hair in a bun, Bridgit, the one Vera had wanted to smack earlier. She seemed sincerely pleased that the room was better than two-thirds full as the two of them peeked through the doors. Both were aware that they owed the crowd of middle-class Indians, expatriate Americans, and local academics to a grave misunderstanding, but neither was going to mention it.

This moment was worse even than confronting Tyson at the airport—only now did Vera feel truly a fraud. Nervous, irritable, she strode to the podium. The small auditorium might have been on any college campus in America, the kind of place she'd given dozens of readings in her career. She had nothing to be ashamed of. She was sweating despite the air-conditioning.

"Good evening," she said brightly. "I'm honored by the invitation to read to you, and I'm delighted you've turned up to hear." A few people applauded politely, unaware of anything amiss. Vera smiled bravely past confused looks and harsh whispers from others.

Once she plunged into the first poem, however, the audience settled and so did her nerves. Now she was on home territory at last. She relaxed and read well. Once or twice, glancing up, she spotted a face here, eyes there, a pensive smile, listeners who were with her. Such delicate connections were all she sought from any public reading.

Earlier in the day she'd tabbed the selections she'd read from her book and a new manuscript. Yet the pages were in fact mere prompts—as always she was reciting from memory. And she had the odd sensation that she was observing her own work from something like the distance she'd been seeing Delhi since her arrival. The poems were hers yet separate too. They pleased her. Their workmanship, their sensibility and insight, the knowledge they demonstrated of the craft, all of this pleased her. What more did she have to say than she was sharing this evening?

That question startled her for a moment, and she stumbled, reciting a line twice. Was this enough? she wondered. Did this mean she'd finally matured as a poet—or that she was finished as one? The prospect suddenly seemed unclear, unnerving, the footing of her career treacherous.

For forty minutes she held the audience and then ceased, smiling, sipping at a glass of water. A long, pleasant moment passed as both she and they took stock. No better evidence of success than such silence. Could anyone from USIS complain now? The applause when it broke was warm, dissolving only slowly into a fluster of people rising, chattering, making their way up the aisles. Among those who ventured forward to thank her, a woman in a gold-and-crimson sari waited her turn. "It was delightful—a wonderful treat," she said, proffering Veera's book for an autograph, despite the back cover photo of a noticeably different woman than the one who'd been reading on this podium.

NO AMERICAN official was stationed in Jaipur to welcome Vera as she descended from the train into a blast of desert heat and scalding sun. Instead, an Indian in gray trousers, blue shirt, and a short black tie hurried up to her on the platform. Someone at the American Center in Delhi must have tipped him off about whom not to expect.

"You are Miss Vera Kahn? The poet?" he said. He seemed uncertain about whether to shake her hand. "I am Dr. Kanthan, head of the English literature department. We are so very delighted you have made this arduous journey to grace us with a reading. It is the event of the year for our students. They are so very, very excited."

"I am too," she said, and allowed him to lead her toward a car. She welcomed the dry heat and cleaner air of Rajasthan— though the congestion in her head and chest stubbornly re-fused to clear away. The train's first-class compartment had been sealed tight for the entire journey, its air-conditioning oppressive and only partially effective. She much preferred this, even though sweat was already prickling along her arms and legs.

No one had mentioned any plan or particular schedule, but she was rather surprised that Dr. Kanthan drove directly to a small bungalow, which, she soon gathered, was a guest-house. Without switching off the car, he stepped out and pulled her bag from the backseat. "The remainder of today is for you to rest and perhaps to visit something of our most beautiful city," he said. "Tomorrow morning, 9 A.M. bright and early, I will fetch you here to the university. It will be a grand treat no doubt." With a little wave of his hand, he was back in the driver's seat and pulling away.

For three days Vera had yearned for some freedom, for some time alone, unshepherded by Tyson or anyone else. But now that Kanthan had so unceremoniously abandoned her on the hot asphalt, she wasn't so eager to be on her own.

Her room was spartan but adequate, with a heavy AC unit in the wall. Black scorch marks around its plug made her nervous. She'd sleep later without it running. In the meanwhile, she had no intention of remaining cooped up here. Strolling once more out onto the road, she spotted several bicycle rickshaws huddling in a patch of shade a hundred yards away. A dark-skinned old man with a turban and no shirt was cleaning his teeth with a twig. He spat and looked up at her as she approached. "City?" she said. He nodded.

The rickshaw gathered speed enough to bathe Vera's face in a dry breeze. The old man pumped slowly from one leg to another, standing, his legs young and thin and powerful in their rhythm. As they passed through an ornate wooden gate into the city, he glanced over his shoulder at her. "Go," she said with a smile, and waved him on.

Through the streets and sprawling market they wove, sometimes quickly, often slowed to a walk. A bright pastel pink wash covered almost all of Jaipur's buildings as if defying the surrounding blankness of desert and gray dust. Likewise, the Rajasthanis themselves dressed with a far greater exuberance than people in Delhi—scarves of orange and flaming red, scarlet cotton shifts and leggings.

Spying one woman, no youngster but with beautiful dark eyes, a persimmon *dupatta* over shoulders and head, walking two children by the hand, Vera careened with a fresh surge of joy. She'd never been anywhere so beautiful, so full of life, that was strange to her and yet palpably real—ordinary even in its strangeness. She was also keenly aware that she could only hover outside, riding a rickshaw like any tourist, and watch.

Along one avenue stretched the stalls of spice merchants with their careful heaps of cardamom, stalks of ginger, bright orange mountains of other spices and seeds. Swaying around a corner, she found herself sweeping among the silversmiths. Trays of bangles and earrings, rows of goblets and cups. In the back of larger shops, Vera could make out young men work- ing the metal, tapping with mallets, etching with an instru- ment that looked like a razor.

"That's what Andrew would love." The thought startled her. It had been months and months since she'd thought of her former husband. But it came to her now that *he* was the one who'd always hankered to visit India—a desire that seemed extravagant and childish to her when they were young. Northern Italy, perhaps, if he insisted on traveling. Jamaica if it had to be exotic. Wasn't it enough they managed to steal a few days together in bed in New York, a city where the pub- lishers had him chained? India—they could have their pick of East Sixth Street takeaway, hauling the cartons and little cups of chutney right into their tangled nest of sheets. Or if he stole out to California every few months, why shouldn't that count?

She wondered, possibly for the first time, whether she should have taken his name after all. He'd shrugged, said it didn't matter. Had it mattered? Over time, a continent apart, they'd forgotten each other or failed to keep up with the stiffer, more mysterious adults they were becoming. Vera looked about her. Andrew would love Jaipur.

Every few minutes the rickshaw wallah glanced back for directions. He seemed increasingly suspicious—his trade was to ferry riders from one place to a specific destination. Such casual touring as this made him uncomfortable. Finally, in the middle of a square, he climbed off the bike. Without quite looking at her, he held out a hand. "You pay now. I eat." He scooped his fingers at his mouth to help her understand.

For a moment she considered exploring the city by foot. But she still felt a bit light-headed from the deep-rooted cold in her chest. "No," she said, shaking her head. "Take me back, please—I will pay you." The old man shrugged as if he'd merely been seeking this reassurance and mounted his cycle once more.

More quickly now they whizzed through the streets, up an alley, and out a different gate into Jaipur's more modern precincts. Disorientation soon dizzied Vera. Vaguely uncomfortable, she had no sense of their direction. Had the old man understood her?

Several ancient buses were jammed haphazardly into a lot. Some stood empty, waiting for future assignment, one or two abandoned entirely. Others, arriving or departing, overflowed with passengers squatting on the roof with bags and parcels or clinging to doors and window bars.

Hardly slowing, the rickshaw wallah swung wide around a corner and peddled along a narrow lane, past a row of low derelict buildings. Scabby trees covered in dust threw a paltry shade here. It wasn't cool, but the sudden escape from the sun seemed to silence a harsh and terrible sound that had been ringing in her ears.

In the sand along this lane, dark bundles lay scattered. She couldn't quite make them out. Large and small, they'd been dropped casually in odd contortions. Off to the side, a stick collapsed in the dust. Vera turned her head toward it. And still it took a moment as she was being driven past to realize it was a leg that had fallen. Above the haunch lolled the uncovered head of a young woman, jaw slack, eyes naked and blank and unfocused. Now Vera could translate: men, women, children, sprawling motionless, sparsely covered in scraps and rags. Their entire absence of movement was horrible, testimony to an equal absence of hope or purpose. What had brought them here? What were they waiting for? Were they waiting for anything?

Rage at the deception flooded through her—the beggars in Delhi had been toying with her after all. Those young mothers holding infants and banging on car windows near Connaught Circus wore bangles on their arms. Those babes had flesh on their bones.

Not the sordid shapes lying here in the sand. She spied a shoulder—a small boy's shoulder—no more than socket and bone. These shadows made no appeal. Indifferent in their lethargy, they didn't notice this stranger rolling past. Had they called out, she might have flung her bag, her ring, the clothes she wore. Instead, she sat frozen and horrified.

The rickshaw wallah took no more notice than he had with earlier marvels on this improvised tour. Shade and convenience were his only purpose in fetching his passenger along this particular route.

But the vision of such casual detritus pummeled her. The exhilaration she'd been feeling only moments before disappeared like smoke in a sudden gale. Tourist, she'd already been borne safely past, the only trace a sickness in her belly, a spot on her soul.

BRIGHT AND early as promised, Dr. Kanthan fetched her from the guesthouse. She'd taken a simple dinner in her room and then spent the hot night tossing with dreams she couldn't recall.

The University of Rajasthan stretched across a large swath of desert, its concrete subsiding in reddish sand and ragged patches of wild grass. Kanthan led her first to his own office, where the eight other members of the English department were already gathered. The one woman among them rose and stepped toward her. "Dr. Shukla," said Kanthan.

"We are so happy you have come to visit us," she said. Her hair was pulled taut. A streak of henna marked its severe part. Vera had seen looks before like the one Dr. Shukla offered her. Senior women in American universities shared it. They'd broken the bastions first; they'd made a place for themselves, suffered what had to be endured, compromised too deeply in order to survive, and would brook no latecomers, wanted no sisters or sympathy. Their claim was too precious. "Please, you will take a cup of tea with us before your talk?" she asked. And handed her a cup, a saucer of sugar biscuits. Vera didn't dare refuse.

She'd been asked by USIS to prepare a lecture for occasions such as this, and so a few minutes later she entered a large bare room packed with at least three hundred students. Perhaps thirty-five chairs were reserved for faculty and administrators, all but swallowed by the crowd. Most students sat on the floor. At the front of the room, a bare wooden desk and chair perched with cold authority on a platform. But Vera couldn't bring herself to sit in that chair. Giggles exploded and were shushed as she propped herself on the edge of the desk. "I'm more comfortable this way," she said with a smile, hoping to win them over. She coughed, wishing she could clear her lungs even for a moment.

Certainly the students were smiling and eager, willing to

accept anything this visitor might offer. "My talk today," she said slowly and clearly, "is called 'The Best of Times, the Worst of Times: The Contemporary Literary Scene in America.'" She glanced up from her paper and saw them eagerly nodding, these hundreds of young people. They were gazing so intently. Without warning, a surge of dread swept through her, leaving ash in her mouth. Bone deep she knew, only now when it was too late for anything but to soldier on, that this was the wrong talk for the wrong audience. She'd intended it as a light introduction to American themes and authors, with diplomatic bows to Rushdie, Desai, Roy—Indian writers who'd been fashionable of late. But the students before her had no clue what she was talking about, not enough context to imagine a context. And she could tell from their eyes, gazing at her with fascination as though she were an exotic creature babbling some strange gibberish, that they could hardly understand the sounds she was making. It wasn't that they didn't speak English: their English wasn't hers but a language whose sounds were trained to a different clef altogether. Sitting amid department colleagues jotting diligent notes, Dr. Shukla stared up with a grim triumph at her helplessness.

When Vera finished—she ceased speaking somewhere in the middle of the talk, middle of a thought, middle of a phrase—a ripple of polite applause passed quickly. But then, to her amazement, the students surged toward her. "Miss Vera," a brash boy cried out, "please sign for me." He thrust a pen at her. Laughing at the joke, she autographed a scrap of paper. "Miss Vera," crowed two or three girls side by side and giggling with excitement. They, too, pushed pens at her.

"Miss Vera, Miss Vera," swirled calls from all sides. A throng of dozens seethed toward her. "Miss Vera!" shouted another boy. "Sign this book—*please*—you must!" She found herself backing away, herded toward a wall. No one came to her aid. No sign of the faculty. It seemed Kanthan had abandoned her once more. Arms flailed about the celebrity, all waving pens and markers and pencils. Someone's pad struck her accidentally, dislodging her glasses. She clutched at them.

She was shaking her head, waving her hands, chagrined at the adoration of this mob. Besieged on all sides, still she could recognize the scene as ludicrous. "You don't want this from me," she kept saying over and over. "I'm just a teacher, a poet."

It was clear that at some level they all knew this, but it didn't matter. She was American. She'd been brought to see them and for them to see. When had they ever been visited by someone from beyond Rajasthan—when would they ever again? She was signing notepads and the frayed covers of textbooks, shirts and even bare arms and hands, all thrust demandingly into the path of a pen. The students kept pushing forward with desire but without intent. They'd pinned her against the wall and still they pressed tighter. It was hard to breathe. Just a little panic giggled in her throat.

"Miss Vera, Miss Veera, Veera." The sounds grew confused in her ears. Whose name were they calling? Even here the mocking pursued her. "Veera!"

"HOW YOU holding up?" asked Walter Tyson, reaching to give her a hand off the train at the Delhi station.

She shrugged because the answer wasn't easy. How could she explain the buffeting her own ambitions had subjected her to? His glance quickly took in the dark shadows around her eyes, the loss of flesh along her jaw and throat—his sudden concern a more reliable gauge than the mirror in her bag.

"We can slow all this down if you need. The symposium in Simla can manage without you—and you're supposed to be having some fun too. How about I arrange someone to run you to Agra."

"No. Thanks." She shook her head and didn't cough. "I kind of like the working just now. I'll go back to being pure tourist at the end." She didn't want to confess that lingering in Delhi seemed impossible—she needed to keep moving. She also didn't want to let on quite how pleased she was to see him. Oh, she was confident she could manage on her own, but a lift to the hotel was certainly easier this way.

"Okay," he said. "Better get some sleep then. It's an early start tomorrow. Train's at four thirty."

"Can I get a taxi at that hour?"

"No need. I'll pick you up on the way. Didn't I mention the symposium's my baby?—months and months getting the arrangements settled. So this leg of your tour, we'll be traveling together."

It was only after they'd sleepily switched trains at Kalka that the sky lightened enough for the world to gradually grow visible. They'd begun to climb now, and the air was fresh and cooler. In the lingering darkness of the mountain train's old-fashioned compartment, thick stands of pines seemed to cluster close to the rails like a ragged blanket. But the trees fell away along with the darkness of night, and as they moved from hills into the first smaller mountains of Himachal Pradesh, she was surprised by long vistas of naked reddish and yellow rock. No telling whether the train had already crept above the tree line or whether men had long ago scraped these slopes bare of stumps and brush and soil.

The rails stretched where the mountains allowed, not blasting their way through but clinging to each bend, sometimes dipping, sometimes climbing sharply, always searching for the next pass, dragging the train higher. Long ago during an undergraduate history course, Vera had happened to read about the summer capital of the Raj—a quiet retreat in the distant skirts of the Himalayas where the British sought relief from the furnace of May and June. Her distant studies hadn't prepared her for this: a jagged landscape of high peaks and blasted ridges. How desperate for relief the British must have been to carve this railway all the way toward Simla, seven thousand feet high and misleadingly called a hill station.

Walter Tyson's small pair of binoculars perched on a shelf by the window. Looking up from the book in his lap as the train jolted sharply around a bend or soared for an instant at another crest, he'd gallantly offer them to her first. Twice, and then again, she couldn't bring herself to say no, delighted by the rock and sky. She studied the landscape and she found herself, rather as a surprise, studying her companion.

"Any must-sees in Simla?" she asked for the sake of hearing his voice again—she hadn't really bothered to listen to it before.

"Not much beyond the mountains themselves, as far as I know," he answered with a smile over the rims of his reading glasses. "There's the old viceroy's palace, of course, and a famous monkey temple too—supposed to be worth the walk."

Vera nodded. Whatever adventures she might have conjured for herself in the frantic weeks between the mistaken invitation arriving and her own departure, some wild sexual fling hadn't figured among them. Oh, well, perhaps at the margins, as a never entirely not-present hope or possibility of possibility. Middle age had brought her some relief from the

humiliating urges of youth, a relief ratified daily by the young
men, the *boys,* in her writing and literature classes who gazed
at her or through her as if she weren't entirely visible. Nor did
the harried, pallid men in her department cause her pulse to
race with any dangerous temptation.

Relief from urges. She shook her head now and immediately glanced up to see whether Tyson had noticed—she
didn't want him thinking her any crazier than he might already
suspect. Relief came at a price: a withering, a numbness on the
tongue that wine and poems in small magazines and nights
out with her sister never entirely chased away. If she hadn't
come to India looking for a fling, no doubt somewhere in the
impulsive deception lurked a desire to fly free from that lingering taste of mortality for a few weeks at least.

Walter Tyson. She smiled at the thought, deciding him a
kind man, with his granny glasses perched at the end of his
nose, with his slight paunch and the prissy way he rolled his
cuffs back with such care, once, twice. Ever since his initial
shock at the airport, denying she might be who she claimed,
he'd been quite thoughtful. Could there be any more to it than
professional responsibility? She wasn't sure. She doubted it. It
didn't matter.

Maybe if she could ever shake this heavy cold in her lungs
and the light-headedness dogging her, maybe then it could
matter.

Simla clung to a long, sweeping ridge in terraces of markets
and brightly colored houses and shacks. Like a haphazard
bookshelf, these terraces were articulated along three or four
narrow streets, one stacked above another. As Walter Tyson
and Vera Kahn emerged from the station, she was surprised
by a cloud of diesel exhaust and soot hanging low about their

heads. Traffic was snarled worse than Delhi, trucks too big for the streets wedged growling one against the other.

"Are you up for a short hike?" shouted Tyson in her ear. "A porter can fetch our bags, and the hotel should be walkable."

"Absolutely," she cried back.

The station sat at the bottom of the town. They set off at an easy stroll. Yet even before they'd begun to climb toward the next street, she was feeling the altitude, panting heavily. She tugged at his shirt.

Distracted or daydreaming, he was startled at her touch and immediately abashed. "Sorry—sorry. Do you need to stop for a minute? Should I grab a taxi after all?"

She shook her head. "No. I'll be fine." The acrid smoke hovering in the air stung her eyes and throat and congested lungs.

Tugging out his binoculars as if he'd just noticed something, Tyson pretended to study the rather limited view west and south, the landscape through which the train had passed, giving her another moment or two. When they set off again, it was at a more leisurely pace, and she could manage it, just.

The hotel was new and pleasant, not very fancy. That suited her fine. The scholars and teachers who'd been invited from across northern India to a symposium for which one Vera or another's visit was the instigating opportunity hadn't yet arrived. Dinner was scheduled as the first official function. And lunch wouldn't be served for another two hours. Despite the cough she tried to sneak away into a handkerchief—the altitude, no doubt—she was restless. She wanted to see something of the town, the mountains. "Care to explore a little bit?" she asked Walter in the lobby after the porter delivered bags to their rooms.

"Oh damn, I can't right now—after lunch, for sure?" he

said, looking disappointed. "I'm meeting the hotel manager about preparations for the next two days."

His straw-colored hair, thinning to be sure, still fell with a hint of boyish wildness. She was quite pleased at his reaction and smiled at him in a way she hadn't yet—hadn't in years—and headed off with a little wave in any case. She didn't want to waste what was left of the morning.

After a couple of easy switchbacks, Vera found herself on a road gradually rising. At one twist in the pavement, just below the mall, a sign marked the spot beyond which Indians weren't allowed to trespass during the days of the Raj. All about her, of course, Indians were strolling, pushing, hawking souvenirs. The only creatures not allowed beyond this marker any longer were cars and other motor vehicles. Their absence made Simla's mall, a spine of macadam along the top of the ridge, quite pleasant. The stinging cloud of soot and smoke remained trapped in the terraces below. Up here the air was fresh and even chilly, with a quick snap of wind.

Other colonial vestiges remained intact. A small stone theater, where, according to the plaque, amateur performances of Shakespeare had once been staged, now offered Hindi films and touring concerts. Banks and other looming gray-stone edifices mimicked the architecture of other distant precincts in a vanished empire. Yet at a peak in the road, next to mounted telescopes where for ten rupees one could get a clear shot to the north, a large bust of Indira Gandhi commanded the city.

But what a disappointment: the Himalayas themselves were shrouded in haze. Looking out across long valleys and lesser peaks, Vera could make out nothing beyond. The haze didn't appear terribly thick—the day's light simply seemed to fall short before it could reach the great mountains. Even plunking coins into a telescope yielded nothing.

Frustrated, she strolled farther along the mall. Narrowing gradually and climbing again, it soon turned into a lane running past private residences with high gates and bungalows guarded by lounging men in khaki and berets. At one bend in the road, a fresh fit of coughing brought Vera to a halt. When it finally passed, she was left with a blossoming headache. She nearly turned back in despair. But just above her head and nearly hidden by the branch of a tree—only by chance, only right here should she notice—a faded monkey urged her with all six arms to keep climbing. Intrigued by the sign, as though the message were hers alone, and unwilling to skulk back to the hotel so early, headache or not, she remembered Walter mentioning a temple.

She expected to discover it over the next rise, but nothing lay waiting for her but another sloping bend in the path—pavement had disappeared a hundred yards back. A first smudge of dirty snow appeared at the base of a pine. Other travelers were picking their way up from the town as well, she now noticed. Mostly young Indian couples attired in silken shawls and well-polished black shoes, they wore the shy, eager grins of newlyweds. Apparently a visit to Hanuman's shrine offered an auspicious beginning. So be it—she welcomed the company, the occasional conspiratorial smiles thrown to her by young brides. And, guiltily, she also wished she'd waited for Walter Tyson's company.

She was panting again, straining for thin air. At home, treadmills and twice-a-week aerobics kept her in decent-enough shape. She brushed away a glaze of sweat from her lip. If these young couples could manage the climb in saris and stiff shoes and suit coats, she could too, middle-aged Westerner or not.

Any pretense of a casual stroll had long since disappeared. The slope had grown steeper, more treacherous. Rough-hewn steps had been hacked into the rock, but these were slick with old ice. Beside them a gully of packed mud and scattered stones offered better footholds.

Gradually a prickly sensation of being watched put Vera on edge. Sharply she snapped her head to the side, then again up into the trees, trying to catch a glimpse of the spy. Out of the corner of her eye, she noticed the dull brown rock twitch alive—a monkey swung by one arm from a tree branch and dropped to the ground. Once recognized, dozens appeared out of the thin soil, young ones darting and tumbling over each other, older, much larger monkeys staring at the human visitors, appraising them with hostile indifference. As patches of snow along the route became more frequent, so did the monkeys.

Forewarned, many of the newlyweds had packed along popcorn balls as offerings. Once these were tugged free, the monkeys approached more boldly, screeching and demanding their due. One young bride fumbled with a paper bag of loose popcorn. She giggled nervously. Her husband, embarrassed by such behavior, stood stiffly beside her and pretended not to notice. A great gray male ambled toward the girl with its hand outstretched, impatient and querulous. She struggled not to drop the bag, clutching it against her chest, trying to extract a handful. A few grains splattered to the ground. Too proud to scrabble for stray kernels, the angry monkey hopped forward and with a scolding shriek snatched the bag from her hand. The girl shrieked too. Popcorn peppered about her feet. Her husband strode silently, furiously away.

As the peak in this ridge finally drew close, Vera panting hard as each step skittered treacherously across loose gravel and ice, a pack of teenage boys seemed to emerge from the rock as well. They hovered about a large clearing. "You need a guide, miss," one boy announced with a shout to Vera. Thirteen or fourteen, he was cocky and very handsome, with long lashes and delicate dark skin and a clove cigarette dangling from his mouth. Dramatically, he tossed it into a mound of snow. She couldn't hear the hiss. She shook her head.

"I'm okay," she said.

"Miss, you need a guide for the temple."

Again she shook her head and trudged forward, yearning only to reach the damn temple so she could tag it accomplished, catch her breath, and begin the hike down to the hotel. Could she make it back in time for lunch? The question occurred to her, and suddenly she was ravenous.

A blow slammed her head and shoulders from behind. Vera staggered forward, startled, terrified, trying not to fall. An attack? One of the boys? A heavy weight was riding on her back. Lurching, hunched over, she struggled to keep her balance. Something rubbed past her ear. A small hand was reaching from behind her head. It clasped angrily at her eyes, closing on her glasses and snatching them away. Eerie and disorienting, the moment froze her. The monkey leaped from her shoulders and scurried away.

Monkeys were screeching, boys were shouting. The one who'd offered his services—for bodily protection, she now understood, rather than for particular guidance into Hanuman's mysteries—raced after the animal. Vera was already picturing her appearance at the seminar, how foolish she would look staring out vaguely at the Indian scholars, attempting to recite from memory her talk on the worst of times.

Fuzzy shapes were scrambling higher off the path. The boy halted for an instant at the top of a boulder to hurl a chunk of ice at the monkey, then leaped in pursuit once more.

Vera couldn't make out just when it happened, but the animal must have surrendered at last, flinging its trophy away. Because abruptly the boy was back, shoving the glasses into her hands.

"Here, good lady. I save them for you," he declared proudly.

"This deserves a big reward," suggested another voice helpfully at her elbow.

The lenses were smeared, the frame wrenched awry at one corner as she tried to reestablish the glasses on her head, hands trembling.

"You must do something for him," offered still another adviser.

Vera was aware of tourist couples watching. Gratitude, relief, embarrassment flooded her with warmth. She shoved a hand into her pocket and tugged out something more than a hundred rupees. Hardly equal to her relief, yet far beyond what the rescue warranted, she knew. Wouldn't the others despise her being such easy prey? The boy didn't hesitate, didn't wait for her to consider, but sealed her generosity by pulling the bills from her hand with a cry of "Thank you, dear lady," and a whoop of glee. In another instant Vera was abandoned, boys and monkeys and tourists vanishing with the conclusion of this particular show. What cut had the monkey earned? she wondered.

Ahead and through a thick stand of trees, she glimpsed the gray bulk of Hanuman's temple perched on a rounded knob. Shaken by the attack and its abrupt reversal, she felt no yearning to delve any further. Her mouth was dry. She coughed and coughed again, harsh and deep, a fit that doubled her over and wouldn't let her snatch a breath. At last it eased.

Hesitant, teary, afraid of triggering another attack, she limped to the far side of the clearing's bare rock and snow. She needed to gather herself before braving the descent into town. And casually looked up.

Startled, Vera fell back a step as if she'd been struck again. Distant and impossibly close and impossibly massive, the Himalayas loomed high above the world. No trace of haze protected her any longer. Glasses damaged or not, she made out sun striking rock, shadow caressing snow with a clarity that snatched the last air from her lungs. Earlier, on the mall in Simla, haze erasing all sight, she'd tried to imagine just where on the horizon these mountains might scratch the sky. Here and now, her vision restored, the Himalayas towered above any such human measure.

Yet this view wasn't exotic. It wasn't alien. It simply was, with a certainty of overwhelming fact. Had she been chasing illumination on this journey? No illumination here, beyond the sun striking the mountains themselves. Each stage of her journey so far, each powerful jolt that jerked her between joy and despair, might have been in preparation for this moment, softening her up so she could see. She saw, yes, and she had no idea what to make of it. Poetry failed to soar from her soul as it might have done when she was younger. Barren, spent, her spirit cowered at the ordinariness of the rock before her eyes and beneath her feet. She felt able to see and she felt small and alone and afraid.

SHE WAS aware that Walter Tyson had summoned a doctor. She was grateful to him, wished she could tell him so, accepted the fact she couldn't.

"It is altitude sickness. No doubt about it," the young doctor was saying. She felt the distant stab of an injection. "With any luck this will do the trick for her, quite quickly no doubt."

She felt very bad that the seminar would be disrupted and Walter put to more trouble. Well, surely they could carry on without her. She wasn't whom they'd been expecting anyway.

"IT IS a puzzle to me. No, if it doesn't work already, another dose will be without effect and as well may be dangerous."

The side of the bed sagged and Vera opened her eyes. Walter Tyson was leaning on an arm, studying her closely. Startled to find her gazing up at him, he drew back. She tried to smile. He lay his hand on her arm—she could feel it.

"Should I get a medevac helicopter up from Delhi?"

She wasn't sure which of them he was asking.

"I think it is a bug I don't know," the young doctor was saying. "It may be one she brought with her."

AS SHE approached the edge of waking, she sensed a light in the room and a larger darkness beyond it. A jumble of quiet voices. Were they close by? Where was she? she wondered, without opening her eyes. She wasn't sure yet, wasn't quite awake. Those voices—were they her parents?

For a terrifying moment, she wasn't sure quite where she was, quite who she was. She was sick—that much she knew. Her face felt hot, her throat parched. But still she wouldn't open her eyes. It seemed far too great a challenge. She wasn't ready. The only certain fact was her own awareness. She took that in. She was a she and the rest of the universe, small or large, was not she, lay outside, beyond her closed eyes. Terrified and determined—with all her soul and all her might, she'd cling. Teeth clenched, she wrestled to hold her own.

THE ELECTRIC light in the room had been switched off, but, coming to herself, Vera saw a grayish light leaking in from beyond the windows. Dawn or dusk, she couldn't tell. Walter Tyson was sitting, arms on knees, in a chair by the window. Realizing she'd awakened, he rose and drew close. His face was dark with shadow and with concern.

"The copter's already landed, but the ridge wouldn't let them get very close. We're waiting for an ambulance to come ferry us up to the mall."

She wanted to smile at him again, at Walter Tyson, but she was weak—when had she ever felt so weak, her body and her head and even the muscles of her jaw so heavy. And yet she also felt light, terribly light, as if the faintest puff of breeze might sweep her away entirely.

"I'm sorry about all this," she whispered, surprising them both.

"Don't be," he said, and touched her arm again. She wished he'd keep his hand on her arm. Just a little while. "It was our mistake, not yours. I should have done my homework better before sending an invitation."

A giggle—did she have the strength for a giggle? "Not that, silly man. You'd have liked my talk." Exhausted, she couldn't say any more.

Tyson snorted, laughing for them both. "One damn talk? You can recite it for me later. Once we get you to the East-

West Medical Centre in Delhi. It's their copter." Prattling on, he was sounding worried again.

Vera guessed the journey back down, even by helicopter, would be all she could manage. Thirsty, she glanced to a side table and, understanding, Walter Tyson brought a cup of water to her lips.

DEAN OF WOMEN

She would have been, must have been, twenty-eight or so. Into the classroom she staggers, musical scores and bursting files and spine-cracked books tumbling from her arms onto the desktop. Her hair is drawn back into a harsh bun, of course—it's as if they have to do that. Little wisps snaggle free at the hairline. And even though her skin is naturally dark—Mediterranean or Romanian or something like that— she seems pale, almost sallow, as if she's been spending way too much time in the library dungeon.

What did I know? College-age men don't know anything. Noses pressed against the glass, they don't have the distance to make sense of the world. No perspective. As far as I was concerned, she was notable, principally, for being something other than a tweed-wearing, dandruff-dropping, somnolence-inducing, establishment-supporting old fart. Not that as an alternative she seemed anything attractive. Really, she dressed as badly as most of them. Browns and blacks and fadeds. And she had these thick black eyebrows that seemed to stretch toward each other and meet, or almost meet, above her nose. Still, it's dead January, first day of the new semester, snow on the ground. And I'm thinking, Music history may not be so dull after all.

I was a junior, twenty-one or so. That's just about when, in college, you start conceiving the illusion that you're an adult. What didn't I know?

- That as long as you're in college, you're no adult;

- That she, Irene Fulbright (can you believe the name?— but true), had been plucked from Berkeley on the basis of a promising first chapter of her dissertation;

- That the senior prof she'd be filling in for had, the day after Christmas, been railroaded by his colleagues into an alcohol rehab program, scratching every step of the way;

- That her teaching experience consisted of grading undergraduate papers for her mentor at Berkeley, the second man she'd ever slept with;

- That at twenty-eight or so she wasn't an "older woman" in any meaningful sense;

- That she was one of only three women on the entire faculty of our small college, the other two being senior dragons of the most formidable type;

- That she was already terrified, lonely, isolated, and miserable, desperately missing that mentor who'd so conveniently arranged to ship her nearly as far from California as humanly possible while making it seem a great gift;

- That women don't possess, deep down further than they can even know, the mystery of all mysteries, something to do with sex but separate from it too, that makes sense of and reassures and makes your own life meaningful if only you can find it out;

- Just about everything else that matters.

So I remember that first day, but then there's a pretty good gap in what comes next. After all, it's been twenty-five years and some. Whatever Ms. Fulbright's value as an oddity, I had plenty to keep me busy, and not just my homework. Homework? Doing it faithfully in those days was considered a betrayal of a different faith. We had the war to protest, which meant a lot more than just showing up at marches and sit-ins, burning draft cards. (The look on the dean's face when we carried him in his own desk chair, like the mock god he'd always fancied himself to be, out of his office, down the steps, and onto the front lawn, that alone was worth my semester's tuition.) Not to mention, whenever I could slip away down by the maintenance buildings, I'd be tinkering with other students' bikes and some faculty ones too, trying to help pay that damn tuition.

And there was my girlfriend. Nancy. I've felt bad about Nancy all these years, and now, in starting to try and make sense of what happened, what do I discover but that the guilt has magically lifted from my shoulders. Nancy. Brighter than I was, for sure. A star of the poli sci department. With one or two professors showing more than strictly professional interest in her success. Who, for all her bra-rejecting and poster-making and handing-the-match-to-me-for-my-own-draft-card-burning, had been so traumatized by the over-the-shoulder expectations of her dentist father and Junior League mother that what she wanted desperately, from me of all people, was escape and security—the MRS degree. Nancy was none too happy about the Professor Fulbright situation developing in my life.

A trajectory I don't recall all that clearly. Except that I was enjoying the music she played more than I'd expected and more than most of my classmates. Mozart and Beethoven, naturally. And she really turned me on to Schumann. No kidding. So I actually began to say things in class—a first for me. And after a while I was lingering behind a bit and we'd talk.

And then we're sitting in the parking lot behind the library. Things must have been developing pretty quickly because it's still winter, cold, with snow on the pavement, and our breath is frosting in the car as we snuggle together. Irene shivers as my cold hands burrow up under her sweater. "Jonathan," she sigh-whispers, maybe the first time she says my name. Anyway like that. And she's making these little mewings in my ear—this is what comes back to me now, as my mouth follows my hands.

Once she sang for me. A private performance. It was in the little bare apartment they'd given her. No accompaniment, no piano or record. She lit a couple of candles, and they dripped onto a milk crate as she sang. Her voice was sweet, low. It rose from the deep of her, disembodied once it came forth, as if she were channeling some spirit separate from herself. More intimate than sex, this was, I realize now, a brief glimpse of who she was.

Except for the trouble I was generating with a girlfriend to whom I hadn't made any grand pledges—whatever she may have persuaded herself—I never imagined that what

Irene Fulbright and I were up to was anyone's business. To my mind, Irene was an older, experienced woman of the world. She confessed that she'd slept with two other men before me. See? The fact that her apartment was more spartan than the dorm room I was sharing with two other guys didn't mean anything. The fact that she was scared and determined and stiff the first time we made love, well, that didn't really register either.

Yes, I knew she was lonely and unhappy, that other professors weren't making her feel welcome. But I didn't get it: that her spending time, more than time, with an undergraduate—me—wasn't due to my intellect or my sensitivity or my shoulder-length locks, but was a matter of desperation.

I have plenty of perspective now.

Not that I was strutting my conquest. Things with Nancy were tense enough. But my friends who knew, they couldn't really decide what to make of me hanging out with a professor. I mean, sure, she was an older woman, which carried some cachet—which was cool. But she was also an older woman, which struck them as, well, kind of gross too.

So if I wasn't bragging about it, neither was I trying hard to keep a secret. Her own attempts to be discreet struck me as cute, a function of her modesty or some other old-fashioned, genteel notion.

Another memory: her slipping along the dark corridors of my dorm one night, wearing this cape sort of thing, only it's tweed or plaid, not black silk like in the movies. The hood was pulled over her head. I'd arranged for my roommates to be gone. Irene swoops in the door, shuts it behind her, kisses me. But then we're standing there, fumbling at each other through buttons and blouses and such. And she whispers, "I'm ovulating." Very significant, her tone. I haven't a clue what it means—whether she's more or less likely to get pregnant.

This is all those years ago and protections were fewer and I didn't even have a rubber. So we never manage to make it across the room to my bed—we're just leaning into each other and fumbling at each other, panting.

Finally she heaves this deep sigh, disappointed in me. I clearly failed the test, whatever it was. "This is crazy," she murmurs. "I can't do this again." And sweeps away with her ridiculous hood into the shadows.

I didn't know it was a secret to keep. Nor, for that matter, did I understand then that, in any event, keeping secrets at a small college is impossible. One way or another, the word got around. Soon her colleagues were shunning her, as if the faculty were some strange sect of Amish. Don't they, the Amish, do that, the shunning? The standard version in black and blue, clumping along in their buggies, lived in the neatly tended farms swaddling the college. The professorial version in tweed wouldn't speak to Irene in the post office. Never invited her for a sandwich at lunch. Never had the courage to admit to her why they were behaving like such self-righteous prigs. It was only much later that I heard the full story. You can tell it still burns me.

Nor did I know that the dean, having reclaimed his desk, required Miss Fulbright to stand in the dock before it. After which he summarily canned her—no hearing, no appeal, no announcement. I knew nothing until Nancy, tipped by her poli sci contacts, sidled by me in the lunch line. "She was *so* unprofessional," she said with just a brush of venom. "I hope you can come to your senses now."

"Huh?" I said, bewildered.

Oh, this part is hard, the looking back. What a lame ass I was.

———

If Irene hasn't come clear in the telling so far, maybe it's be-cause she wasn't very clear to me either. Did I simply not try to get a better glimpse of her, or did she resist? I guess up until the moment Nancy nudged me with her hip in the dining-hall line, I hadn't felt any great urgency on that score. Much less did I realize just how over my head I was.

After an initial brief bewilderment—how could they do this?—I was swept up by a churning rage, a tantrum that heaved me, that wrung me. How *dare* they do this. Male pro-fessors pursued the extracurricular education of women stu-dents far and wide in those days without penalty. It was one of the perks. Hell, anyone could look at the faculty directory and see how many marriages were made (or just as often de-stroyed) by such liaisons. There's a polite word. A word they didn't bother with when it came to a lonely young woman who wasn't on the tenure track and who hadn't yet finished her Ph.D.

I wanted to shake the heavens with a real political protest, crash the columns of the temple about me in my fury. . . .

The dean's secretary wouldn't even let me in his office.

Okay, so I'd charge off somewhere else and demand an explanation, a righting of the wrongs committed against Irene Fulbright. . . .

By whom? Did she want the wrongs righted? Why hadn't she spoken to me before disappearing?

Because that's the other humiliating truth. She never bothered. Not so much as a word, let alone a kiss. Suddenly she was gone. Apartment abandoned, office door locked, the chair of the music department covering her class on music history. (Irene had just started on Chopin's First Concerto.) From the hall I spotted him at the blackboard and never en-tered the room.

Never before had I felt so helpless. My friends were amused but distracted.

It was all so easy, what came next. It seemed urgent all right, and necessary. Privately I indulged the notion that the gesture was, well, heroic. But the point is that somehow I felt responsible. That I'd done Irene wrong.

More naïveté.

Why am I telling this? Partly the story is the running into Irene later. After all, it was the running into her after so very long that got me thinking in the first place. About how what came next, after stomping away from that History of Western Music classroom, became the great fork in my path. Everything changed for me, didn't it? But at that moment I was caught up in a rush, a swirl. I seemed to be watching my life happen, rather than moving myself. I sure didn't sense the momentousness. No perspective.

Destiny? For the better? It'll take a few more decades before I'm ready to pronounce on that.

Backpack over one shoulder, I left the college and haven't been back to this day. Hitched a ride on a country road, another one on the interstate, and three days later made it to Berkeley. Didn't bother to call my folks until I arrived.

What was I after, other than simply tracking down the elusive Irene Fulbright? I'm not sure I could have told you even then. It wasn't that I thought she'd want to marry me. Not even I was naive enough to think in terms of making an honest woman of her. I don't think I thought she was pregnant. She was too careful for that, and that hadn't been why the dean dismissed her.

"So, you're the young fellow that Miss Fulbright has been

writing to me about. Letters upon letters." Professor Edmund
Ehrenpreis looked scarcely different from his bearded and
slightly bulbous kin I'd left behind three days before, except
that his vest and tie were a little fussier, his own beard
trimmed to a keener point, his arrogance monumental. He
was tapping an ancient baton against a pile of music scores in
his office.

"I believe she's actually been trying to provoke me to jealousy," he said. "I gather, therefore, that you and I have had
something in common." And generously saw fit to share a
brotherly leer and a waggle of the baton.

"Nothing in common," I said. "Has she come to see
you?"

"Ah. No. No sign of her, I'm afraid. Until this moment I
didn't know she'd fled the wilds of Pennsylvania. Not that I'm
surprised."

And that was that. No sign of her. I looked up some of
her friends. Dared question the all-powerful secretary of the
music department. But no one had heard from Irene. Or not
that they'd confess to me.

I was stumped. Going back to school, if it occurred to me,
would have seemed unimaginable, as if I'd already been translated to a different existence entirely. And I couldn't possibly
return to my parents either, despite the increasingly frantic
pleas of my mother. She had good reason to be frantic. Not
that she could have protected me.

The decade was about to turn. It was a heady time to be
where I was, the age I was. Nothing seemed hard. The room
and a mattress over someone's garage in San Francisco came
easily enough. The part-time gig in a bike shop—they were
thrilled to have someone who already knew a derailleur from
a free wheel. I settled, but I was waiting, watching. Here's

what I see now: that I never really gave up on the idea of the search—I'd simply come to a stage where the path faded from view.

Burning a mountain of draft cards hardly crippled the government's draft machine. The army had little trouble zeroing in on a bike shop or the boy who'd so foolishly surrendered his deferment before it expired. This, too, I accepted as some sort of necessary penance.

For what?

One year and seven months in the Delta. Any notion of penance evaporated pretty damn quick, let me tell you, along with longings for or guilt about Irene Fulbright. Hell, I was grateful for the occasional sympathetic and slightly gloating letter from Nancy until—get this—she married a poli sci prof in grad school and abandoned her doctorate. No more letters from Nancy.

I'm standing here in my own shop. Three guys work for me. I've trained each of them—they've got to share my vision about how you make a bike. And there are plenty of worries these days. About health care costs. Social Security. About the purists who shell out for handmade steel frames with lugs that are lovingly brazed at each joint—whether they'll keep paying three times what the corporate boys charge for composite or aluminum. I'm doing what I'm doing and it all seems so inevitable, so carved out of a solid block of possibility.

But now that we're looking back, thanks to Irene, I find myself thinking about that sharp swerve in the path. I can almost imagine it as literal: a little gravel trail I'd never noticed before, veering away from the winding spine that strung together the brick and stone and clapboard buildings of my old college. Curiosity, boredom, the zeitgeist—how's that for a college word?—maybe the reason was no more than Professor Fulbright's strange mewings in the parking lot. Reason or not, I poked my toe out onto that path, curious about where a little detour might land me—and *whoosh*. A year and seven months of fear and heat rash worse than anything you can imagine and a right hand that can't quite grip a spanner. Well, if that's the worst of it, other than the occasional visitation that still will come late some nights, I'm one lucky pup, you bet.

There'd be no more of this story—has it been a story so far?—if my beautiful, dark-haired daughter, Jessie, hadn't settled on the notion that she wanted to go to a women's college on the West Coast and that I should therefore find a way to send her. Well, orders are steady, cash flow is pretty good—maybe I should add that fourth employee?

Much as I enjoyed the California scene during those brief months of my wayfaring exile, it's another place I never returned to, not once they shipped me off for basic in Texas. I just kept going east: Texas, Virginia, a short stint in Germany, Vietnam. One year, seven months.

My wife, Jessie's mother. I haven't really mentioned her yet. Perhaps there's reason enough. Dorothy. Nice old-fashioned name for a nice old-fashioned sort of girl. We've been married twenty-seven years. You want cliché, you want cornball: she was a nurse in the VA where they worked on my hand and arm. She met me her first day on the ward. Good thing. Another week or two and I wouldn't have seemed so special. She hates when I say things like that. But see, maybe I've learned some things along the way. Dorothy.

Jessie, Dorothy, and I drove two thousand miles to northern California. Man, let me tell you, it's not the same. I swung a detour through San Francisco and past the old bike shop. Hey, maybe I'd get them to order one or two of my beauties, right? Me, still naive: the frowsy shop I remember so fondly is long gone. Sushi counter and garden center on the ground floor of a soaring high-rise of condos. I never even turned off the car, just swept slowly on by. No need to say anything to my girls.

Hillbury College is splayed across the top of a hill, cliff really, with the ocean a long toss below. Redwoods and palm trees cluster just shaggily enough across the campus you don't mistake it for a golf course. The buildings are Spanish style, of course, whitewashed stucco with red tile roofs. It's too damn precious by half, but I can't say that to the girls either because they were already smitten.

The Admissions Office had its program down cold. Coed in shorts and a polo shirt, hair pulled taut in a ponytail, she was walking backward along white shell paths, talking all the while, telling stories about Hillbury College to the thirteen parents and girls who took that hour's tour. I followed along, hands in pockets, wishing I could feel more grumpy but pretty impressed instead. And the sun was nice.

And then we were back in the admin building, Jessie interviewing with one of the college seniors. Dorothy disappeared out to find the stables—horses *her* secret love. Ha.

I had a cup of tea in my lap. I was trying to fade invisible in this big wingback chair, more uncomfortable than a stiff saddle. And I glanced up, no reason, as Irene Fulbright came striding down the broad curving staircase from loftier offices above.

Me, I was surprised. Surprise enough, isn't it, that I should recognize her after all these years? It was her dark eyes, of course, and of course her nose and the shape of her mouth, the architecture that suddenly has you recognizing someone. Her personality, her character expressed through expression, mysteriously but unmistakably. She was wearing a tan pantsuit with a cream blouse open at the neck. Professional. Impressive. I was impressed.

Irene? She was surprised too. Her first glance ticked into a kind of frozen smile and then she was sure. And isn't it even more remarkable that she recognized me, given I've done more changing? I look like a guy who makes bicycles for a living.

"Jonathan?" she said, grasping at the heavy knob at the bottom of the banister. Deans don't dare miss the last step on a staircase.

I was thinking of all the things I should be saying, and there was nothing to say, so I nodded.

She held out her hand like I was the father of a prospective student. I fumbled up from the chair, spilling the tea, nearly dropping the damn cup from the hand that doesn't work while trying to grasp hers with the one that does.

"Hi," I managed profoundly at last.

She was silent for a moment. Without any awkwardness, she took my left hand in her right. She didn't ask what the hell I'm doing at her school—not that I had any clue it was her school. She looked up at me, her eyes crinkling with amusement, but searching my own, one to the other.

"My daughter is visiting. She loved this place before ever seeing it. So, you know, I figured we ought to see it."

"Naturally," she said, and I wasn't sure how to take it.

"Irene," I said with some exasperation. "Or should it be Professor Fulbright?"

"I'm not quite sure what it should be. Not professor anyhow." She laughed. "Not for a long, long time. Dean, maybe."

She shook her head and her eyes crinkled more, and her lips—she was wearing lipstick—smiled at me. "No, it better be Irene for now. Aren't we old friends?"

"Old friends? Jesus, Irene, I went *searching* for you."

"Shhh." She wagged her hand and smiled in at least eight directions. She gestured for me to sit again and settled herself on an ottoman at just the right angle, her knees together, her pumps in perfect alignment on the floor.

"It's been a long time," she said, and patted me on the knee.

I nodded, still trying to take this all in.

"You're here with your daughter?" she continued ever so brightly and professionally. "And your wife?"

I nodded. "Dorothy." I swallowed. "How about you?"

"No," she said. "No wife for me. Did have a husband. Two actually, though not at the same time."

"What about your music?" I asked. I'd been saving that one a long time.

She shook her head. "That's something I might thank you for—pushing me off that particular career trajectory." She was still smiling brightly, but her words were softer and a little bit fierce. "I came away from Pennsylvania knowing all kinds of things about myself that I hadn't been brave enough to face before. Oh, I knew already my voice wasn't concert caliber— that's why I went for the Ph.D. But it was only after my little experiment at your school that I could admit I didn't have the temperament to be a scholar. Too dusty, too lonely."

"Didn't that disappoint your mentor? Ehrenpreis, right?

She blushed and gave a little laugh. "Didn't you know, Jonathan? He was the first of those husbands."

The difference in our ages, six or seven years, so impor- tant before, meant nothing anymore. Hell, I was the grayer of the two. But here she was still making me feel the younger, the naive one.

I snorted angrily. "Well, the bastard lied to me. I went to him first."

She nodded. "I was lying low for a while. It took me five years more to realize I didn't have the temperament to be a musicologist's wife either."

She looked down. I looked down. We sat in an awkward silence for a moment.

"What happened to your hand?" she asked at the same instant I said, "I went looking for you."

"I went looking for you," I repeated.

"I know."

"Because I just said. But I wanted you to know."

"I did know."

I glanced at her again. Nodded. "But you didn't want me to find you. Okay. Well, once I'd gone off in that direction, there was no going back. Fork in the road, you know?"

"No. No going back, is there?"

"Vietnam."

"Sorry?"

"What happened to the hand. One year, seven months in the Delta."

"Ah. I wondered but never knew."

"No."

Again we sat in silence.

We'd finished, Irene and I, hadn't we?

Out from an office bounded my darling Jessie, more rapturous about this place than ever. In from the stables came Dorothy, a glow on her face too, and I could make out that she was not a little envious of her daughter.

"These are mine," I said to Irene. "Jessie, who'll be here in the fall if you'll have her. And Dorothy."

"Oh, we *must* have you," said the dean, shaking the hand of one and then the other.

"I knew Dean Fulbright in college." It felt like a confession.

"Can you believe I was his teacher?" she said.

"No," cried Jessie and Dorothy together.

EVEN IF the old bike shed had long since disappeared—where in a different lifetime I'd fiddled with ten-speeds and those upright English jobs the academics peddled as if they were in Oxford—the area around Hillbury has plenty of high-end cycling shops. It wasn't hard to scare up a distributor. I should have done it before. These frames I make are better than good. They're also more expensive than I have any right to ask, which only makes them hot in a place like California. And I was pushing the process along with some urgency.

Urgency.

Now that I'd be heading back out to the Bay on business anyway, just weeks after our family visit, I might as well hand-deliver Jessie's enrollment papers to the college. That's what I offered to Dorothy, ever so casual. It felt flagrant and mocking. It allowed me to feel worse about what I was up to.

Had I drawn a single breath without thinking about Irene Fulbright in the three weeks since we'd left Hillbury College? My chest started to tighten even before we made it back to the car. And ever since, I'd felt harassed, haunted, raked by my own desire to see her again. I couldn't let on, of course—how could I admit it to anyone? It was ludicrous, I admit. A man

my age. And what was I after? I don't think I could have told
you.

But everything else in my life seemed like shadows. I was
stumbling through the paces of my day distracted, easily annoyed—much the same as when Jessie was a newborn, a
preemie by a month, and there was so little sleep for either
Dorothy or me.

I'd never been unfaithful. It never occurred to me
other than in the most hypothetical way. I was so grateful to
Dorothy. We were a fine match from the start. And we had
such a good life, her allowing me to build my bikes while she
helped deliver other babies in the community hospital.

This time at least, because I had some warning, I gave her
some warning and called from the back room of a bike store
in San Carlos.

"What are you doing?" she demanded.

"I thought, since I'm out here on business, maybe we
could have dinner."

"You're kidding, right?"

Of all the responses I'd imagined, that wasn't one. "Not
actually."

Her exasperation only seemed more evident through
the phone. "Fine," she snapped. "I'll meet you in the city at
seven."

"Well, I have to drop off Jessie's papers anyway."

"Not on your life. Just give them to me at dinner. Seven."

One confession after another. That's what this feels like.
Here's another: sweaty, shaky, I felt nervous like I hadn't felt
since, when? College? Probably. I hadn't brought a tie—would
the place she picked demand a tie? Jesus.

I walked halfway across the city from my motel just to burn some time and I was still half an hour early. And the guy at the front desk, he laughed when I asked about a tie. This is California, he said. Still, there were plenty of guys at the bar in ties and the ones who weren't, well their clothes made it seem all right anyway. So I asked for a beer just to take the edge off. It was a bad idea. Made me sweat more and sat hard in my stomach.

I saw Irene coming toward me, and that's when I understood that she wasn't the same person I'd known. Just her stride—head up, confident, self-assured, take-no-prisoners. Compared to that vision of her in the dark corridor of the men's dormitory, a hood pulled over her head. She'd been *terrified*. Which I didn't comprehend either until this moment in a San Francisco restaurant a quarter century later.

What with ordering a glass of wine, a bottle of sparkling water, dealing with napkins and waiters, Irene was managing not to look at me. She wouldn't even glance my way. But none of it hid the scowl. Dark and ominous, it knit her brow, and I smiled, imagining I could spy the faint shadow of her carefully plucked eyebrows swooping toward each other as they had when she was young. That thought—the memory of who she had been and the awareness that she, we, were no longer young—let me breathe again for the first time in what seemed weeks. I almost laughed. I was that giddy, suddenly.

"This is nice," I said.

She shot me a hostile glance. "Nice," she said.

"Not just the restaurant. That too. Great place. You must have been here before? No, I mean seeing you again."

The glance scoured me. She didn't bother to speak this time.

My nervousness was gone. So, too, was the brief elation.

I buttered the edge of a bread stick, no easy feat with a frozen hand, and wondered what the hell I was doing here. And that's when I got a little angry too.

"Irene," I said. "I don't know why you're so pissed off. All I wanted was to see you again. You know, catch up some more. Have a meal."

She sighed with exasperation. "The catching up we needed we did already. It took all of five minutes. What more do you want to know? What more *is* there to know?"

I sat silently. We drank our wine. The service was slow.

"Jonathan." She gave another dramatic sigh. "Anyway, it's not you I'm angry at. It's me. It's not enough you show up and throw me back all those years—you've got me sneaking out to a secret rendezvous for chrissake. I hate it, not just the doing it but the wanting to."

"Could have fooled me."

"What the hell, Jonathan. What the hell."

It wasn't an evening of great conversation. For that matter, the rest of the meal sort of disappears. What I remember is the hotel room off Union Square. Actually, no, not the hotel or the room either, not from that night. And it wasn't so long ago.

What do I remember? The smells of her. The texture of a small knot of hair that had snagged around my finger. The taste of her hair, the salt and sour of her skin. I remember the surprise of tumbling together as if we'd been falling all this while, years and years, toward this moment.

We slept some. Must have done. Because it was five thirty and her jostling me. "Time," she said, and kissed me.

"Don't forget Jessie's papers," I murmured.

And then I'm lying there, alone and wrecked. Wrecked

like I hadn't been since lying in a VA bed after a year and seven months in the Delta. The shivers and shakes, the night sweats waking in the dark hospital ward—they were all worse than the hand itself, healing most of the way.

At the VA a sweet little nurse came along and helped me back to myself. We were married. I was happy, yes, I was. Happy as anyone has a right. Twenty-seven years' happy.

Happiness is good. It's precious. What could be more important?

And I'm lying in that San Francisco hotel room. Wrecked. Not happy. Happiness had nothing to do with it.

At twenty-one what did I know? We've already been through that. The answer, remember, is Nothing.

But feelings I had plenty, with raw desire a trump that tugged me and tossed me wherever it led. It led me to Nancy, and it led me to Irene.

Out in the Delta I was feeling plenty too, but not the same kind, that's for sure. Boredom. Is that a feeling? Yes. It is. You can suffocate with enough of it. And fear. Plenty of fear. Not much point in talking about that, except that it's real and hard as brass between your teeth. Allowed myself to be tugged and tossed some more too, in a down-and-dirty sort of way, on leave in Tokyo. Love? Yep, felt some out there. Though it's no good talking about that either, what you feel for a radio operator or a medic or the new guy whose name you don't know but gets sent to point first day and by that night he's being choppered away, what's left of him.

Then some time of not feeling very much at all.

Then twenty-seven years of happiness.

Here's the story. At last. It's me lying in that king-sized hotel bed. During the night some part of me had come unclasped.

After all those years. I lay scorched and exhausted, and I was so full of Irene Fulbright I felt like twenty-one again. Except with perspective now, and a kind of simple joy that I never had at twenty-one. How many people *ever* get to know? That's what I was wondering. I was lying there, panting again, itchy with hunger for her.

"Irene," I said.

"This isn't smart, calling me here," she whispered.

"You're in your office, right? Who's to know?"

"That's not the point."

"When can we get together—can you meet me tonight?"

"No, tonight won't work."

"Irene."

"Jonathan—what the hell are you doing? Don't you need to get home?"

Though it sounds stupid to admit, that stumped me. I didn't have a clue what I was doing.

"Jonathan?"

"Yeah?"

She sighed. "Okay. Okay. But this is not a good idea."

"Sure," I said.

Not a good idea sounded better than *Tonight won't work.*

I had plenty of time that day to think. Partly I was thinking about my unsupervised crew and about how many bike frames were actually being assembled and lugged, about the cost of the motel room (I'd paid for the one night in the Union Square hotel and checked out). Sure, I thought some about Dorothy too. I hadn't checked in with her for two days. Probably the longest stretch in all the time we'd been together. I don't think she'd have started worrying yet, but she'd guess that something was up. What makes it harder: I've never been able to lie to her. And telling the truth, well, it wasn't time for that. Sure, I felt guilty. But the guilt also seemed to stand off at some distance from me, something akin to the credit card tab I'd have to settle later.

I was also thinking about Irene. Couldn't stop thinking about her. The exertions of the night before had quenched nothing. The unclenching had only increased my hunger. If anything, I yearned for her more than ever.

I wanted to think about the future, but I couldn't make out the path more than a couple paces in front of me.

If she'd done it the night before, I wouldn't have been so surprised. But we'd agreed that I should gather a simple picnic, find a nice bottle to go with it, meet her in Golden Gate Park, a small knoll of grass she described precisely. I showed up early again. But that's me. And by the time she was an hour late and the sky was darkening, I'd eaten my share of the chicken and finished a fair bit of the merlot.

I guess she expected me to behave like an adult, take the cue, and go on home.

Why couldn't I do that? It would have been easier on my dignity, certainly now in the telling. Maybe the pattern had been set too long ago. What choice had I but to pursue her once more? At least this time finding her wasn't the challenge.

I even bought a tie so that when I showed up at her office next morning I wouldn't feel out of place. Hell, that and a denim shirt—clean and ironed—I figured I could pass for an academic. Irene's secretary, a black woman with her hair pulled back tight and wearing a charcoal suit, knew nothing. She only seemed surprised because I didn't have an appointment. I said I'd wait. I settled in another of those incredibly uncomfortable chairs in the outer office. There was plenty of reading material about the college. Jessie, my daughter, would be arriving here in a few months. I felt giddy and disoriented.

But I didn't have to wait long. Irene tried not to storm out toward me when her most recent appointment left her office, but she stormed out toward me, striding briskly, this big mask of a smile on her face that showed just how furious she was.

"Hi," I said with a shrug.

"Please, come on in," she smiled. "Would you like Charlene to get you a cup of coffee?"

"That would be great," I said.

But she slammed the door behind me.

"How could you come here?" she hissed, trying to keep her voice down.

I shrugged again and squirmed, but truth was I was so happy to see her and be hidden away in private like this, the two of us. "You must have forgotten we were going to meet down at the harbor. Yesterday."

"Jesus Christ, Jonathan. I didn't forget anything."

"Well, okay. Then what happened?"

Maybe it was my tone, but she turned icy. Which is what she wanted—it put her back in control. She turned away from me, walked to the other side of her desk, and settled in the high-backed leather chair. "Nothing happened. Or what happened happened the night before and it was a mistake. Surely you can see that." She might have been explaining some kind of demerit to a hapless student.

"Irene," I said, hapless and miserable.

That's enough—I don't have to do this. I'm not going to play out the rest of that scene because it's all so predictable—I understand that now, of course—and it's all so humiliating, for me. It would have been nobler not to have gone to see her, I suppose. It would have demonstrated my restraint and self-control. But at that moment, I didn't have any self-control. I just wanted, needed to see Irene Fulbright again. I guess I needed the sharp, nasty, humiliating scene in her office too.

After leaving the dean's office, I wandered across San Francisco for a day or two on foot. I had to keep moving because I blazed. That's the only way I can put it—I flamed with yearning for Irene Fulbright.

Notice, I'm not saying love. I'm no kid. I knew it wasn't that.

I wanted to *be* with her. I wanted to swallow her up.

I don't know what in god's name I wanted.

Except that I couldn't stop thinking about her. The way she'd been almost thirty years before, the way she'd been in the hotel a couple nights ago.

No, it wasn't that either: it went back to the first sight of her coming down the staircase in the college admissions building, her stumbling a little bit at the sight of *me*. It was as though she'd flicked a switch and this electric bolt rang along my spine. Thirty years' worth of desire was kindled. I was kindled.

If I'd been young, who knows, maybe I'd have laid siege to the college, battered her door with glorious, outlandish melodrama. I could have played music underneath her window and sung for her the way she once sang for me. There's an image.

Me, how the hell was I going to pluck a guitar?

I didn't have any illusions. Irene wouldn't hesitate, not long anyway, before ordering security to run me off the campus. Followed by a quick restraining order from the local magistrate.

Instead, I walked the city. At first I noticed almost nothing, the blaze was so fierce. I must have looked like one of those guys from when I'd hung here in that impossibly distant decade, the almost respectable, almost derelict loons, staggering about and endangering unsuspecting motorists. But as my lower back began to ache, and as the stabbing began high under my collarbone, and as my knees—they were feeling it too—began to stiffen, the blaze slowly faded. The fever passed and I came to myself. That's what it felt like. I found myself looking down into the branches of a very particular tree, with a very particular texture to its green leaves as it reached up to me on a hill above Golden Gate Park. I was just there again and Irene, she wasn't there. It was a clear, warm day. I noticed that. And if I felt weak and a little disoriented, and more than a little foolish, the fever had done me some good too. It had cleansed me, burning away an old skin. I fairly tingled.

Why can't I lie? I wish I could lie.

Dorothy nodded and turned away. She was already in her nursing uniform and in a hurry to get out the door. An extra hurry now that I'd told her. I'd flown the red-eye to Philadelphia and driven home directly. This world was just as I'd left it, Jessie off to school already, the dog walked, the house tidy, ready to be abandoned for the day. I stood in the kitchen but felt as if I were peering in through the screen door. I wanted back into my life.

If I couldn't lie, you know, make up a big, fat whopper of a tale and let it fly, there was no choice but the truth, all of it. So that's what I gave my Dorothy. She nodded, right? I could see the pain register in the corners of her eyes. The squint even though the room wasn't all that bright. But she didn't give away any surprise. And if there was pain in her lovely eyes, there was also a new hardness, a kind of shell. I wanted in there too, but she wouldn't let me.

"Mrs. Downey's baby is due," she said. "I've got to go."

I would have preferred some good yelling, a little clear rage. But that's not Dorothy.

I haven't gone into the shop yet—you can't call it a factory—that'll have to wait. The kitchen seems hard and cold, but that's where I'm best for now. I'm in a kind of limbo, not even probation, waiting for Dorothy to play the conversation out with herself.

And yet, and yet. I'm sitting on a straight-backed chair at my own table and I feel that I've come to the end of something. Chastened, I've caught up with myself at last.

CHILDREN OF GOD

A soccer ball lies in a dusty patch of the *maidan*. Even with a fresh scuff on one side, the blue panels are bright and the white ones glisten in the rare, sweet dew of the morning. Sandip Kumar, trudging hand in hand with his younger sister on one side and his father on the other, stares angrily at the ball. With a quick tug, he tries to escape. He wants to kick the ball so hard it will fly out of sight. He knows his family will never allow him to retrieve this ball, never pick it up with his hands even. The sweeper's boy, Ganga, has stolen it, has made it his own, playing with it.

Sandip's father squeezes the boy's fingers tight and hurries his children to the bus stop on the main road outside the Greater Kailash enclave. He doesn't notice the startling green of the short grass and high pipal trees. Early February, and the sky rings a deep blue, no shadow of the murderousness the sun will carry in six weeks. Buzzards have been chased away by flocks of small jade parakeets. Roses and poppy blooms explode. But if Kumar's children miss the school bus, he will have to drive them halfway across the city, a nightmare this time of morning.

Kumar hurries his children along too so that he will not give in to temptation and rage, not in front of them, and kick that bloody ball himself. Already this morning his coffee and newspaper have been spoiled because his wife forced him to lecture the second sweeper, Radha. The first time he has ever spoken to her directly. Perhaps the first time he has noticed her particular existence.

"Yesterday the ball was stolen from the boy's room," he said to her angrily but awkwardly. His Hindi is rusty and he suspected she couldn't understand anyway, terrified and barefoot in front of him, trembling, one hand clutching a strand of dirty *dupatta* in front of her face. Before him she cringed, panting or whining like one of the pariah dogs that also afflict the compound.

His wife could control herself no longer but rushed forward to shriek at the girl. "You have polluted the house, all of it. Shame. Shame. I will throw you in the alley dust where you come from. You will never sweep in GK again. Never. Listen to me—here you sweep bathroom and back hall only. You, we do not want you even to wash dirty clothes. You took the ball. We know you or your boy, this *badmash* Ganga, one of you stole it." Maya Kumar stood hands on hips, chin thrust forward like an angry wasp.

"Enough," Kumar growled. His wife's anger had annoyed him. It spoiled his coffee and *Hindustan Times*. Such village notions of caste and pollution matter only to her and her mother. But stealing he cannot ignore, and for the neighbors' sake as well, he must save face. "One chance more, that is all. You hear? Anything else disappears, I will summon the police. I will smile when they break a *lathi* on your back. And the

boy—no more of him, your *badmash* boy. You understand?
He is dirty and smells bad. He is too old to follow you. If I
see him again, both of you will leave, both." Sighing, he tossed
the napkin onto his plate—his wife knew this would mean ill
temper for the day—and stormed out to gather the children.

The little terrier bitch, set off by such commotion, was
yapping and yapping on the flagstone porch, where a leather
leash bound her to the iron fence. So nervous was the *mali* at
all the shouting and barking and fury that as he heaved his
heavy water bucket from pot to pot on the porch, watering
the family's plants, his bare feet slipped on wet stone. The
bucket flew into a wall. A small tree capsized. Water tumbled
across the porch. The *mali* slapped helplessly at it. As the
flood crept toward the front gate, the terrier's yapping grew
fierce and hysterical. Kumar, dragging the children toward the
bus, sloshed through the water, shoved the dog aside with half
a kick, charged ahead into the narrow street. A *subji* wallah was
pushing his cart along the pavement, singing his tomatoes and
onions, but this Kumar failed to notice as well as he brushed
past.

One by one, in clusters of two and three, children drift toward
the playground on the *maidan*. They are sleepy still, not too
hungry yet. A few wear sweaters or vests discarded by their
mother's employers, but their legs and feet are cold in the
damp grass and dirt. For now the playground is theirs. They
claim it. The boys see the soccer ball. It belongs to them now
too. The others will never want it back. All night they dared
leave it here so no one boy will claim it, and in the grass it still
lies waiting for them. They smile and spit. Ganga, Radha's
son, eyes his trophy but veers away. Flirting close then swerv-
ing away. Toying.

They are watching the ball and each other watching the ball, and they do not yet notice another boy who is strolling on the pavement with his *ayah*. The stranger spots the all-but-new ball and tugs free of Jaya's fingers. The playground is safe—no cars allowed—and she is bored and sleepy. This boy heads directly to the ball, steps on it lightly, and rolls it under his foot. With a sharp stab, he kicks it across the grass to the other children, who are now staring at him.

Ganga snares the skidding ball with his foot but stares at the *ferengi* shyly, uncertainly. He is very beautiful, this visitor, with shaggy hair—shaggier even than Ganga's—hair so white it seems to have no color at all. A color that hurts the eye. And *his* eyes are blue and smiling.

But the smile is also a taunt, open and daring. Ganga sends the ball spinning back, but already the other boy, Daniel Ash, is walking toward him.

The *ayah* cries after him. "No, no, Danny sir, no—please. These are not children for friends. They are not to play with." Jaya dashes forward a few steps—far enough to satisfy her sense of duty—and settles on a bench to watch as necessary.

The other children draw farther away. What does this stranger want? Whatever it may be, will they be beaten? Their eyes are dark and suspicious but glint with flashes of longing too. They retreat across the grass. A small pack of boys hunkers on their heels in a patch of dust near the swing set, ragged brown shawls wrapped around them chin to toe.

Only Ganga does not flee. He wants to flee, to fly away, but the taunting grin of the stranger holds him in place, hardly allows him to breathe.

Daniel dribbles the ball steadily toward the Indian boy. He pushes it right up to Ganga's bare foot.

After a long moment, the foreigner draws the ball back

with his toe. "Jeez," he says aloud, and with a quick punch sends it spinning away toward the fence. Without another glance at Ganga, he sets off to explore the playground. Ganga trails along behind. The other servant children scatter away before him, then cluster once more like another flock of small parakeets, this a drab, ragged band.

The swings are lashed together. Only later in the afternoon will the large padlock be removed. But Daniel grabs the bar of a red whirl-around, dented along the rim, and trots in the dusty rut. The whirl-around spins reluctantly, then faster and faster. His head tilts back, his white hair flying, eyes closed, smiling dreamily. The whirl-around tilts too, slightly askew like a top that has never quite managed to topple. Daniel leaps onto it, and for a few rotations the whirl-around carries him.

Grinning mischievously, he waves at Ganga. "Come on!" he cries. The other boy hesitates but doesn't need to know the words, then runs and leaps onto the metal. Daniel pushes again with his left foot, driving them both, faster and faster. Off he jumps, catches himself, and continues to push the whirl-around with both hands as it flies by.

Still aboard, Ganga holds tight, his face revealing nothing. But he's scared. Not of the whirl-around. Long master of this toy, he can fly clear whenever he wishes. But the *ferengi* boy— Ganga is drawn to him and afraid of him. He recognizes mischief and power. The boy has snatched the ball from him as easily as he himself crept after his mother into a house yesterday and smuggled it free—soiling it forever—from Sandip Kumar.

By five o'clock the afternoon is cooling once more. The morning's children disappear like smoke from the *maidan*. They have retreated to the safety of the alleys and the tight fists of shacks that gird GK like a coarse rind of some desert fruit. Only Daniel Ash wanders slowly across the grass, dribbling the soccer ball in boredom. He insisted that Jaya bring him here again after a nap in the afternoon heat. Both his parents are working, but they haven't yet found a private Indian school that will admit him this late in the year.

From the mouth of an alley behind the small temple, cloaked by shadows, Ganga sits and watches.

Soon other children appear still wearing school uniforms, drifting in from all sides, loud, bursting with laughter, claiming the playground as their own, girls curled tight in conversation, boys jostling each other and tossing cricket balls from hand to hand. Servants release the swings. The seesaw is unlocked too.

None of the children will give away the secret right off, but all have noticed the blond stranger. Like a breeze, whispers spread the word through GK before most of them have even reached the fence. Shyly, they study him from the corners of their eyes.

Of them he seems oblivious—worse, he is indifferent. The ball alone occupies him. Bored, irritated, he scuffs it into the hard-packed dirt near the pavement. In fact, Daniel is very well aware of the others, aware that they are watching him, whispering about him. Why does everyone here *notice* him? Everywhere his parents have dragged him, to offices and shops and homes of their friends, people grin at Daniel, they stare at him and pinch and squeeze, offer candies, will never, never leave him alone or stop watching.

Sandip Kumar is among the last to arrive, and he strides directly up to Daniel. The other children fall silent in astonishment. This is not the Sandip they know, a quiet, sulky boy who pouts and stares at the rest of them. But Sandip and Daniel have already met—their families have spent an evening in the same room—because the Ash family is renting the house next to the Kumars'. It belonged to Sandip's grandparents, but not long ago his Babu died and Grandmother moved in with them, sealing herself in a white sari alone on the upper floor.

"That's my ball," he says with a shrug, hands in the pockets of his navy blue shorts.

"Yeah?" says Daniel with a shrug of his own. With the outside of his foot, he nudges it indifferently toward him. Sandip hesitates.

"Sandip, no, no—you mustn't," scolds his sister, who has been eyeing them enviously. Uma makes a face. But she replaces it at once with a flirtatious grin for the blond boy who now lives next door.

"You can have it," Sandip says with a sigh. "I'm not allowed to anymore."

"How come?" says Daniel with fresh interest.

"They stole it from my room, one of them did, and Papa will not allow me to touch it."

Daniel says nothing, but he taps the ball again toward Sandip. Perhaps he hasn't understood. Perhaps it's a challenge, a test.

Sandip is tempted. Beaten and bruised, the ball still draws him. But he knows Uma is watching and will happily report to Papa. But why, he wonders, can this American play with the ball so easily? Will he get in trouble? Will this mean that now they will not be able to play with him, that he, too, has been soiled by the contact? Must he go through a cleansing at the temple?

Even as the thought occurs to him, he knows that none of this will happen, that touching the ball makes no difference for the American. The rules are different. This boy can be polluted and it will not matter. Papa is also pleased to have the money for rent. And more: renting to an American family, all but having them live in your own house, this brings glory that thrills his mother and sister. The rules are different and he resents it.

Daniel senses something of this as well. With that mischievous smile, he picks the ball up in his hands, tosses it spinning high in the air, and catches it. He punts it, high again, higher and higher, until it lands in the grass twenty yards away, children scattering away from its reach. The boy hiding behind the temple rises off his haunches, tempted to dart out and capture the ball again.

"Ganga." His mother hisses from behind, slaps at his head, catches him by the ear. He casts one last glance at the *ferengi,* and then the pain from his mother's clutch whips him deeper into the alley.

Next morning, as Daniel is heading through the back hallway from his bedroom, a heavy booming blow strikes the metal door onto the alley. His mother fumbles to unbolt and unlock the door, and tugs it open for Radha, who comes to sweep the bathroom and this hallway as part of the arrangement with the Kumars. She leaves her plastic sandals on the stone threshold and pads into the hall. Already the small, wiry woman is chattering endlessly to Daniel's mother, who, because of her professional studies, speaks Hindi. Daniel, hardly noticing, now notices the Indian boy from yesterday morning squatting patiently on his haunches in the alley, a ragged brown shawl drawn tight around him against the cold, as the door swings shut once more. Not for a moment does Daniel doubt that the boy is waiting and watching for him.

He hurries into the family living room and shoves one spoonful after another of American cornflakes and milk into his mouth. Jaya, the *ayah,* hovers at his shoulder, making a show of such attention for the boy's parents as they rush about, dressing and snatching up papers and briefcases in preparation for work. Soon they have departed and Jaya's attentions, too, have wandered.

Daniel slips away into the back hall once more. Jaya, having switched on the small TV to a Hindi movie, will assume he has gone to the toilet or into his bedroom. Radha is scrubbing the stone floor of the bath, and Daniel quietly sneaks past. The heavy door is bolted again but not locked. Carefully, stealthily, he swings the bolt up and pushes it forward. The door creaks open. He draws it shut behind him, and suddenly he is surrounded by high walls and barbed wire and packed dirt ruts, a world behind Greater Kailash. Two paces away the Indian boy is watching him. He hasn't moved. He isn't smiling. Daniel, fighting not to shiver in the cold, hunkers down next to the boy and doesn't smile either.

A fire of twigs and dung flickers a few yards away. An old man is warming himself, lean shanks thrust nearly into the kindling. Daniel nods at it. Ganga hesitates, but the other rises and heads to the small blaze. The smoke is heavy, the air hard to breathe, but a dull warmth does hover close. Daniel squats. The old man, chewing toothlessly at something invisible, eyes him but doesn't move or speak.

Soon Daniel has soaked enough warmth or grown used to the chill and he rises. Without a sound, Ganga sets off and Daniel follows him deeper into the maze. They turn a corner, two, coming upon other fires scattered here and there. Each bend of walls and dust is all but identical. Disoriented, Daniel coughs, looks back, sees nothing familiar or singular. A heavy cloud of coarse smoke leans on everything. He has no idea where the Indian boy is leading him, what there is to show, but he eagerly follows as if to discover some potent secret he will never find on his own.

Ganga has no particular destination in mind. All he yearned for this morning was a glimpse of the white-haired *ferengi* boy—he never expected him to enter his world, couldn't even dare hope it.

Together they wander past a cluster of shacks backed against a concrete wall that bends in an arc for a hundred paces. On the other side is a sewer trench. In this cold weather, the stench is muted, cloaked by the ever-present smoke as well. Each hut is patched out of mud and cardboard and scraps of corrugated tin, including the one where Ganga and his mother live. He wonders whether the *ferengi* boy will sense anything, will want to see. But Daniel is watching everything carefully without seeing, without sensing, and Ganga suddenly does not want to draw him into the darkness of their hut, to show him they have nothing to offer, not even chai, with his mother off working at this hour. He's imagined sharing his secret treasure of pins and pens, half-smoked cigarettes, and the tiny glass bottles he's collected, one way or another, and hides in a box tucked behind a mat at the wall. But now he realizes this, too, is impossible.

A peacock hen screeches invisibly, startling Daniel. He trots around the corner and discovers several birds scratching in the dust, pecking at a small roost of garbage dropped next to an anonymous door. A male spreads its wings and lifts heavily to a rooftop overhead. Delighted, Daniel waves to his friend. Ganga follows but doesn't understand what the *ferengi* is upset about.

Ahead on the path, he spies two of his friends hunched

intently. He almost pats the stranger's arm but hasn't the courage, doesn't know what the response will be. Will he be beaten for risking a touch? Phlegm gathers in his throat at the thought, and he spits heavily at a wall. But Daniel has spotted the other boys too. He tugs at Ganga's thin shawl (Ganga grins to be answered so quickly, a thrill shooting through him, but the other boy doesn't notice), and they hurry to find out what in the dust is worthy of such attention.

Ganga's friends are squatting on their heels, one wearing a blue sweater vest with a wide gash at the shoulder. The other's brown shawl, identical to Ganga's, is wound tightly about his shoulders and knees. Only his dark eyes move. They are quick and alert. Beneath them, a butterfly swatch of pink skin, a birthmark or scar, stretches from cheek to cheek across his nose as if the top layer has been seared away.

Blue sweater has a stick. He jabs it into the jowl of the pariah dog, which isn't quite dead at their feet. It twitches, muscles pricking involuntarily. Its eyes are crusted shut. Scabs cover much of its lean gray body.

Daniel watches, horrified and slightly sick to his stomach, fascinated. Again blue sweater stabs with indifferent cruelty. No twitch this time, no sigh, nothing. Between one torment and the next, death has worked its transformation. No pretense remains that what lies before them is anything more than loosely gathered sticks covered by a stained rag.

For the first time, the boy with the butterfly mask moves, a hand appearing from beneath his shawl to grab one of the dog's hind legs. Without a word or sound, he rises and sets off down the alley, dragging the carcass behind him with some matter-of-fact purpose that is all mystery to Daniel. Blue sweater follows lackadaisically.

Ganga watches his guest, uncertain. Daniel is uncertain too—he is sickened and excited all at once. He knows he has witnessed something as ordinary as the dust and smoke about them, and yet it is disturbing, thrilling. He would like to see more, but he doesn't know what and he doesn't know how to ask. He turns his eyes to the other boy, who wags his head from side to side reassuringly, imploringly.

Still unable to fathom the stranger's reaction or desires, Ganga sets off down another alley. Without warning, they emerge abruptly behind the temple and onto the small *maidan* of Greater Kailash. The *subji* wallah brushes past Daniel, pushing his wooden cart on the cracked pavement toward the next row of houses. His tomatoes, eggplants, and onions glisten red and purple and green in the morning light.

Startled, Daniel feels more disoriented than in the maze of alleys. Haven't they wandered leagues and eons from this life? Can reappearing be so easy?

Ganga has reclaimed the blue-and-white soccer ball. Its sheen is fading, but he feels they are on safe ground once more, as if the familiarity of yesterday's game reestablishes the harmony of the universe. The ball scuds toward the blond boy. Soon Daniel will return to his house, where Jaya will shriek and sob and say never a word to his parents about his disappearance, her terrible failure. This already he counts on.

By the middle of the afternoon, Sandip Kumar's mother has already heard the tale, and the moment he returns from school, she sets upon him with a flurry of outrage and dire warnings. He grimaces as he drinks his cup of milk, listening to her all the while, his dark eyes narrowed to sullen slits, his head drooping.

Before he even reaches the playground, he spies the American boy besieged, nearly overwhelmed by the children of GK. Shy hesitation has disappeared today. The girls, all of them wearing Western skirts, are coyly holding hands with each other and offering this visitor sweets. Their brothers race about, kicking the blue-and-white soccer ball as if they're innocent of its history. Yet for all their flailing and shouting, they never stray far—without ever quite looking at him, they hope to lure the American boy into their game.

Sandip's fists clench in the pockets of his shorts. "You mustn't play with those servant children," he shouts glumly.

Daniel stares at him. "Why not?"

"You just mustn't. They're dirty; they cheat and steal."

The ball skids close by and Daniel's foot snares it. He picks the ball up and shoves it at Sandip. In that instant Sandip sees that the boy's blue eyes have flared with hate. Regret and longing fill his throat and turn swiftly to bile, to ashes. He can hate too, and the surge of it releases him. Sandip lets the ball drop to the ground, but kicks it cleanly to Vijay Singh and joins the game. The American runs as well, swept up in the shouts and passing, and tumbles in grass and dust, the hatred a secret pact between the two.

As dusk gathers, as mothers and servants call the children to dinner, as Uma gives up trying to tug Sandip away, as Jaya goes to fetch Daniel's father to order his boy home in turn, for a long, oddly quiet moment only the two of them are left on the darkened *maidan*. Sandip says nothing, makes no gesture. He stoops to pick up the ball and bears it closer to the other's face. As Daniel watches, wary, the Indian boy pulls a small clasp knife from his pocket. With a quick thrust, he stabs the leather and the ball sighs. Sandip rips hard with the blade, widening the gash into a nasty grin. He flings the suddenly heavy, lifeless ball toward the alley behind the temple. It thuds with a halfhearted bounce and lies still. Daniel says nothing. Chilled to the bone, he turns away and trudges home. The evening has suddenly grown too dark to make out whether anyone else has seen.

Already Daniel and his parents have grown used to the startling variety and volume of sounds rising in the narrow streets of Greater Kailash, the car horns and cries of beggars and peacocks and always more horn blasts. Yet the wailing and raging shouts that wake them early next morning are too alarming, too close at hand to ignore. Daniel's father tugs the front door open, but it is Daniel who slips out first and peers through the fence that separates them from the Kumars. All there is bedlam. Uma is sitting on the stone porch weeping. Maya Kumar shrieks and wails, her hair loose, hysterical. Sandip stands brooding and sour as he watches his father angrily saw with a kitchen knife at a leather strap. Someone has wound it around the top of their iron fence. It is stretched tight—this is why Kumar must struggle to get a clear angle with the blade—around the throat of their terrier. Its limp body hangs five feet above the flagstones, tongue swollen, eyes abulge at nothing.

Daniel's father, a step slower in recognition, stiffens abruptly and roughly tugs his son away from the fence, herding him back into the house they are renting. Much as he and his wife have wanted their son to experience the real India, not some sanitized version created for tourists and diplomats, he hopes to protect the boy from such sights as this. But Daniel, sensing his father's impulse, knows it is too late. Two days have sped him along, forced him like a winter flower. He is much older now, unshockable he thinks, almost a different person. He nearly pats his father on the arm—he imagines doing it—to reassure him.

The day is long and quiet. Daniel's parents have delayed going to work. The incident next door, nothing so horrible in itself really, has upset their equilibrium. Daniel hears them making plans at the small dining table. Perhaps the Embassy School is the best option after all. Political friends can use their influence to find or create a place for him there even at this late date. Jaya trails after him throughout the house. She will hardly let him out of her sight this morning, especially with her employers at home. No Hindi movies for her today.

No thumping on the alley door either. This morning Radha never arrives to sweep. When Sara Ash inquires next door—she has wanted to go anyway, to offer sympathy and any help—Maya Kumar tells her (in Hindi because she remains shaken, nervous, on the verge of tears and rage) that Radha has disappeared, that she's probably returned to her village for some festival or family matter. They will find another sweeper.

When Sara passes the news on to Daniel—also that Uma and Sandip have been kept home from school as well, perhaps they can play later in the day—his heart sinks. His friend will have gone with his mother. Yet it occurs to him that returning to their village is perhaps a wise course. He nods to himself. The momentum of desire and violence that gathered so quickly and now has broken like a powerful wave across three families scares him.

"He is the one, your *friend*," Sandip says bitterly. "He tortured our little dog to death. No doubt of it."

Daniel doesn't reply. What can he say?

The two boys are trudging across the *maidan*, brought here by mother and *ayah* as if this is their hearts' desire and worth any sacrifice. Middle of the afternoon: the playground is deserted, one universe of children already fled, the other not yet arrived. Before they are aware of it, the two almost tread on the sunken shell of the soccer ball. It remains where it landed the day before. But the ripped leather has quickly turned gray and stiff, as if before long it will disappear into the soil in the natural course of life and death. The two of them veer abruptly aside.

Walking with the American so close, almost hand in hand, Sandip is aflame with longing and anger. He wanted to be friends with this strange boy, to run his hands through the golden-white hair. He would have shown him secrets and been rewarded with friendship. But Daniel Ash has rejected him for Radha's son—untouchable, wild, dirty—a thief he will become or a *badmash* altogether.

What did the two of them do while he was in school? What had the devil boy shown him? Sandip pictures the brown hands and long fingers caressing the soccer ball, *his* soccer ball, and a cold rage sweeps over him again—a sour triumph, too, as he remembers gutting the ball with his knife. He wishes, yes, he could stab this golden boy, hurt him, open his flesh so he will sigh like the ball and bleed into the earth. So caught up in the fury and the vision is Sandip that he trembles invisibly. His teeth are chattering. He glances at Daniel Ash, afraid the give-away clatter may be audible. But the American boy is caught up in his own thoughts, hearing nothing—which only enrages Sandip still more.

Reluctantly they arrive at the whirl-around. Neither puts a hand on the bar to spin and bring it to life, no matter that the

adults wish them to play. They stand in the dust, staring awkwardly at the tilted, dusty toy, their heads bowed, as if joined
in close accord. Suddenly both glance up, sensing something,
startled, as if a high whistle pierces the air, one only they can
hear. Together they spy a flash of cloth in the mouth of the
alley behind the little temple, a blur of browns. Daniel's eyes
open wide. Sandip's darken. His fists tighten in the pockets of
his shorts.

But no one appears. The two boys linger on the *maidan* as
the other GK children arrive after school to shout and run
and play, into lingering twilight, resisting the first calls for dinner. At last, still together, they drift toward their side-by-side
houses. They have hardly spoken in these several hours, and
yet, taste of tarnished metal on their tongues, they have com-
muned after all: resentments and angers ache into clenched
teeth. They understand each other now.

Daniel is restless. He paces through the small hallways of the
house, his face hot, his feet cold. After a dinner of eggplant,
rice, and chapatis prepared by Jaya that he hardly touches, his
mother asks him several times what is wrong. His father
finally snaps at him when Daniel knocks a small wooden
Ganesh onto the floor. What can he say? How can he explain?
It's impossible. "I'm sorry," he murmurs under his breath, and
retreats to his room. "Get some sleep," his dad calls after him.
"You've got school tomorrow. You obviously need it."

Daniel hears a light tapping at the door and his heart leaps.
He slips on his bathroom sandals and races out of his room.
But it is the front door that Jaya has already tugged open, so
he knows it will not be Ganga. To his surprise, Sandip peers
in, gesturing to him as if Jaya is not even there. This time

Daniel thinks to grab the shawl his mother bought him, and reluctantly, curious, follows him out into the chilly morning.

Without a word, hardly bothering to notice him, Sandip leads quickly on. He turns a corner and then another, and suddenly they are in the alley. Daniel is surprised by how well the wealthy boy seems to know the alley world, how confident and comfortable he appears, as if the Kumars own it too. He glances over his shoulder just in time to see Radha bang on a heavy door, which opens to admit her. It may be the Kumars' or some other house entirely, but clearly she has not fled to her village after all. She kicks her plastic sandals into the entryway and bangs the door shut behind her.

Already Daniel is lost once more and disoriented. He must put his faith in Sandip—this he doesn't like. The sun hasn't risen high enough to peek over walls in this maze, and the smoke from countless small fires is thick and acrid. Daniel's eyes sting.

With the muted stink of a sewer as marker, he recognizes a long, sagging stone wall. Ahead in the dust, two boys are squatting intently over something. He can't be sure they are the same two he saw when Ganga was his guide, not until he makes out a ripped blue vest. The other's brown shawl hides everything but his eyes and a butterfly scar, pink across his cheeks. To their side a small fire of twigs and dung smokes a dull blaze. Between them in the dust lies another collapsed bundle.

Daniel knows at once, knows bone deep before he can even make it out distinctly, though crumpled on the ground, Ganga is hardly a greater bag of broken sticks than the dying dog. Clumps of hair have been torn from his scalp. He eyes are swollen shut and his lips are bleeding. He is panting lightly, each breath racking him. Instead of gouging with a stick, the two other boys have brought water and are clumsily bathing his face with a scrap of cloth. They glare fiercely at Daniel when he draws close, as if he is somehow to blame.

He stops short, sickened, angry. Is this my fault? he wonders.

Furious, he spins round, ready to fight, to lash out with fists, to bite and kick and shout. But Sandip has already abandoned him. He is striding away quickly, hands driven deep in the pockets of his shorts, his shoulders hunched. Two older boys, teenagers who work for Kumar, have fallen in behind Sandip, slouching along like trained dogs. In another moment, all three have disappeared.

Awash in anger and regret and dismay, Daniel is breathing hard, close to tears. Even if he wanted to follow, it is too late.

The chill of the morning cools him, chills him, and he hugs himself. The labyrinth resists his gaze. He is not sure whether to go right or left or keep true ahead. Once more he has the feeling that he's aged decades in a few hours. Yet he also feels alone, more alone than ever before. Not scared. No. Sadder, lonely, but not scared. There will be no explaining this to his parents. Not what happened, but how it's changed him. Will they even notice, since it's all inside, that he's not the same boy?

The first step lies before him, through the dust and smoke of the Greater Kailash alleys, to find his way home.

YEAR OF FIRE

On a slow night, a warm night, Natalie would perch on her bar stool, propping first one foot and then the other on the next stool over. It was a different pair of stiletto heels each night of the week. She'd rotate through them, gold to lipstick red to candy pink. So she'd be leaning forward, foot cocked precariously as she touched up her nails (which already matched the shoes du jour). And since it was a warm night and she was between sets anyway and there were no customers to flirt into buying her the Fox Hole's version of champagne, she'd let her blouse hang open. You might could see through it all buttoned up, she'd say, but it sure weren't no friend to any breeze that way.

Duncan Boothe was tending bar and his wife had left him and he was doing his best simply to wipe down the bar and clean a glass or two and try not to stare or imagine what he could be doing with Natalie. On one of those nights early on—he'd only been at the Fox Hole for a month—Natalie shook her head and laughed.

"Shoot," she said. "You're a cute guy, Duncan, you sure are. Sweet too. I'd take that problem off your hands—the one in front of you—but then I'd have to be helping out the other guys who work here. Know what I mean?"

He nodded, frozen but his face hot, wondering how she'd made out the problem, what with the bar between them. And sweet he didn't feel.

"It's the funniest damn thing, the way you boys go ape over a girl's boobs." She was shaking her head again, thoughtfully. "Never made any sense to me, but I guess I can't complain. Not for that, I'd be working with my dad over at the Six Mile Ford plant. Most likely I'll wind up there anyhow, once they've dropped." Most all of Natalie's sentences lilted up at the end as if she were asking a question. "Fatty tissue—that's all they are, you know? Just sacks of fatty tissue. I learned that in junior high. In Roanoke, before we moved up here for the work."

Duncan was still nodding. But after a while, when he realized what she'd done, he was grateful to her. She'd set him free. *Fatty tissue*—it's all he needed. For the rest of that year, he was able to spend four nights a week with Natalie and her friends without wrestling that particular problem, most of the time.

Later that same night, she came back to him and his problems. "So why'd your wife go and leave you? What was her name?" She dragged deep at her cigarette. "Ginny, wasn't that it?"

"Jenny," he said.

"Yeah. Ginny. You all must have been fighting bad. You didn't smack her, did you?" Natalie looked him up and down. "No, you ain't the type. I *know* the type."

She knew the type. Twenty-four, two kids, her second husband already flung free. Duncan had gotten some of her story already. But how did she come to hear about Ginny/ Jenny? Had he let something slip? Since when had he become the object of study? It made him plenty uneasy, the tables turned.

HE DIDN'T have the Fox Hole in mind when he launched his first clumsy researches by wandering down to Eight Mile Road and Woodward Avenue a few weeks earlier. But Jennifer had already decamped; his classes at Kingsmount Academy wouldn't resume before Labor Day; he wasn't writing poetry, or nothing but crap. So when a faint flutter of inspiration tickled him, bourbon-induced or not, he figured there was time to kill and nothing to lose. A book: that's what he could do. It would be an exposé of sorts. Not literature. Something more journalistic, about life in a bar like this and the girls who worked there, and the guys who drank there, and maybe something about what the life in the bar could say about life in a city that had just torn itself apart. Who knew, it might even make him some money. Teaching in a private school paid nothing, and his family, the Boothes, had ceased supplementing his income months before.

Eight Mile was where the city ended and the suburbs began. Those couple of blocks along Woodward Avenue, the main north–south artery, were a kind of no-man's-and-everyman's-land of liquor stores and strip joints, cheap motels and, on the other side of the avenue, a sprawling public cemetery. Up until that summer, most of the traffic headed south from the still-sparse suburbs to the professional buildings downtown and to auto plants across the city, to the Grand Circus Theater for a movie, to Greektown and to Hamtramck for Polish pizza. But one July morning, the traffic jolted to a halt in amazement and terror and then fled, once and forever, in the other direction. Caught up in the sharp tidal surge, other white families who still lived in the city followed swiftly behind, away from the riots that over several days had burned out great swaths of the old black neighborhoods.

In the wee small hours of that first morning, the cops had raided a blind pig, one of those unlicensed neighborhood joints for drinking and playing cards. It wasn't a big deal to begin with—those raids happened most every night. But this one went wrong—white cops bungling and then shooting to cover it up. The city exploded. Who would have guessed it had been seething with black anger and despair for months and years? Not the police apparently.

Not Duncan Boothe. A straight drag fifteen miles up Woodward, Kingsmount Academy might have been on another planet. What did any of this horror have to do with the handful of faculty and their families who remained on the sprawling estate through the summer? Along with the others, Duncan and Jenny followed reports of the riots on one of the school's big black-and-white television consoles, witnessing the chaos and destruction on the tube like the rest of the nation. It was distant, the burning city, remote. Yet it was also so disorienting—this was *their* city after all, not Newark or Watts. Like everyone else, downtown was where they shopped, stood in line for new movies, ate Chinese egg foo yong, watched the Tigers play ball.

It was as if the napalm flames half a world away in Vietnam, which they'd also been witnessing on television, had suddenly burst from the safe quarantine of the box before them. Duncan had been living in dread of Vietnam, afraid of a plunge into its swamps and tunnels and firefights against his will. This is what kept him yoked to teaching at the school, where his family's local influence had managed, so far, to re-place his college deferment. Which meant that Duncan had his own full measure of anger and despair.

The burning city seemed sinister and fascinating, impos-sibly distant and yet near at hand, and somehow it just didn't feel real.

Except that Michael Rosen, about to be a senior at Kings-mount, lived with his mother not so far from downtown. Early that same first morning of the disturbances, he'd jour-neyed by bus, only slightly ahead of the crest of violence and its faster-spreading repercussions, up to the school library for what was to have been a single summer's day—he was giving Jenny Boothe a hand with new entries in the card catalog. It was Jennifer, hearing the news first from an English teacher who rushed in to share and then on her radio in the small of-fice off the main reading room, who called Michael from the card catalog to listen with her. Together, silent, heads bowed, they followed the early reports.

His neighborhood was a mix of elderly Jews and recently arrived blacks, and it wasn't all that far from Twelfth Street and the fires that were creeping from charred block to block, with invisible snipers on the roofs, with milling, angry crowds shouting at the cops when they weren't looting, weren't dying. Michael's mother was trapped there, or more likely in the hos-pital where she was a delivery-room nurse. They couldn't get any word. Again and again he dialed the heavy black tele-phone on Jenny's desk, only to be met with the grating signal for tangled circuits or, more disconcerting, merely a hollow silence. Nor was there any way to slip past the National Guardsmen ringing the city like a tourniquet and find his mother for himself. Not that Jenny would let him try. A couple of times he threatened to set out on his own. But the buses had ceased running after several were seized, burned, their stricken hulks dragged into barricades. He had no car of course. Jenny would have wrestled him to the ground in any event. Michael had no doubt of that and neither did her husband.

So they took him in for the time being. It was true that their cottage at one end of Faculty Row was dark and cramped at the best of times. Duncan was certain that had they asked the headmaster, Henry Hopkins, he would have made a place in the empty dorms for one of the school's star pupils. But Jennifer wouldn't have it. She and the boy had become friends over the past couple of years. In between classes he would drift into the library's office and they'd chat about this and that. After a while he even managed to satisfy his daily work duty—each Kingsmount student, no matter how privileged, had some such responsibility—by shelving books or reading the stacks. Jennifer wasn't about to abandon Michael Rosen to an empty dorm, not knowing whether his mother was safe, not knowing whether his house would survive. So in the late afternoon, the three of them hiked to Faculty Row together. As they entered the home, even before starting dinner, she tucked some sheets into the couch and strung a blanket across a line in the small living room as a measure of privacy for the boy.

DUNCAN HAD stumbled in on them once, a year or so earlier. Jennifer and the boy were sitting face-to-face in her office, next to the leaded windows overlooking the quad. Deep in conversation, they flustered when Duncan appeared through the door, as if they'd forgotten where they were, as if he'd caught them at something. And, yes, a pang of resentment—

of raw jealousy—did flare in his throat and chest and thighs. Because they were intimate, this sixteen- or seventeen-year-old boy and Jenny, twenty-four or twenty-five herself. Michael was pale, tall and rail thin, gawky, with a big head and a shock of dark hair and dark deep-set eyes. Jennifer's reddish blond hair was gathered back in a haphazard ponytail, stray wisps defying any rubber band. She had a broad face, lightly freckled, a pixieish nose, and grayish blue eyes that at that moment with Michael, seemed full of warmth and gaiety. And without seeing it, he knew she had a little cleft, an ancient small scar on her upper lip. It was that tiny flaw that Duncan had never had an answer to. It had slain him in college, overcoming Jenny's steelworking father in Ohio and her impatience with his own lack of either an ability to do hard work or a clear ambition toward something else.

They, Jenny and the boy, were intimate but not sexual. Duncan knew that. Sex was never the issue. He understood it thoroughly and almost wished it weren't true—that they'd trespassed in that more predictable way so he could at least possess that to lord over them. Because jealous he was. When had Jenny and he last shared that kind of intimacy?

"Are your grades so good you can afford to skip study hall, Mr. Rosen?" he demanded, sounding every bit as mean as he felt.

Startled, blushing furiously, the boy gangled to his feet and fled, glad to get away.

"He *adores* you, Duncan. Why can't you see that?" Jennifer said.

The truth of this was not a surprise. Over the past couple of years, Michael had signed up for any course of Duncan's that was available, from poetry to journalism to the Victorian novel. He'd done very well and his grades reflected it. But there was something more about the boy, a neediness, a hanging on every word, that Duncan found distasteful. He supposed the boy was looking for a father figure or at least an older brother. But that wasn't a role he sought. It demanded too much. Kingsmount didn't pay Duncan enough. Why not let Jennifer do that too, he thought bitterly.

"Adoration's not what I need," he snapped, mean again and sad and wanting to reach out to her and just not able to.

Afterward, a day or two later while he was marking some papers at the kitchen table, Duncan realized what it was he'd also spied in that instant of bursting in on them quite unintentionally—what it was they shared. The insight struck with a marrow-numbing clarity. So obvious, how had he not seen, not understood this before? Jenny and Michael were bound to each other precisely because they both felt like outsiders at Kingsmount. They didn't belong, didn't fit in, no matter how hard they tried. (Unlike him, Duncan Boothe, scion of the founding family.) Bound by this burden, they'd adopted each other. Yet—and here was the irony—the boy wanted desperately to belong. Not Jenny. She'd never felt at home.

At Princeton she'd been foolish enough to believe Duncan's impersonation of a poet—one of the roles he'd inhabited over the years. He grew his hair long, let his Brooks Brothers collars fray. He played acoustic guitar quite well. She was tough, prosaic, political—and passionate. As the antiwar movement began to grow, she attended rallies, carried petitions. For his part, Duncan had no problem with any of her beliefs, not that he took them all that seriously either. He certainly didn't defend the war—and had no intention of joining the fighting if he could avoid it. Torching his draft card in a slight drizzle outside her residence hall was an impulse, an inspiration—it worked magic, brushing aside her reservations about who he really was.

That last year in the East they were happy, and the world seemed open and beckoning, full of possibilities. It was only much later, looking back, that he might have realized that Princeton had not been the launchpad to greater things, glory as a poet or success in real estate or on Wall Street, as everyone anticipated for him, but rather the apex of his personal trajectory. After graduating, a gradual slide began, unanticipated and unperceived at first, as back to Kingsmount he brought his bride. This was all he could think of, falling back on the influence of his family—his indomitable mother—to replace his deferment from the draft. Him returning, the not-quite-prodigal son, not yet anyway. He was one of the elect, one of the Boothes.

Jennifer loathed his family, especially his mother. She was a Boothe by marriage, but now that her in-laws had passed away, she was more Boothe than mere blood might ordain. She ruled husband, family, Kingsmount, through checkbook and ruthlessness. What wasn't to loathe?

LESS THAN a year after he intruded on them in the library, it was a hot, muggy July and the industrial city only fifteen miles south was on fire. Michael Rosen was trapped on the right/wrong side of the barricades, and they took him in. The decision wasn't Duncan's and he didn't make the offer, but in truth most of the time the boy's presence in their lives over those few days wasn't a burden. Most of the time, of course, they weren't actually in the cottage together, tripping over one another. When they were, say, at dinner, the situation seemed natural enough, almost a regular little nuclear family. Jenny would be bustling about assembling some kind of casserole of noodles and cheese. Michael would stand and watch helplessly, wanting to help her. But the kitchen was too small.

After a bourbon, however, or after a second one, Duncan would be watching the boy watch his wife or her showing him how to test the pasta or where to find something in a book, and suddenly having Michael in his house wouldn't seem so natural or okay. Little intimations would detonate behind his eyes. Them and their damned intimacy, their shared understanding. Him and his damned failures. He clenched his teeth to keep the rage hidden.

On the second evening, after a quick bourbon for Duncan, the three of them strolled from Faculty Row with a few of the other families up to the campus. Naturally, some of the other teachers had televisions of their own, but already they had developed this little ritual—it seemed they should be witnessing the city's destruction together in one of Kingsmount's common rooms. Weren't they a community, after all?

It was one of those evenings in midsummer when the light lingers, fading so slowly that it can't possibly disappear entirely before dawn. The estate was green and lush, the heavy-leaved chestnuts bending under the weight of their own glory. That day, however, the reality of the catastrophe had first begun to intrude even on Kingsmount as something more than an abstraction, a story. The stink arrived, invisible at first, followed by the coarse, gritty testimony of smoke and cloud overhead. So as the families strode through all the summer majesty of elms and oaks and cypress, past the Scandinavian sculptures and fountains, and through the modern Gothic boys' school architecture to Marquis Commons, the acrid fumes hung faintly in the air. Some covered their mouths and noses or tied kerchiefs around their children's faces as if they were playing cowboy bandits. Some simply breathed, drawing the stink into their lungs as if this were their due, their fate.

For a long time that evening, the small gathering of twelve or fifteen adults (their younger children playing outside on the lawns) sat in solemn horror, watching the great box of the television, no one saying much. The sound was turned down as well. Scenes flashed across the bottle-thick tube, water arcing through the air toward buildings aflame and crumbling, Molotov cocktails arcing through the air and landing in a blast of fiery splinters, ragged scrums of protesters or looters splintering away from police batons and tear gas. Occasionally they'd spy a sniper on a roof or a body flopped broken in a smoking lot.

"Hell of a way to accomplish a little urban renewal," Duncan muttered, half to himself. It was merely a throwaway joke. Smart-ass irony. Not very funny, not very subtle, bad taste of course, lousy timing. But how big a deal? He wasn't even trying to lighten the mood. He never really intended anyone to hear. But out it flashed like a dark fist clenching all his anger, his resentment, the black despondency that for months had been tightening its grip around his throat. The black-and-white images of their city being wracked by protest, violence, and flame, like the fellow images of destruction half a globe away, might have been a projection of the despair gnawing his own soul.

Jennifer heard. (He didn't realize until a moment later.) She'd been perched next to him on an overstuffed couch, but now she drew away as if sniffing something worse than the smoke settling its ash invisibly about them. Shock, disbelief scarred her face, not so much for the brutish comment itself as at the sudden eruption of recognition that it had brought her: as if the fist had physically struck and she knew him for what he was.

He felt a yellow-green sick, a shudder. Or better: not a shudder but a hard thud to his chest that rang hollow, except for the lard of self-pity that seemed to sit heavily in that cavity. He knew in an instant that something was more than just wrong. Jennifer was staring at him as if she hadn't actually seen him for a long time. Most disturbing was the faint smile—out of sync with the look in her eyes—that flickered about her mouth with a hint of relief. This had been one of those rare and unexpected moments when a stiff key turns in the soul, a decisive click that changes everything.

IT TURNED out that Michael Rosen's mother was perfectly safe. After another day or so, that's what they discovered. Grueling shifts at the hospital had swept her along fourteen, sixteen hours at a rush. Given the sudden flood of wounded and ailing, they'd shifted her from delivering babies to a ragged sort of triage in an emergency area that had spread across most of the hospital's main floor. Naturally, Mrs. Rosen was plenty worried about Michael too, hoping he'd reached Kingsmount safely before the surging tide of violence crashed over him but unable to know for sure. Finally, in a momentary lull, one of the other nurses was able to slip away to her home in Lincoln Park, where she could place a phone call to the school's switchboard.

And that was that. Two days later Michael went home—his neighborhood had been spared, but the streets were littered with debris and largely vacant, the smells of wet ash and urine blowing in from a few blocks away. The summer withered. Jennifer and Duncan watched each other stumble through the dying paces of a routine that seemed empty, that made them miserable. Duncan watched too with a numb passivity, seeing the choreography play out with an apparent inevitability, lamenting it, and feeling sorry for himself.

Again and again he recalled that single frozen moment after he'd betrayed himself in Marquis Commons by speaking aloud and how Jenny recoiled on the couch. Perhaps if he'd reached out to her just then? But he wasn't capable of reaching out. He knew that for many months now she'd been the one reaching out toward him, again and again, and now the futility had sucked her dry. They stumbled through their paces. No more blowups. No more fights or really much conversation of any kind. They were kind to each other in their shared misery, even thoughtful, sensing that it would soon be behind them.

And then in the deeper heat of August she was gone. A single bag. A bus ticket. She took hardly anything with her. There wasn't even the need for a forwarding address, at least initially, because she didn't know where she'd be going after a short stay with her parents in Youngstown.

EIGHT MILE and Woodward. The border, a ruptured membrane between city and suburb, between before and after. Between black and white too, but not all at once. The city had always been divided into discrete neighborhoods, a kind of de facto arrangement of race and ethnicity that had kept things under control, mostly. The gathering pace of white flight to the suburbs didn't change that all at once. But where the city ended was less an imaginary boundary than before and a deeper scar.

Duncan thought a book about a bar like the Fox Hole, the girls who worked there, the men who paid to drink and watch them, might say something about what the city had been and what it was going to become. Except the Fox Hole was the fifth place he walked into, and by that time he wasn't saying a word about writing any damn book. And truth to tell, what Duncan Boothe really wanted was not to be at home without Jennifer. What he really wanted was to be as far as could be managed from Kingsmount Academy without sacrificing his job or, the truer truth, sacrificing his mother's protection from the draft. He told Serge, the manager, that he needed the money. That much was true too. Serge looked at his khaki pants and faded blue Oxford shirt and shook his head.

"You know how to pour drinks."

"Sure."

"Sure," he said, skeptical. "I pay you out of the till," he said. "No taxes and no complaints from you. Got it?"

"Sure."

"Sure," Serge said.

IT WAS the middle of the year and he was trying not to get fired, but not trying very hard. He slept through one class, forgot to show up for another. His lessons were increasingly improvised. He'd spin out rambling musings on books, usually novels he'd read in college, rather than those assigned for a specific period on the rigid school syllabus. Papers he handed back late or with a grade and few if any comments. He wanted to be almost anywhere other than Kingsmount Academy, where the legacy of his family and the invisible watchfulness of his mother pressed on his chest like a heavy stone, forcing the breath, the life, the wish for life from him.

But his dread of being drafted to fight in Vietnam pressed back just as hard and he was frozen. What horrified him wasn't a fear of pain and oblivion or a moral opposition to the war itself—any political outrage had largely departed with Jennifer. But after all his years in a boarding school environment, he just couldn't bear the thought of military life, the inspections and hierarchies, the pandering and the humiliations. Whenever he imagined it, a cloying, clawing sense of suffocation overwhelmed him.

At first the notion had been that most of his research would be complete before school began. Maybe a couple of hours a week after that until he'd gathered enough material. But tending bar at the Fox Hole had gradually become its own addiction. He hardly struggled against it. The mindlessness and the easy familiarity with strangers were an escape from Kingsmount, an escape from himself. One night a week, then two, then four, then five. On his feet five, six hours a night, not thinking, not explaining, pouring beers and cheap champagne, listening to stories, signaling the bouncer (Serge often did double duty in that role) when one of the girls needed a hand or one of the drinkers needed assistance in paying a tab and making it to the door. He wasn't thinking and he was drinking less himself, when he wasn't home. He still maintained the notion that this was a research project. That a book would come of it eventually. Of course, the notion was purely his own, since he couldn't confess the plan to Natalie and her friends, let alone Serge. And he surely didn't dare spill these beans in the hallowed vine-covered walls of Kingsmount. Except that he did. He let it slip.

One morning, early, it would have been a Thursday because the school paper had appeared and been distributed in the dorms the night before, he was meeting with the student editorial board to critique this latest issue, column by column, story by story. He'd been appointed faculty adviser the previous year, probably because the headmaster felt it was just deserts for Duncan Boothe's manifold failings as an assistant coach of any sport—soccer, cross-country, hockey, even football. By his second year back at Kingsmount, he'd escaped those duties entirely because none of the regular coaches would have him.

So it was Thursday morning and it was early, and he was both exhausted and slightly hungover, not having returned home from the Fox Hole much before the time he should have been rising. He looked a wreck, rushing into the seminar room with (an illegal) mug of coffee. All eight boys were waiting for him, several half-asleep, most nearly as mangy as he, with collars twisted, ties knotted askew, shirttails hanging over belts. Among them sat Michael Rosen, editor of the op-ed page for his senior year.

If he looked no more tidy than the rest, he was alert, awake—judgmental. The boy might as well have been drumming his fingers on the long wood table, as if Mr. Boothe had kept them on pins and needles for hours. Judgmental, and so goddamned earnest. That's what annoyed Mr. Boothe all to hell. Yes, Rosen was more mature than most of the others, smarter too. Yet there was something so ridiculously naive about him as well, and innocent, and easily shocked. More easily shocked even than Jenny.

"Sorry," Boothe muttered. "I was out late."

Some of them were already spreading the newspaper open on the long table and didn't much care. Others were nodding. Michael was nodding. Somehow Boothe didn't like the import of their nodding. By now was this their working assumption about what he did, stay out too late, probably drinking?

"It's a book project I'm working on," he began, startling himself. "I was doing research—basis of all good journalism, right?" He shouldn't have begun. He was yammering now, wanting to justify himself in these teenage boys' eyes, as if that mattered or were possible.

"What kind of research?" one of them asked.

"I'm undercover, sort of, working in this bar. Down in the city, see? Actually, it's a strip joint. I'm going to write about the lives of the people there, the ones that hang out, the ones that, well, work." Now he was confiding in them, hoping to impress them or at least make them believe. And he was watching himself prattle with a kind of paralytic horror, as if he were loping toward a cliff with no hope, no real desire to stop.

Surely now he had their attention.

"Wow," said a couple of them together. "Jeez," from another. Michael didn't say anything at first, but he looked amused or maybe contemptuous.

"Seriously," Boothe said.

"Yeah. Cool." This from Michael at last. "We'll have to come visit when we turn eighteen."

"Then I'd have to kill you," Boothe said, soaring with a kind of rapture and despair, the cliff already far behind, above him.

Several giggled nervously. "Wow," one of them said again. But smiling or impressed or frozen, their faces showed that they weren't sure he was kidding. Neither was he.

IT WAS a year of fire.

He'd been balancing a glass with some melting cubes on his chest. A night off from the bar. The small black-and-white television was flickering silently, but he wasn't really watching it. He was lying on his couch, smoking, a tower of student papers teetering next to him on the floor. Unmarked, yellowing at the edges, they were already three weeks overdue. Duncan's cigarette flicked them to life while he dozed. Yet only because these papers were so close at hand could the flames scorch his fingers and wake him, sort of, before the smoke could kill him. Up he blundered, disoriented, batting and swatting and stumbling, and the little fire became a big fire. Up went the school-owned cottage. Down came the school-owned cottage, and with it the few possessions, including the TV, he still jointly owned with Jennifer. If she ever returned for her share, there'd be little cause for argument over who got what.

Almost before the local fire crew had finished extinguishing the last embers of the blaze, Henry Hopkins planted Duncan on the other side of the Kingsmount estate, in a small room that had once been the gardener's quarters in the lodge. Hopkins seemed to want to get him away from the other faculty and their cottages before further accidents could happen.

Did the headmaster have any sense of the irony? Boothe wondered. He doubted it. Henry Hopkins didn't do irony. But surely had he considered, he might have realized that Duncan Boothe would have spent much of his childhood playing in this same lodge and roaming its gardens and passageways, even the gardener's room with the gardener's belongings still smellily scattered about. After all, it had been the Boothe family home for six decades until, while Duncan was at Princeton, first his grandmother died and then, more swiftly than mere physical health might have intimated, his grandfather followed. His parents remained in their more modern house on an adjacent property. The lodge passed as per trust and deed into the hands of the academy.

Ten months after the riots, nine months after Jennifer went away, eight months after starting at the Fox Hole, the stink lodged deep in his throat and lungs, the acrid rasp of burning wood and linoleum, rubber and pumice and who knew what else from a house in flame. He'd tried hot showers in the gym. He'd tried mouthwash and inhalers. Come the last two evenings at the Fox Hole, he tried heavier doses of bourbon even than usual. His snout had always been too damned sensitive.

Yet after three days, the smoke still coated the inner surfaces of his skull. It even seemed to muffle the early morning alarm clock, which only slowly managed to drag him out of dark dreams he was relieved not to recall.

Otherwise, this morning he felt just fine. He was in a remarkably buoyant mood.

No way did he trust that mood. He wasn't that foolish. It was phony. How could someone whose life was totally screwed feel so goddamned perky?

He didn't shower because there was no shower in the tight quarters, just an ancient rust-stained bathtub in an outhouse. Grabbing the black academic robe that disguised just how soiled and tattered it had become, Duncan hurried across the estate toward the school campus. He tried shaking his head to clear it, but that wasn't a good idea—it spiked the headache that had only begun to retreat and brought on a faint wave of nausea. Even so, the giddiness remained intact.

He was giddy, gleeful, shaky with a kind of joy. Then the diagnosis came to him with a sudden stab of certainty: shell shock. That was it. The insight delighted him. He chuckled and thought about lighting a cigarette. But for once drawing smoke into his throat seemed a bad idea. Well, the last cigarette had been a bad idea too.

As he tromped through the wet grass, it occurred to him for the first time that his banishment to the lodge was Henry Hopkins's final warning, the headmaster's way of serving notice that he could drift no further. That grandson of the founders or not, son of Dorothea Boothe, now president of the foundation, or not, he, Duncan Boothe, would be dismissed with the next screwup or failure or dereliction. No doubt—and this he realized now belatedly as well—his mother would have approved both the banishment to the gardener's quarters and the implicit warning, thus drawing one last step closer to fulfilling her own threat to wash her hands of him if he didn't steer a straighter course.

So why was he in such a goddamned good mood?

Shell shock.

Only such a diagnosis could account for it. Wife gone. House gone. Career on the rocks. What else might explain the giddiness, the lack of concern, the lack of despair? He found little satisfaction in being able to diagnose himself. Or in recognizing the abundance of irony here too: teaching at Kingsmount had indeed managed to protect him thus far from the draft. His friends and classmates, the ones who'd already enlisted or been yanked out of their lives, they needed all the pleasantnesses of Vietnam to summon their own versions of shell shock. Those who survived. What talent had he!—he could muster such dislocations of sense and spirit while protected by this idyllic estate outside a city that had burned the previous summer.

With these thoughts the giggles gradually dispersed, replaced by a bone-deep weariness. Family pull exhausted, academic excuses exhausted, if Hopkins sacked him, he might very well wind up lugging an M16 through swamp and jungle, after all, translated from the flames of a city, a house, to the flames of napalm and cordite.

As if to prove that his high spirits were nothing but phantoms (or more bluntly pathological), the May breeze shredded the last of them, assisted by a dew that soaked the grass and quickly his shoes, by the purple azaleas and the hanging pagoda blossoms on the chestnut trees. By the time he reached the central campus, he was miserable once more and thoroughly sorry for himself. Rather than lifting, his headache was thudding with dull throbs. He was too late for breakfast, but he could snag a mug of coffee in the dining hall as he hurried past. Coffee he needed in the worst way.

But there wasn't time—if he hurried, if he sprinted for it, he just might slip through the chapel door at the very tock of eight. (No one, but no one, was allowed in after that fell moment when the heavy door swung shut.) The brief service, like the assembly for announcements after lunch, was one of the school's daily rituals. More than a good-faith gesture, Boothe's attendance was expected. No doubt his absence would be strictly noted by the headmaster. But he needed that coffee. Even the quick trot across the quad seemed too much to face without it. And here was the dining hall, the first building he would pass, no one waiting there to slam a door in his face or grimace at his appearance.

Dark and massive, with a high-peaked ceiling and hanging lamps, the great chamber might have been modeled on some fantasy of an old mead hall or a medieval English college, except that it was also entirely modern, the brick and stone all in loving repair and very much of a piece. A gaggle of local women was scattered about the long tables. They wore starched aprons and little white hats that looked like ducks floating in their hair. Ignoring the intruder, they were piling dirty cups and plates on huge oval trays or wiping down the wooden surfaces. He shoved through a swinging door into the kitchen and poured coffee from a great cauldron that had been cooking it for hours. Mug in hand, he shoved a shoulder back out into the quad and halted. No reason now to race. Eight o'clock had come and gone. Tock.

Across the way and under the Marquis Hall arch, he spied a student standing alone. Duncan felt sour enough to veer in that direction and scold the boy for skipping chapel. But within a few steps, he realized it was Michael Rosen. He was smoking, casually, flicking tufts of ash at the brick arch. The impudent gesture annoyed Boothe, as Michael Rosen so often managed to do. He seemed to be flaunting the rules and not caring who witnessed it. Yet they both knew that Rosen's insolence here was an illusion, a pose. As a senior the privilege of smoking was his, as long as he did so outside. (Younger boys would sneak off into the estate at night for their round of fags.)

For his part, Michael gave no sign of surprise that this teacher was truant from chapel. He flicked an ash. Along with the half-dozen other Jews at Kingsmount, he received a special exemption from this particular ritual. The others would be scattered about the school, waiting for class to begin in half an hour. But from Duncan Boothe's perspective, Rosen seemed to be hovering outside the chapel, exempted but still in some way excluded as well, apparently longing to belong. That's what Duncan had always suspected—that the boy wanted it both ways. Wanted, beyond everything else, to be hugged to the belly of the community just as he was, warts and all, Jew and all. This morning he was wearing blue-and-green tartan slacks, tassel loafers, a crisp shirt and tie under his navy school blazer. It was all perfect, and not one item seemed quite to fit, like pieces jammed together from different jigsaw puzzles.

"You're mighty turned out for a school day," said Boothe.

The boy shrugged. "No big deal." He tossed his stub behind a bush. "My birthday." Shrugged again.

"Eighteen?" Boothe said. "Big day."

Another shrug.

There was something perverse in his need to extend an awkward conversation that neither of them wanted. "You and your pals going to celebrate?"

Rosen didn't respond. Then he asked, "What do you hear from Jenny?" and glanced at Boothe directly for the first time, his eyes dark and defiant.

Stung, startled, he felt his face flush with anger. He'd never suspected the boy had it in him.

"She know about the fire?"

Not trusting his voice, Boothe shook his head.

They, the two of them, hadn't spoken about Jennifer for nearly the entire academic year. Yet they were both thinking about her the whole time, missing her the whole time. Boothe realized what he should have known: that the boy must have missed her about as much as he did, if in a more uncomplicated way. But there was something new that day to his tone—defiant, razzing. Michael Rosen was taunting him.

Boothe, amused and aggravated, almost laughed aloud. Taunting *him*—letting him have it back for a change, instead of mooning around as he had all these years, like some puppy he'd slapped with a wet newspaper. But rather than laughing, Boothe shook his head again. That dead cigarette butt peeking out from behind the shrub looked pretty good.

For three days now, the ash in his mouth had made sense of the year for him. It was satisfying to taste the shape of nightmare—a neat trajectory from fire to fire. But now he realized it was wrong. What shaped the nightmare of his last nine months was the living with Jennifer's absence, so potent that it had become a kind of presence. Yet he denied it, ignored it, refused to wrestle it.

And he was responsible.

There was no denying it. (He shook his head again and the boy stared, wondering but not saying anything more.)

He'd driven her away. Probably because she was the best thing that had ever happened to him and he couldn't bear it.

He'd been missing her with every breath and doing everything under the sun not to know it.

The boy had been missing her too.

What kind of a bond was that between them? Not a happy one. But still.

Here was Michael Rosen in his birthday getup. Eighteen and insolent. With sideburns and a little fuzz on his lip. The boy had been growing up. So Kingsmount was a success for him, after all. And Jennifer's absence had only helped toughen him. It gave him some irony—a good gift. He'd needed the irony.

Boothe wondered whether he'd changed too, and the answer came to him: not an iota. Fire to fire, he'd been frozen in misery and self-pity and self-satisfaction. Not a hint of change.

The boy was leaning against the Marquis arch, hands in his pockets, not looking at Boothe any longer. And that's when the last rush of intuition swooped—*he* must have heard from her. Michael must have received a message. A phone call? No, more likely one of her notes with the peculiar *o*'s and *a*'s and *q*'s. Only once here at the end of the year? Or had she been faithful to him throughout the long exile?

Boothe yearned to know and surely the boy was eager to tell him, to confirm the humiliation. But what would this particular knowledge bring him either way? Would it help him change? And he couldn't bring himself to beg.

IT WAS a slow night, a warm night, and Natalie was in the middle of a fifteen-minute set, dancing on a raised platform only slightly larger than one of the tabletops on the main floor of the bar. Because the only customer was Harold, a foreman at a nearby steel-stamping plant who stopped in at the Fox Hole most every night for a couple of boilermakers, head down and deliberate, Natalie was performing for Desiree and Blossom, the two other girls on duty. They sat at the bar too but were swiveled around to the stage, leaning back, calling out to Natalie, applauding each bump, each grind as the pink see-through blouse made its way to the floor.

Duncan Boothe was tending bar, and she might have been dancing for him too, with the same playful earnestness as for the other women.

"Yeah, that's what I'm talking about, girl—you a star," cried Desiree.

"Give it to 'em, baby," called Blossom, who was distracted by a flaw she'd only just detected in a long white fingernail.

Natalie was grinning at her friends, working hard for them, a slight sheen of sweat on her face in the bright lights, blue and red and white, beamed from above. But her eyes had a faraway quality too, and Duncan suspected she'd started using again, despite all she'd promised Serge. He knew she'd been sleeping with Serge, but that wouldn't protect her ass. If he found out she was back on the stuff, Serge might beat her up so she couldn't dance or he might just throw her out entirely. Serge wasn't the sentimental type. Either way she'd have trouble feeding her kids, not to mention her habit. And given the recent layoffs, she'd have trouble landing a job with her father at the Six Mile plant as she'd once predicted.

The last few months had not been kind to Natalie. Age had swept up on her quickly, with a hardness about her eyes and toughness to her skin, and a weary, wary watchfulness that could slough off in a moment all the way to indifference. In the last month, she'd begun wearing a heavy blond wig while she worked, trying to suggest some connection between her own accent and the bustier claims of a country-western star.

Duncan watched her on this night and was saddened by all of this. His own concern surprised him. And while he was thinking such thoughts, he had to admit that any lingering pretense that the Fox Hole would provide a slightly titillating insight into the larger life of a broken city had long since disappeared. Black girls might dance here, but never, ever would black patrons venture this far north to the very border of the city to see them. For the first few months that Duncan had worked at the bar, the occasional single businessman in a gray suit or even a clutch of three or four of them, usually already drunk, would stop by. They were raucous in a forced, self-conscious, show-off way, and after a couple more drinks and bets and dares, they'd usually try and grope the girls. But here was Serge's great gift—he could handle them, dissuade them, without using the force he could or even pissing them off. Usually there'd be an extra tip—plenty generous—tucked into the G-string of the woman involved. But these after-business dinner parties no longer tumbled through the door. It had been weeks since Duncan laid eyes on any of the old solo businessmen either. Now it was only the local workers, guys like Harold, who drank hard, who might watch the girls dance, but resisted every come-on and watched their pennies too.

So Duncan had already come to think of this as an evening of surprises. Except he wasn't all that surprised when Michael Rosen walked in the door. It seemed in rhythm with the strange blasts of the universe. The school's ancient red pickup truck sat parked at the curb behind him. Spying it, Duncan wondered how he'd managed to swipe the keys. The boy was resourceful. Duncan silently gave him credit. He was also angry—not surprised, but very angry.

"Hey," said Michael with a nod as he slipped up onto a stool. "I'd like a beer." He held out his license to prove his age.

Boothe said nothing, didn't glance at the card. He held a straight glass to the tap. He set the beer in front of the boy and turned away to rinse some other glasses.

"I warned you I'd come," Michael said to his back. "I thought it'd be fun to see where you work for real."

Boothe didn't respond. He wiped the counter, slid a clean ashtray over to Harold, and emptied the butts out of the old one.

"How's the book coming?" said Michael ever so pleasantly.

"Look," said Duncan, rubbing hard at some spot in front of him, "on this turf you're a customer. Nothing else, nothing more. Just drink your damn beer. See what you want to see and then get out. I'll pretend I never saw you."

"Really? That's swell—you'd do me the favor. You won't snitch. Thanks. Yeah, thanks."

"Fuck you," he muttered, turning away again.

And here was Natalie in front of him, coming to the end of her act. She bent over, breasts dangling, to pick up the pink blouse. Desiree and Blossom whistled and clapped. Natalie did a quick curtsy toward them, but already the lights had gone off and she looked weary, vacant, a long shift at an end. The routine was for her to slip away behind a partition to a bathroom in back, put her shirt on, and then return to tease customers into buying drinks. But there were no customers to flirt with and the routine was dead. Stepping awkwardly off the stage in her spike heels, she stood still for a moment, her shirt clutched waist high in her fist, her breasts hanging before her. Fatty tissue.

Duncan wanted to put an arm around her, to wrap the blouse protectively about her shoulders, to sit her down and comfort Natalie.

"Makes sense now," said Michael, "why you'd give Jenny up for this."

Serge had them both out the door in about twenty seconds. He wasn't gentle. He didn't have to be. It wouldn't take him long to replace the bartender. The only thing Duncan took with him from the Fox Hole was a bar towel that he pressed to his face to stanch the flow of blood from his nose. He hoped it wasn't broken.

For his part, Michael's bottom lip had split in a dark gash and one eye was already closing behind puffy bruises.

But it was over now. The sudden, furious squall had caught them up, thrown them against each other, and spent itself and them. It disappeared as quickly as the initial explosion. Together they walked to the red pickup. Although his own car was parked in the alley, Duncan climbed in the passenger side and rested his head back against the seat. The bleeding eased. Michael got in behind the wheel and leaned his swollen face against the cool metal for the time being.

"Can you make it until morning for the infirmary?" Boothe asked, his voice nasal and muffled.

Michael nodded without lifting his head. "I'll tell them a story. Don't drip any blood in the truck, okay?"

"Right."

Neither of them moved for a little while.

"Sorry," said Michael at last. "That was pretty stupid."

"Don't tell me about stupid."

"Right."

When Boothe climbed down from the truck, it took the boy several tries to get the engine to catch. Finally, jerkily, he pulled out onto Woodward Avenue. It was after midnight and traffic was light. The red pickup swung across three lanes and headed north. One wheel threw off the angry howl of a bad bearing. The brake lights flashed once and then the boy was gone.

DESERTS AND DOWRIES

"My father is coming to explain," she says as if I am too stupid to understand in any other way. As if I am stubborn too and will accept the song of truth only from an authority beyond challenge. I groan—can I help it?—and my wife glares at me with contempt and triumph before turning back to her pan of hot oil. With long fingers she releases perfect little tufts of dough. Chapatis puff and blossom like golden butterflies skimming along the surface.

(IN SAUDI I have a cousin, an engineer. In Dubai my mother's brother sells electronic goods, carpets—even trades a little gold. This I have been told.)

"YOU SADDEN me with this coldness, Amitav," Gulu says, his eyes brimming mud behind thick lenses. "You are family now and this you do not understand. You are a son to me and what I own, everything in the world, is as if it were yours already."

(*And what I have is to be yours, even if it is not mine.* This I do not bother to say.)

"My daughter, my joy, has asked me to speak. To help you because you do not help yourself." The old man sighs and buffs the heel of his palms again and again across his thighs. "Your brother's apartment should come to *you*, Amitav. By right and by tradition and by law, yes, Vijay's flat belongs to you. This woman has no right. She takes advantage. She should go back to her own family, now that her husband is dead. What kind of woman is she, not to feel shame for how she behaves?"

This woman. Reena. My brother's wife, my dead brother's wife, Vijay's wife.

(IRAQ, IRAQ—plenty of jobs there, rumor whispers. No one goes to Iraq anymore. The Iraqis are too crazy even for desperate Indians. Americans bomb and shoot for sport. Yes, but in Iraq I would be far beyond reach. I smile, I dream.)

MY WIFE'S father shakes his head again, so sad is he for me. A little man, shriveled, Gulu is very ugly. His skin is blotched, his nose a gnarled hook. A very frightening man is Gulu Tagore, known and feared throughout many sectors of the capital. Now he sits in my chair, in my house, a pillow under his stocking feet. His left big toe, dark and evil, pokes free through a shameless hole. My wife, curled on her knees beside him, kneads his feet.

Somehow, by magic or by force of will, after this daughter who was married to me he spawned six sons, each larger, more fearless and ruthless than the last, each more stupid and eager to do their Babu's bidding. *Badmashes* they are. Because of their fists only and their knives and the blood they have puddled, laughing, as if it were rich *gee* for cooking their feast, is Gulu feared when he suggests, so coyly, a ransom price for his shoddy concrete. Buildings will crack and crash across Delhi when the time comes.

Six sons and in his old age arrives another daughter. Sita he names her no less. Sita, yet she is almost as ugly as the demon himself, and now he has arranged her marriage. Who would agree to a match with this girl but someone too old to care? Only an ancient friend of her father's. A sergeant of police who has worn out two wives already in bed, in kitchen, in beating his clothes clean against the rock of their own lives.

And Sita's dowry? The sergeant, old friend, must also be a fool not to know Gulu. Will Sita's Babu empty his own pockets for this princess of his heart? Gulu Tagore, wealthy man who wears ready-made from the bazaar, his pockets are empty. He stashes his loot where no one will ever find, police sergeant a hundred times over.

"Reena has legal papers," I say. "She lives in Vijay's apartment with her son. Vijay's son Rumi. The house belongs to her, not me."

Sadly Babu shakes his head as if I am very slow. I do not want to be frightened of him.

MY CYCLE I do not dare leave outside in this neighborhood, even chained. Dogs run here, darting from alley into dirt road, scavenging, howling, and boys run here quicker, cannier than the dogs. One is hurt, the others snatch what is left. So I use the key I never surrendered and enter Reena's flat, lifting the bike before me.

No sign of Rumi. This, almost, surprises me. I know the boy will not be off at school or working for money, not so long as his mother will care for him, fifteen years or not. She punishes herself and rewards him with his faintest whim.

Out of the sun I shiver. It is cooler in the flat and dim, shutters closed, curtains drawn—almost airless. I do not turn on a light or fan. I do not need to. For I know this home, every crack and joint of the stone floor, every cushion, just where Krishna dances tucked in his corner and wreathed in flowers and paste. Nothing has changed since this was my home too.

To this flat I came to live with Vijay after our own Babu died. I was thirteen, Vijay nearly thirty, a big man with a laugh as big. Always, always he glanced over my shoulder, never at me. As if someone, a secret shadow better worth his knowing, was trailing behind me, stepping through a door just then.

Vijay's wife, Reena, was a young bride then, hardly older than me, but me she treated like a child, playing mother until her own son could be born. Me Reena sang to and fed, made me do my homework; me she stroked and laughed at, as if I were truly a child and not thirteen, fourteen, fifteen.

Vijay it was who trained me to bookkeeping, arranged my first job, arranged my marriage too—and died three days before the wedding. No sign, no telltale: off to bed he goes, yawning whiskey and tobacco. And never waking. The doctor shrugged. Reena, hysterical, dragged him to the flat too late for anything but magic or mourning. Even when I touched fire to Vijay's lips at the crematorium—my duty, Rumi too young— he smiled a dream, as if this spark might wake him at last.

Delayed three months, the wedding still stuttered and sputtered the empty figures of a dance. Agony upon agony for me and for this girl I just now was meeting, older than I'd been promised, claw already clutching my arm. Her brothers bought friends for me, howling then, all of them, playing pranks on me, pinching and yelping, me feasting without appetite, grinning and praying for the long night to end, and then my new bride showed me—*taught me*—my duty.

Did Vijay intend what he had done? Was it a brotherly prank too? Perhaps he knew Gulu Tagore or owed Gulu Tagore? Did he figure that, once married, I would not, could not claim Reena for my own once he died, that ancient tradition of a brother's responsibility?

Do I not know her flat is also my due by tradition?

How much does *she* understand?

Urgently I must pee. It rushes on me, never since I was a young boy so fast. My bowels groan. Clutching myself to hold the flood back, I scuttle out past the kitchen. A single toilet shared by several families crowds against a gate to the alley. Plunging forward, still rushing, I explode a spray against the dark hole, gasping with pain and relief.

Returning, I slip past the small kitchen. It, too, remains unchanged, dark, emanating a sour smell that dismays even the roaches. A scourge second only to barrenness this truth in a home: Reena is a terrible cook. Like a tone-deaf musician, a color-blind painter, she betrays herself with *dal* or *channa* or *sag*. Even her rice is a sticky mass, sour. How can I confess to my wife—she is such a magician in our kitchen, as if to taunt me—that I prefer ruined food?

"RUMI?" CRIES Reena, alarmed at finding the padlock hanging limply on her front door.

"No, no—it is me, only me," I shout rushing to meet her.

Reena's eyes widen, but she says nothing. Quickly she sets down the carton of milk she carries and pulls her *dupatta* over her head and across her throat modestly, as if I am a man she does not know, not family.

"Sister, hello." The sternness in my voice surprises both of us. Her eyes spread wide again. I am proud of myself and struggle not to grin. This is good—such bearing, such control.

Confused, Reena hesitates. Perhaps she considers kneeling forward to take the dust of my foot as if I am an elder from her family's village. I am honoring her with a visit. Oh, how wonderful, that she should take the dust of my feet.

Instead she studies me, her head cocked slightly. Slowly a mischievous smile grows. A single crimson bangle catches against her wrist. It catches and trembles. "Amitav?" she says. "What are you playing at?"

"Nothing. I am playing at nothing," I snap.

She nods and drops her eyes. But now, silent, she swoops the milk up and into the kitchen. Her *dupatta* falls from her head across her shoulders, but she neither covers her hair again nor removes the scarf entirely. To me this is a signal of my lot. No longer am I an intimate, a brother—but neither will she treat me as an older man of the family and worthy of respect. Alone I stand by the door. I am inside but she has not invited me; she has not welcomed me. I am not sure whether Reena merely endures my presence or takes me for granted or is—secretly perhaps?—pleased that I have paid her a call.

As she opens windows and switches on a fan to stir the air in the slightly cooler evening, Reena looks weary. A black smudge bruises her cheek. She has spent the day as *ayah* caring for an American child after it returns from nursery school. But even with her new salary from the Americans, Reena cannot afford a sweeper to clean her rooms. Her money goes to Rumi. This much I know. And from him it disappears instantly and without trace as if she has dribbled it directly into the sand.

At last Reena disappears into the kitchen once more and returns with a pan of *chi* and two cups. She sets them on a low table, pours, and, finally, glances up to me. She says nothing. I say nothing. But I sit on a low stool before her. Reena's hands are large but delicate. They flit and settle calmly, efficiently, like dark birds in the evening. They are beautiful hands. For herself she keeps the cup with the broken handle and honors me with the other.

Miserably I nod. Yet I am so happy to be here, bowing with Reena over tea and out of time. If only she would let us stay this way, sipping tea silently, forever.

"He wants the flat," I blurt out as if we have been discussing it all along. "This flat. For Sita's dowry."

Reena's eyes widen with fright. She tugs her *dupatta* close about her throat.

"Gulu says that by all rights and tradition this flat must be mine," I rush on, unable to stop myself, confessing and wanting to hurt her at the same time.

She is shaking her head. Or, no, her head is weaving back and forth as if she is listening to a sound, wail of a pipe beyond my ear, pitch beyond hearing. Or as if she is keening the sound herself, a flame of despair that fills only her own throat.

"I lived here as my home. This was my brother's flat. When Vijay died, you should have gone back to your own family. This is what they say, Sister. And Rumi, yes, should come to live with my family." I am improvising now—no one has ever mentioned the boy. Him, certainly, I do not want, though by tradition, too, he is more than my nephew now that Vijay is gone. Rumi is my new *chota* brother, and I am responsible for him. I sound stern. I want her to hear the worst of it.

Shrugging, I smile and spread my hands, once more her valiant defender. "What are we to do? I do not want this place, Reena. This is your flat—how could I steal it from you?"

Still her head is weaving. Does she hear me any longer? Can she even see me, her eyes so dark and deep and liquid, ah, so scared? The crimson bangle trembles on her arm.

"WHAT DOES that woman say? Does she understand what must be done?" my wife demands without looking up from the rice she is separating into camps, clean grains on one side of her board, husk and chaff and insect scruff across the way.

"What is for her to understand?" I shout. I stamp my foot but still she does not look up. "It is her flat, not mine. What should she understand?"

She nods with a little smile to humor me, as if she knows not to take this tantrum too seriously—otherwise her Babu and his sons must learn of this foolishness, and this is something she does not wish for me unless I am a fool indeed. I know her so well and she knows me and no words are even necessary. I stamp my foot again peevishly. The rice dances and dies on the tabletop. My wife picks the grains clean with her little smile.

If Reena had thrown herself wailing on Vijay's pyre (even though we used the electric crematorium to save money), this and this only, a *sati,* would satisfy my wife and her family.

Give them a chance perhaps her brothers will arrange it themselves, quick flash of oil in the kitchen, a cooking accident. How convenient for Reena to disappear by flame or bus or oxcart back to her family's village.

MY WIFE, acid and knowing, beckons me to the phone.

"Master wishes to speak with you," says Reena on the other end. I can tell someone is standing next to her. This is how she speaks of her boss, the American, as if the Raj still lived.

"Yes? About what?"

She is panting. I can hear it. She is caught between frights, the man her boss inches from her, Gulu lurking in the shadows about us all. "Master will talk with you about my flat."

This I've guessed. My stomach rocks queasy already. What have I to do with any of this? Why must I speak? But there is no other way, no chance to refuse.

I sigh. "So, okay. I will speak to him."

"No," she gasps with horror at my suggestion. "Not on phone."

"What, he wants me to come to his home?"

"Never. He says you or no one, never to come here." This time quiet and steady. "He wishes you to meet him tomorrow at the International Centre near Lodhi Gardens. Four P.M."

"Tell him I have a job. That is not a good time."

"Correct. Four P.M. in the garden." The phone clicks.

WHY SHOULD I go because he, this American, beckons? What can he want with me? I spout and spume and rage, all without a sound or movement, my wife watching me. Only because Reena wishes it will I go.

(CANADA. SURELY I must have cousins in Canada who will shelter me and find me work. Bookkeepers are very useful. Canada—I might as well wish for the moon.)

MY SCOOTER'S clutch is broken yet again. Once I beg the afternoon off—half day without pay I cannot afford, risking dismissal—what choice but to ride one bus and transfer. A block short of Lodhi Gardens, I pry my way through arms and newspapers and body steam, leaping away and stumbling into the road. I want to breathe and gather myself after the oven press of the bus. But the sun beats on my head and I am sweating. Everyone in Delhi sweats on a day like this, except for the retired diplomats at the International Centre, the rich men, the professor women in saris fit for a wedding or wearing Western clothes, and the foreigners, *ferengi*.

For me the humiliation of walking up the long drive: arriving on foot, not even in a scooter taxi. Private cars brush my legs as they rush toward the circular entrance far ahead. Servants spring smartly to open doors and salute.

Sprinklers cast casual rainbows across the green lawns— Delhi's summer mirage—across beds of English roses. Me the sun wilts. I imagine hurling myself against the rainbows. But as if they read my thoughts, the private guards in khaki and berets, rifles slung over their shoulders, eye me suspiciously. I imagine it would cool them, relieve their own discomfort, to pummel this unwelcome intruder with their long wooden staves. Intruder I feel. Servants notice me only with suspicion as I approach the inner gardens.

"You're Amitav, I suppose?"

Startled, I stumble, wondering where the voice comes from, cast like magic. Just then the American steps from cool shadows in a doorway to the library.

I nod. "You are Mr. Andresen, yes?"

He does not hear or sees no reason to answer. I have begun to offer my hand, Western style, but quickly I pull back. I have seen this man before, often, from the street outside his house. I will be waiting to offer Reena a ride home on my scooter as if all this is most natural and convenient from my office, or bringing her a message from Rumi, content just to catch a glimpse of her even if she does not see or understand. Oh yes, Mr. Andresen I have seen on several occasions, but he has not bothered to see me either. I am a stranger to him now.

He gestures that I am to follow him and I trot—I must trot—at his heels to the tearoom, another oasis of cool light. Next to each other, we settle onto large rattan chairs. The cushions are so high I must scoot forward or my feet will dangle in the air. I am parched, desperate for water. But he does not think to order us water or tea. Perhaps this is his way of demonstrating his power. Perhaps he is merely rude. With Americans both are possible.

"I understand you're trying to throw your sister-in-law out of her house," he says without ceremony or preparation. He is a little man by American standards, but his voice is deep, accustomed to authority.

"No, sir. Please believe, this is the last thing I should wish. This terrible affair has nothing to do with me."

Startled, skeptical, Andresen stares, his mouth hanging slightly open. Only now do I notice his eyes bulging like one of the mongrel dogs that scavenge our city. "She *says* you're her dead husband's brother and you're claiming the flat."

Shaking my head, shrugging, I meet his gaze. "It is my

wife's father who wants to do this. Sir, he is a very bad man. A *badmash,* as we say. His sons, they are very violent." My throat is so dry I can hardly speak. "The flat this man wants only for dowry."

Andresen finds my confession distasteful. He purses his lips, slack and rubbery they are, and looks over my shoulder as if he is Vijay returned. (Why have I done this, exposed myself to a man such as this?) "Well, whether it's you or your father, you should know it's not going to happen. It better *not* happen, you understand? Or you won't have just a defenseless widow on your hands—you'll be dealing with me."

Puffing himself up, so full of himself. I would like to see Gulu's sons crack their staves on his ribs.

"You should also know I've helped her out with the rent—she was frightened the government might toss her out themselves. Well, we're not going to let that happen either. Since I've got my own financial stake in this thing, you and your father better think twice about meddling. Do we understand each other?"

I nod, but the blood is pounding in my chest and in my ears and my face is flame. Why does this man pay Reena's rent? How can she allow this? What does he imagine possible with a poor widow? What do I imagine possible? I imagine beating his rubbery lips and face with my hands, with stones from the earth, with fire from the heavens.

But my fury slips away from me like a sullen prowler ashamed of his lot. I do not know what to say to a man who cannot hear me, fury or no. Andresen also is a bully, but one who finds me too insignificant to torment beyond this casual humiliation at his International Centre.

He and old Gulu deserve each other, and they will dance a little dance without ever meeting. Once I report that this *ferengi* is involved, Gulu will grow purple. He will chew even more betel than usual and spit in my house, saving face, a bully whose bluff has been called. Reena's flat will be saved.

But Gulu will need more to save face. This, too, I suddenly foresee, oh wonderful prophet that I am become. The tyrant will still need his victim. That victim, prophet and savior of Reena—she who does not care or know or guess, ah, Reena—that victim will be me.

A shiver shakes me as if fever has swept me up. Will the *badmash* sons beat me or haul me through the lanes and alleys in a cart of garbage and dog shit?

No, no, for that will shame their older sister as well.

No, I realize, Gulu will have his revenge through her. My wife will be my wife, my fate my fate. Nothing will change.

Abruptly Andresen heaves himself off his cushion and strides away as if he were Lord Ram himself—a puny Ram—and I an easily vanquished demon, discarded and insignificant. A waiter shuffles to our little corner, snapping a towel at motes of dust, impatient for me to disappear as well.

For a moment I glance about, not so much envious as mesmerized by this place, its luxury, its air-conditioning, its gardens. And I notice, tucked away behind the servants' entrance, an electric bug killer, glowing blue. Even here, even here, flies dare intrude! Delighted I clap my hands—startling the waiter—as if to warn the flies away and am released.

Away I rush, knowing now what I must do—prophecy yet again—and head down the long drive. Here are the roses, here the green lawns, and without looking back I plunge into the precious rainbows. Immediately my thirst disappears. The water is warm. Only by their weight can I tell my clothes are soaked. My hair washes into my eyes. Can this be me? Never,

never would I do such a thing. A shame, an embarrassment! Glorious.

At luxurious last I glance at the International Centre and spy the guards moving toward me with their staves. Yet in their eyes I spy unease. Perhaps they think I am mad. With a wave, a little dance, I rush away to dry in the sun. Perhaps I will walk home, a madman in the sun.

(PERHAPS, BEFORE I am quite dry, I will ship out to Saudi and offer my services there.)

MT. PLEASANT

The glider was gliding smoothly above the buckling gray boards on the front porch, and Alison's head rested against its back, her eyes half-closed. This was the first moment in two days she'd taken to rest, what with the mess, the trash and detritus and havoc the renters left behind them in what had been her grandmother's house. Two days she'd spent with her father bagging up trash, sweeping floors, washing grime from the bathroom. So now, when she sensed a motion on the sidewalk below, for an instant, quick as a breath but still an instant, she couldn't figure out who it was lugging two huge, awkwardly bulbous pumpkins toward the steps. The sight only became more ludicrous—shocking—as she realized the old man staggering with the load was her father.

She didn't rise to help him. Even here, his parents' home in the District, Simon Forester couldn't bring himself to relax persuasively. Saturday morning, work behind them, and he's wearing a laundered white shirt with a sweater-vest, khakis pressed razor sharp, black loafers. *Black* loafers. Alison snorted in disbelief and leaned her head back on the glider, not even pretending not to see him. Too many sixty-hour weeks as a tax attorney, she figured. Or maybe he'd always been this way? She wasn't sure. Was he afraid one of his clients might spy him off duty five hundred miles from the office? Or that someone here in his old neighborhood might recognize little Simon Forester and not appreciate all he'd achieved?

Once or twice, sometimes even three times a year from before her earliest memories, her parents used to visit this small brick house in Mt. Pleasant. This was where they came for Christmas, and once her mother even arranged a seder, two families crowded together. And after their divorce she'd continued to come, either with her father or, until Grandmama died when Alison was twelve, on her own. No place on her earth had she felt so at home, so unquestioningly welcome. She knew every cubbyhole where she could hide, every creak in the narrow stairs. The musty shadows of attic and basement. She'd learned to tuck seeds along Grandpa's neat rows in the back garden and, after he died when she was ten, how to plant pansies that would make Grandmama clap her hands and break a brief smile.

Looking back, a decade and more, she felt a sharp ache — she hadn't felt that way even for a moment since. Not at either parent's house, not through four years of college. Certainly not now, between boyfriends, between jobs, between places to live.

Yet she felt frozen on the front porch. She couldn't bring herself to step out into the street. With the house scrubbed clean, waiting for her father either to rent it again or finally recognize that it only made sense to sell once and for all, this was a city where she should be able to set off and feel comfortable. At least a dozen friends from college lived here now. Any one of them, boy or girl, would be delighted if she called, would rush her to museums or nightclubs or walks in Rock Creek Park.

Even on her own, Mt. Pleasant was the perfect place to blend, deflecting whistles from men on corners with brown paper bags by their heels, poking her head into small markets filled with Asian or Latin American flours and spices. Alison ran a hand across her eyes. Here she *should* feel at home— with such a mix, such a confusion everywhere. Light-skinned, with kinky hair that might pass for an expensive perm, *she* could pass either way in Mt. Pleasant and no one would care. No one but her. Grandmama never made her feel half anything, only loved whole.

"You could give me a hand with these, girl."

Shaking her head, she didn't even open her eyes. "Come on, Dad. Haven't we done enough hauling the last couple of days?" She winced then, and tried to hide it, at the sudden eruption of her mother's voice.

He seemed not to notice. Perhaps it only struck him as natural—which would be worse, as far as she was concerned.

"Hey, it's Halloween tonight," he said. "That's always been a big thing around here. We might as well do something for the kids. I picked up some bags of candy too, back in the car."

Sighing extravagantly, Alison sat up and shaded her eyes. But her father had already completed the job before asking any help. The two pumpkins perched on the top step while he stooped to spread newspaper on the gray boards. How she resented that! Him asking only as a reminder of her own shortcomings and selfishness.

He would never pass for anything but what he was. Black man, yes—a professional, a success. Alison wished that everything he'd achieved might not be so easily measured in his clothes, the starch and those damn loafers, not to mention the self-conscious, almost prissy way he wore them. His hands too, smooth and so beautifully black, almost purple, with their long, elegant fingers and bright pinkish nails—were they manicured, she wondered, or trimmed and shaped and maybe polished too by himself or his properly white wife? She loved those hands and hated him for them.

"Better off turning out the lights and hoping no one comes," she said. "We're as likely to get a nasty trick of toilet paper in the tree or a stone through the window, whether or not you've got candy for them."

"Not here, Allie. I don't think so. Kids are still decent around here."

"Sure they are," she said. "You haven't lived in Mt. Pleasant in, what, forty years? And you know *just* what these kids are like. Better than anywhere else. Which is why you left in the first place, right?" Furious, panting, Alison watched her own petulance sweep her away as if she were a sour adolescent again. "I'm not sitting around here tonight with a basket of candy on my lap waiting for rotten eggs or worse to be thrown in my face."

She was goading him without quite intending to. She wasn't sure why. But her feelings had been building toward this for a long time. She wasn't sure why.

He'd blow up. The prospect frightened her—he could be very fierce—but it was also exciting, dangerous. Her throat and chest tightened. She could taste it on her tongue. This would give a leverage she longed for.

She wasn't sure why.

But he didn't blow. He turned from her, cold rather than raging, and Alison almost cried out. For the second time she felt uncertain of who this was before her, this suddenly older man, gray at his temples, hair worn nearly away on top, this man who could turn from her so entirely. He unbuttoned each sleeve, folding the cuff back three times. He pulled his father's horn-handled folding knife from his pocket and sat on the top step of the porch next to the newspaper and pumpkins.

The glider was gliding once more, Alison unable to abandon the spot. She watched as her father sawed a circle in the crown of the first pumpkin. After tugging it free, he shoved a hand inside and scooped out the stringy guts, handful after handful, seeds and all, onto the newspaper. He wiped his hands and picked up the knife once more. Now came the face. The tendons in his wrist flexed as he worked the thick wall of the gourd.

What would it be—a comic mask or a horror show, triangle eyes and jagged teeth? She had no expectations because, she realized with a pang, she'd never witnessed this before. Could that be true? Did memory simply fail her? Surely they'd carved pumpkins for Halloween while she was young? What kind of hole was this in her memory?

No expectations. But what she didn't expect was the easy virtuosity of his labor. This man's temperament lacked any artistic play, at least in her experience. And yet a jack-o'-lantern of wit and flare was emerging, with magic curves to the eyes, a puckered mouth threatening to explode with laughter.

At last Simon Forester replaced the crown at a jaunty tilt and set the jack-o'-lantern in the left-hand crook of the step. A candle would come later. With a large white handkerchief, he wiped the knife clean. He wadded newspaper around the damp guts and carried the package inside. The screen door slapped behind him.

Bits of dirt clung to the rump of the second pumpkin. Blank, unfinished, it sat on the porch of the old house, betwixt and between.

BALKED ECLOGUE

She's not at all as you've imagined her, Robbie's mother, as she takes your arm almost at once—after one glance at your face at the front door—and helps you upstairs to the guest room. No trace of expensive, horsey tweeds, no polo casual or pearls at her throat. Just a shapeless mustard-colored sweater and some billowy jeans.

"Come," she murmurs, "just drop your things. I'll bring them up in a bit. Poor thing, that's right, just a little farther. That's it, Alison." As if she's testing, tasting your name aloud. She's heard plenty about you too, no doubt. What was *she* expecting?

The hallway is treacherous. It's reeling about you. You can hardly keep on your feet. The nausea swooped up out of nowhere while you were on the train, pasting your forehead with an oily sweat, setting your teeth achatter. But you flagged a cab (where was Robbie? why didn't he meet you at the station? where is he now?) and made it, clinging, all the way out to this old house you've heard so much about.

She's got you firmly by the arm, steadying the world, as you lumber toward the canopied bed. "You go right to sleep. Sleep as long as you need. It's the best thing, and you're very welcome here. You're my special guest."

"Mrs. Chambers," you manage through teeth and thick tongue.

"*Shhh,*" she insists. "No need to say a word. Not a word. We've plenty of time later. I'll bring you some tea in a bit." She pulls back the covers for you and slips out the door again to give you some privacy and fetch your bag.

You're wrestling against the corduroy skirt, pushing it off, tangling legs with the panty hose you're not used to. You want to cry aloud in anguish and frustration. It's now, of course, that Robbie arrives, with a knock at the door after he's already charged into the room. "Hey, babe, I hear you're sick or something." He brushes your sweaty hair back off your forehead and pushes close for a kiss, a quick thrust of tongue in your mouth. "Come all this way, you can't be sick now." He fumbles a squeeze at your breast—it hurts—and you push him away in disgust and fury. You're wagging your head dumbly because you can't even manage the words.

You're furious with Robbie because this is him—not showing up when you need him, barging in when you're not ready. He thinks it's funny. Or no, he thinks it's a mark of intimacy, that he can do this. Or maybe he thinks it's erotic. But it's not—it's pushing into your private room when you're not ready for him, when you're not protected; it's him insisting on more than his rights, breaking down walls that are your walls, your integrity, that no one should get to break down. Most of all, however, you're furious with yourself because your heart has leaped up at the first sight of him and your tongue danced even for that faintest of seconds with his tongue. Even though you've come all this way to tell him it's over, that the two of you are over. And now you're happy to see him, if only for an instant, and you're too sick to tell him anything.

You've slept, but for how long? Is it night or day? The shade is pulled down at the window. The only light leaks in through the crack at the door. It might have been ten minutes you were asleep, or ten hours. You're disoriented. You're awake and you're sick with a vertigo that pummels you if you even turn your head on the pillow. The room slops and swooshes, and you feel it at the root of your whole being. Nausea rises with bile on your tongue. Vomiting would probably help, but you'd have to get to a bathroom and that's beyond imagining. Easier to cradle your own stomach and lie with your head still.

You're awake and that's the worst of it right now. You close your eyes and the universe reels. There's no escape from the dizziness and nausea, no escape from your own consciousness.

The room is too warm and it's hard to breathe and you feel caged in here. The room is a prison, your illness its bars pinning you to the bed. The sheets are starched, but already they've lost their crisp coolness. Already they stink of you and your illness. The room is a sickroom.

It has been a sickroom before. You sense that. The smell isn't only of you, but of others who have lain here over the course of generations in Robbie's family. Some no doubt have died in this room.

The house and his family. How often he has spoken of them to you. It's why—here's the truth, finally admitted— you agreed to come here now, even though it will be only to surprise and hurt him with your leaving. You wanted finally to see this place, the rambling old house, nothing so special in itself, he's sworn. But a place that his fathers have returned to, by chance, by intention, by desperation, for six generations. It's a rootedness that is breathtaking and alien to you. You envy it, are drawn to such a notion of place and family. And it terrifies you too—the thought makes you want to run hard and fast and far as far can be.

But all you know of the house is this one room. You can't even recall clearly the front hall or the banister and stairs that somehow you climbed. This room. Warm and sickly sweet, the fresh wallpaper striped mauve and green like something out of a bygone century, those damned starched sheets—who starches sheets? This *is* the house. You don't need to see more. You lie panting and hot, a pool of sweat staining the world. You can't close your eyes and you don't dare move your head.

Robbie's back and he's talking again, and you're not sure when he arrived or just what he's saying. The nausea has you cramped in on yourself. Robbie's trying to be solicitous. He's put a cool cloth on your head—you're glad but you can hardly feel the cool—and he's talking. If only he would stop talking.

You moan, but words don't take shape. Shaking your head to chase him away is a mistake—the room rolls and careens and a belch croaks out of you, deep and long and rank, leaving you dazed. Robbie pretends not to notice the stench. Please, *please*, you beg him with your eyes—*stop talking*. But typically he doesn't, he can't, fathom what you're saying to him.

Why are you grateful he's here, talking or not? Why have you hungered for him from the start? Is it that he's nothing like you? Your eyes are open and you can look at him and he's so, well, preposterous—with the blond ponytail and the un-ironed polo shirts and the nose that's strong and pure. You hungered to eat him alive the first time you saw him and, if you could imagine eating anything at all right now, you'd still like a good chew.

Yes, except something has changed. You still want him, but the obsession you used to feel has passed, like a fever lifted. Last week at a party, just any party, you happened to glance across the room and see his hand slip inside the expensive white halter of a girl almost as tall and blond as Robbie. You saw her eyes close for an instant, and you imagined his fingers tender on her nipple, pink and taut as a pencil eraser. Not like your firm dark aureoles.

Why has he wanted you? You moan again, sick and wanting to avoid the thought. But there's no closing your eyes and he's talking again, something about the house and the family most likely. And you've always suspected the answer: that you're different too, half black and half Jewish and ever so exotic. You were a sip of something dangerous and alien, not like the nipple on the other end of his fingers, just where they belonged. Something clicked. Something was lost. And you were free.

He's been gone only moments and now he's back, sitting next to you on the bed with a little gilt frame in his hands.

"This is so cool. I really wanted to show this to you, babe."

Light crashes off the glass into your eyes. You can't really make out what's there, just some kind of soiled and ragged envelope behind the glass.

"We found this up in the attic when the new insulation went in. Too bad there was no sign of the letter itself. Just the envelope, look, from R. E. Lee, President, Washington College, addressed to my great-great—I think that's right—granddad. Maybe there's one more *great*. Who moved here when the college was founded and built this house."

You lift your head to see and see only a smudge on the envelope, shards of light stabbing you again. The motion sets you off, maybe it's Robbie who's set you off. The room rolls, your belly is gurgling, swishing, rising, heaving. Suddenly Robbie stops talking midword. He sees it coming but is frozen, poor blond deer in the headlights. Can't even begin backing away. The explosion of vomit covers him, knocks him off the bed and toward the wall.

You fall back gasping, sobbing, your head clearing. The bed is still.

Robbie is staggering out the door as you turn your head. He's trying not to vomit too in reaction, sympathy, disgust. Almost at once his mother, your host, has appeared. She's carrying a bowl of water and a cloth, and she begins, gently, to clean you off. She wipes your eyes, your forehead, at last cleaning around your mouth and neck. In one long motion she strips the top cover from the bed, mops it across the floor, and kicks the mess into the hallway before coming back to you.

She sits next to you and strokes your brow with her hand. Her eyes are gray. They seem to recognize you and understand. With a hand you push yourself up toward her and hang an arm briefly around her throat. For a moment she allows herself not to be Robbie's mother and hugs you.

"Thank you," you murmur, your duty as guest fulfilled.

CHRYSALIS

James Blessingame, District Court Judge Blessingame, slipped out his back door, tiptoed through the strip of garden along the drive, and peered stealthily around the front corner of his house, spying on the old man who'd been casing the vicinity for at least ten minutes.

Only by chance had the judge stopped home during the afternoon. An unexpected recess—the lead attorney in a case before him had gone into labor the night before—provided a rare weekday chance for Blessingame to desert his chambers, drop by the house to gather up athletic gear, and head to his club. Now, his toes prodding a small rhododendron in crimson bloom, he realized his fist still clutched a drooping jockstrap. Glancing about in fear that someone, one of his neighbors, might notice, he stuffed it into a pocket.

Ten minutes earlier he'd spotted the old man strolling casually up and down the sidewalk. The vision was so preposterous that it nearly failed to snag the judge's attention, his mind distracted by an annoying dispute over office space with a senior colleague; by an attractive new member of the bar (black eyes, navy suit so modestly slit it promised rare secrets); by whether to dispense with the workout after all and plummet directly to a rubdown and sauna as a way of dissipating the tension that pricked tiny scalpels into the muscle of his neck. From the kitchen he was gazing absently through the length of his house, through hallway and living room, when he happened to make out the stranger's vague shape through a front bow window.

No, the man wasn't a derelict. Nor did he strike Blessingame as delusional as the judge strode angrily along the hallway. Then he sighed and halted. Someone, he decided, must have played a trick on the old man, twisting him around off Woodward Avenue with false directions. Or he'd failed in deciphering a map and spun himself silly on these residential streets. Or boarded the wrong bus, climbing down at this unlikely stop.

But that wasn't it either. This man knew where he was. Blessingame, peering forward toward the window but not allowing himself to be seen, could make that out too. For some reason—perhaps the old man's bizarre behavior provoked a reciprocal secretiveness—the judge didn't simply charge through the door and confront him. He was curious and wanted to observe just how far the fellow would go.

It wasn't merely being white that cast the stranger so clearly out of place. Some white families—mostly older couples to be sure—still lived scattered among these few blocks of Harper Woods on the northern crease between city and hostile suburbs. Back and forth this one had been wandering, sizing up the neighborhood, studying the house. He tried to appear casual, at ease. Instead, he managed to seem both furtive and painfully awkward.

Once upon a time he must have been a big man with strong shoulders. Yet the hint of a stoop made him seem frail in a gray suit that had grown too full. His hair (he still had that, a full head of it, the judge noted with some chagrin) was iron gray and dramatically swept back. Between two fingers he was fastidiously pinching the brim of an old-fashioned fedora, another failed attempt to make himself less conspicuous.

The afternoon was hazy, humid. School hadn't let out. No one lingered or played in the street, no one strolled along the sidewalk or even peered, so it seemed, from behind windows of the other homes to note the sly old man. Now from the corner of his garden, James Blessingame watched as the stranger nodded, apparently reorienting himself, reacquainting himself. Slowly, slowly, ever so casually, he was edging his way up the front walk.

At the fieldstone steps the visitor climbed stiffly but quickly now, no longer glancing back. Nor, once on the porch, did he knock to announce himself. He perched the fedora like a sentinel on the wicker settee and turned to hunch intently at the door.

Judge Blessingame edged farther out. He couldn't quite spy what the old man was working at. He slipped still closer. The bizarre fellow was scratching—prying with a nail file or small screwdriver at something on the doorpost.

"Pardon me—would you kindly explain just what the hell you're doing to my house?" Blessingame's voice boomed deep.

Startled, the visitor stiffened but didn't quake or collapse. Bracing one hand against the door, he turned to confront his accuser. His left eye seemed damaged—it wouldn't open quite fully. Yet he appeared neither meek nor apologetic. "I'm surprised it's still here," he said as if it were an accusation. "You live in this house?"

"I own this house." Blessingame approached, mounting the steps. "What's that you've found? Why shouldn't it be there?"

"I doubt you'd have any use for such a thing—a mezuzah. But you haven't removed it. No one has."

"Pardon?"

The old man pointed. He scratched again at a small cylinder set in the doorframe at an angle, perhaps two inches long, painted over many times, hardly more than a defect in the wood by now. A fleck of white paint fell away revealing only a slightly paler shade.

"Huh." The judge studied it without drawing closer. "Now I figured that was some kind of buzzer. You know, broken or rusted. Been planning to fix it too, but not till time comes to repaint the rest. Thanks to you, it'll be sooner than I'd imagined. You do know you're trespassing, Mr.—?"

Defiance as well as impatience crept into the old man's eyes. His jaw stiffened. "Naturally I will reimburse you for any damage. Hazzan. My name is Theodore Hazzan. How do you do?"

"I'm sure you will. Blessingame's mine. James Blessingame. Welcome to my house." He didn't manage to keep the irony from his tone, but Hazzan seemed neither to notice nor care. His eagerness to return to the task was paramount.

"What did you say this box is?"

"A *mezuzah*. They're fastened to doorposts and entryways. By Jews, of course. Not your people. By Jews."

"Yes. Yes." The judge nodded. "I remember—the Lord commands the Israelites to mark their doors in Egypt. But with blood, wasn't it? So the Angel of Death will spare their firstborn. I'd no idea they were still doing it. Not this way either."

Hazzan merely gestured with his nail file at the self-evident ornament.

"That's fine, whatever they may do," Judge Blessingame continued. "But no Jews live here anymore, not in this house."

In truth, the unexpected turn of the conversation made him uneasy. He'd known, of course, that this had been a Jewish neighborhood, supposed even that Jews built this very house in which he took such pride. None of that bothered him. It made no difference. He was grateful for the care and solid good taste they—whoever they were—had exercised.

And he had nothing against Jews either. At least not in the sense that people usually supposed or that some of his own friends did. No, it was true he could be impatient with particular Jews he'd encountered in college and law school; later too, professionally and in service organizations trying to salvage something of this decaying city. But such impatience (which he vigilantly, politically secreted away) festered in his chest and jaw only because these particular Jews could be so damn *earnest*. How desperately they'd be keening to do the right thing. No desire even for public acknowledgment of their good deeds and then call it quits. No, they yearned to keep living off the glories of the sixties, marching and riding buses and even dying for the rights of their black brothers. Well, that was fine as far as the judge was concerned. But Jews, at least the Jews he dealt with day to day, knew nothing, knew shit about being black today. And he was sick—this was the truth he admitted to himself only now on the front porch of his own house, peevish and weary and fed up—he was sick of them trying so damn hard.

"Inside lives a little piece of paper," the old man was stubbornly continuing as if Blessingame hadn't spoken. "Parchment actually. A prayer, a blessing."

"Parchment actually." Blessingame again didn't manage to hide his exasperation. "I'm glad for the lesson, but you must understand that this is of no use to me. I assume it's not even proper for the likes of me, for my people as you say, to have one of these things on my door."

He was surprised by his own peevishness. The old man bothered him, got under his skin. Tiny blades were worrying themselves again into the muscle of his neck. And a bone-deep weariness seemed to have welled up, as if lying in wait for such a moment (and loneliness too, but any acknowledgment of that hovered on the horizon of awareness), and opened him raw.

"If this—*mezuzah*—was yours or your family's, feel free to take it. Here, I'll get a decent screwdriver and we'll pry it off for you. I can touch up the paint myself this weekend."

"No, that's not the point," the old man snapped. "And there is nothing to take anymore. Just the case. Without the scroll it's hollow, worthless."

"Empty or not, worthless or not." He wondered how the old man knew it was empty, but he was tiring of this. A sauna and rubdown—the opportunity was fast disappearing. "Mr. Hazzan. What if I remove it myself? I'm not offended it doesn't belong on a black man's house, if that's the problem. Either take it yourself or let me remove and dispose of it, but I have no more time for this today."

The accusation and dismissal seemed almost to strike the old man. He winced and raised a hand, shaking his head. "I must sit." He waved. And lowered himself heavily onto the porch, leaning on one arm, his knees spread awry. His bad eye squeezed shut into a squint that set his whole face akilter.

Good Christ, thought Blessingame, stepping closer, worried the old man might pass out or collapse entirely. That would have worse consequences than mere inconvenience. "Look here, do you need an ambulance?"

"No, no. I'm okay. It's warm today," he said with a broken smile. "A glass of water maybe?"

"You just sit there until you're okay," the judge ordered. He reached into his pocket but realized that the front door key was on a ring still hanging in the back door lock. Hurrying down the steps and through the garden once more, he filled a glass in the kitchen and strode quickly through the house his family and friends had thought him mad to buy— unless there was a girlfriend or plans for a girlfriend, perhaps a family, that none of them knew about. A house this size for a single man, even a man of his accomplishments. . . .

Blessingame came to a halt and pursed his lips. Knowing the old man was waiting for him on the front porch cast a shadow across the sun. Suddenly he felt the weight of years he hadn't noticed settling about him, and the chill of loneliness—of aloneness—he'd been too busy to acknowledge. Yes, in fact, there had been a woman, one in mind when he bought this house. Not that his family and friends knew she existed. She, Marjorie, was an attorney he'd met in San Diego—the law school brought him as a speaker and she'd been in the audience. She asked a tough question after the talk and then another, and they'd thrashed the matter out over coffee, ignoring students and professors standing around impatiently. He'd extended his stay, taken holiday leave. For four days they breathed only each other. And after six months of secrecy and cross-country flights and delicious planning, she'd arranged to join a local firm. No reason to admit to the senior partners why she was making the move. No reason for Blessingame to tell her about this house—it was an impetuous surprise even to himself. He'd signed the contract on it hours before her plane landed, as if the fact of it would allow him to grasp Marjorie close too, before they could discover all the reasons that would drive them apart (a black judge depending on reappointment; a white attorney held to a different standard than her senior partners). Instead, the fact of the house festered into an insupportable burden. She never moved in but visited from her tiny apartment. After a few furtive and disappointing meetings, the poison of those practical reasons leached them even of the language for parting.

The stabbing sadness of the memory startled Blessingame. For an instant he puzzled at the glass in his hand. Then he remembered the old man. Sad and freshly irritated, he tugged the front door open and failed to take his usual pleasure at the heft of its heavy wooden swing.

Hazzan hadn't moved. He was panting lightly. Accepting the glass without looking up, he gulped several gulps of water. Some dribbled onto his tie. He flicked at the beads absently.

"Take your time," the judge said sternly, an impatient nurse with a cantankerous patient. "Rest until you're feeling better."

His lips rubbery and blue, the old man was still panting. He gestured at the door frame. "I came to do something."

"I've told you already—take it. Feel free. No charge. We'll have it off in no time."

But Hazzan was shaking his head. He dug at his jacket pocket. "I don't want it. Just to put this back." Gently he drew forth an envelope and from the envelope, gently, a small ragged scrap.

"Ah," said Blessingame. "Ah." His voice changed. "That, I take it, belongs inside. And you come to have it, how?"

"I stole it."

The judge glanced smartly at the small cylinder buried beneath successive coats of hardened enamel. Why was it that only now did he consider the possibility that Theodore Hazzan was disturbed in some way after all, perhaps a certifiable nut case? "You stole it," he repeated. "Not anytime recent, you didn't."

The old man didn't respond. He was staring out toward the street, his thoughts on something other than this conversation, this distraction.

"Years and years ago. A lifetime since then," he said at last. "We didn't live in Harper Woods, our family. My father worked tool-and-die downriver. For him the day was not a good day unless he could cross the door with his hands black with honest dirt and grease, my mother waiting with a bowl and soap for him to wash first thing. *He* didn't make money enough to live in such a place as Harper Woods."

Blessingame grunted, defensive about his own position here. The Jews he knew weren't tool-and-die, not unless they owned the plant, and he found it hard to conjure the image of this man's father and his righteously dirty hands. Yet he couldn't suppress a confession of his own. "Downriver, you say? Matter of fact, most of my family still live downriver. You believe my dad worked the River Rouge plant thirty-five years?"

His visitor nodded or shrugged—the judge couldn't tell—but the old man seemed hardly to hear.

"Anyway, what's your father got to do with you stalking my house?" said Blessingame more curtly.

Hazzan lifted his hands and dropped them on his knees once more. "I came first to this house when I was seventeen. I needed a job and jobs were hard to come by, unless I followed my father to the union and the shop—and I did not want to leave school. So I did a terrible thing."

"Stealing that piece of paper was so awful?"

The old man wagged his head at the ludicrous notion and then nodded at the door. "I asked the man who owned this house for a job."

"But you said they were Jews. You were both Jews, right?—what was so wrong?"

Hazzan wagged a hand this time. "I could think to ask this rich man because he had once been my father's friend. As a boy I knew him as Uncle. I would hear the stories of them going to *shul*—synagogue, you understand?—as boys together, of waiting on sidewalks and fighting for jobs, of them freezing together in late-night pickets to protect those jobs. For my father this was good, this was life—this battle, this struggle, the hard work and his family. But Uncle Arthur didn't like the dirty hands or the freezing so much. He was a smaller man, with fair skin and delicate hands, a musician. Who can blame him?" Hazzan seemed to be asking the question of some judge other than the one before him.

"With dimes and pennies, help too from his wife's family I suppose, he bought his own tool-and-die shop. It grew—how it grew. What was necessary to attract business he did, and he did also what was necessary to keep his workers from taking too much. No union organized his floor, not ever.

"Perhaps they had fought and argued before—how could I know? I was still too young. But I remember the night my father came home in a dark rage because Uncle Arthur had forced the union out. Who do you think one of the organizers was? Papa said nothing, threw nothing. But his lips were white and he forgot to remove his overcoat. I had never seen him such a way. My mother was actually frightened. Not of him but for him. Never did I see my father's friend again—

never was his name spoken in our house—not until I found my way to his shop and asked for help.

"Uncle Arthur was surprised, delighted to find his long-lost nephew in his doorway, as if *I* was the black sheep who disappeared so long ago. He took me in his arms. And before I knew I should never take his work, he hired me. As a favor to my father, his all-but-brother—that's how he would have it.

"My father! Finally I got up the nerve to tell him—and he stared at me. He stared at me and turned away and—this I had never seen him do, never—he leaned into the street and he spit and he turned away from me."

Hazzan paused. He ran a hand across his face and sipped at the water his host had fetched him. He did not notice that Blessingame, sighing, had settled next to him on the steps.

"This porch—I painted this porch," he continued. "Not sloppy like this, but with love, every stroke. Because I loved this man Arthur Lewis. Can you imagine that? He read—*everything*—and Mozart and Brahms, he knew them like friends. From outside these windows, I listened to him listen. More— he'd stood up to my father and paid the price for his betrayal—cut off like dead. And he built this new world for himself. Well, I was standing up too.

"Those bricks in the walk?" he demanded with offhand defiance. "One by one, a perfect dance from one to the next, I drew the walk and laid those bricks. I can still feel them raw at my fingertips. I knew this house even better than he did. Better than you do. Better!" He was furious, staring now at Blessingame.

With hardly a pause Hazzan shifted ground, but suddenly he seemed stealthy again or embarrassed. He was gazing out across the street. "Arthur Lewis also had a daughter, Elsa, two years younger than me."

"Ah," Blessingame said again, his impatience and boredom kindled once more. For such tired testimony as this, Hazzan's first love, he was to sacrifice his precious afternoon?

"No," Hazzan snapped. "Nothing like that—it wasn't that way. You don't understand. It was for her father's sake. So he would think well of me. So I could watch and study him, even talk with him when there was chance—I tutored Elsa in mathematics, and then, later, I escorted her to concerts and movies. *As a favor to my uncle,* don't you see? He was arranging nothing between us, and forbidding nothing either. Me he didn't take seriously as a threat to his precious daughter. My father's son, a poor boy from downriver, I was too grateful to be any threat. They knew they could count on me. And because he asked me, I was such a good boy, so respectful. Such a fool.

"You expect me to say Elsa was beautiful like a dream. But no, not beautiful. Not even pretty perhaps—I knew it then, but it did not matter. For a long time I hardly noticed her as anything but a child, she was so shy and gray and quiet, a little girl, nothing more than her father's daughter. At first. But later her eyes, they showed me secret fire, dark fire, with a temper too that seemed crazy.

"Naturally—it was part of my job—I would be correcting her little mistakes, with arithmetic maybe, here and there. When with no warning it was this howling storm sweeping Elsa up in a rage and her shrieking at me, swearing at me, calling me names I'd never heard, never imagined, so that I became the young one, naive and innocent. She scared me with those wild moods. And she laughed at my face then and kissed me, and I was the young one.

"Sometimes, when she was cruel, she ignored me or made me walk behind her. But if I dared walk away, oh, she wouldn't stand for that—she flung herself about my neck. She would cling to me and rub herself against me. Here on these steps, she snatched my hair and kissed me in the moonlight, daring her parents to see.

"So, yes, this much you were right." He waved a hand, conceding. "This house itself became our only confidant. We knew its secret places, and it knew our secrets too. I'd spot its roof down the street as I approached, before these trees had grown so tall, either in the daytime to work openly or in the evening, late and secret, and a sweat of fear and yearning spread across my chest."

The judge glanced about uneasily. He wasn't sure in any event that he wanted his neighbors spying him talking this way to a crazy old man, a Jew come back to the promised land no less. But there seemed no way to stop him, and—this the truth that made him most uncomfortable—the story had caught him up as a reluctant witness after all. He needed to hear it through.

But why? he wondered, exasperated with himself now. None of this had anything to do with him and yet he needed to hear it through. Was it the coincidental stories of working-class fathers and sons with aspirations for flight? Or was it the still-vibrating echoes of Marjorie deep in his ear? Once conjured, she seemed to be refusing easy dismissal to safe and distant memory.

"For nearly two years this was our way," Hazzan was saying. "Today, well, such a thing wouldn't be possible. But that was a different world.

"Our secret seemed powerful and strange. We treasured it not because we were afraid but because this way it stayed so strong. We didn't say the words even to each other—we didn't need to.

"Her father, her parents finally they began to suspect. When? They could tell. Perhaps they were not surprised after all. But they said nothing to me. They changed nothing openly. I was still welcome to do my little jobs here and to tutor Elsa. I wasn't going to challenge them then. As long as they would let us be, I would risk nothing.

"We *knew* each other, Elsa and me—you understand? We didn't have to speak even, we knew each other so well."

Blessingame was nodding silently, lips pursed.

"Slowly, so subtly, Uncle Arthur went to work against me with gentle poisons. He never forbid. No, he knew it wouldn't work. Forbidding would only drive Elsa to me. He knew his daughter too. But slowly, over months, he let her see that it was only a choice, simple and clear. That she was to choose between the family and me, between his world and the one I offered.

"But why did he do this? I loved the man.

"Look, you see the sky through that tree, and the road with these houses, and my car down the block, the green one, yes. None of this is as clear to me as my memory of Elsa hurrying along the pavement toward our rendezvous in the sandwich shop over on Woodward Avenue. Her scarf, blue, bright bright blue, the breeze tugs at it and she fights hand-on-head to hold it in place. I'm sitting in the window of the sandwich shop, waiting and watching, and I see her hurrying along the street to meet me. But she isn't my Elsa. She isn't the same girl. Something in her walk. Something in her mouth. Still, she sits down opposite me, smiling, but her eyes, they won't look up at me. They aren't dark with fury and fire and love—they're hidden and flat. I bob and shift and try to catch her out, to make her see me, but she won't see. If she will look, if she will see *me* . . . But she won't allow it."

Hazzan pulled a handkerchief from his pocket and wiped at his nose, his hand trembling. "And what I could not understand then was very simple — that Elsa had made her choice and chosen, well, not me. This made no sense. It has never made sense. With all we shared, all we knew of each other, how could she abandon me so easily?"

Blessingame sighed and rubbed his eyes. An inspiration, an insight deep as his own pulse had come to him in the last few moments as they sometimes did on the bench, but this one gave him no satisfaction. "Sounds to me like maybe that's what your uncle Arthur had in mind, or something like from the beginning," he mused. "Maybe once he realized you and his daughter were — *close* — this could be one final way of rubbing your old man's nose in it, paying him back. Through you, by doing this to you." The judge shrugged.

Hazzan tilted his head to the side, considering. He glanced up at Blessingame intently, head cocked so his good eye, sharp blue, could get a clear look, as if making the man out for the first time. He nodded his head. He shook his head. Then he took up the thread of his story again, as if afraid to let it go just yet. He needed to follow it through as well.

"What could I do? I was in a rage, but against who? I couldn't be so angry with Elsa. But she didn't have the courage to step across with me into another world. I couldn't even be angry yet with him, Arthur Lewis. Not yet. I felt humiliated and ashamed.

"That night, very late, I rode my bicycle out to this house. I didn't know what I was going to do or what I wanted to do. Maybe she would be waiting for me . . . But, ah, I knew

better. I was crazy with pain. But, but. I didn't know what to
do and I had to do something.

"The moon was very full and cold. All she had to do was
look out the window. Any of them could look out—I didn't
hide. Clear as day, better than I see today, I could see these
bricks and steps. Yet I was blind too. I stumbled over there on
the walk and the bike clattered to the ground. I froze. But
nothing happened. Silence. They were mocking me—they
couldn't hear, wouldn't take notice of me even if I was sneaking up like a thief in the night, like a murderer. So, like a thief,
I stole up these steps and my knife pried the mezuzah away
from its place and I stole the parchment out from it and I
pushed the empty case back. I don't think I even knew what I
was doing. A thief, I stole away with the blessing on this house,
and it has haunted me, more in recent years even than then.
We are funny creatures, we men, haunting ourselves this way."

Hazzan fell silent, caught up in his own thoughts, weighing his own words as well as the disturbing notion that the
judge had unexpectedly planted in his mind. "Was I only his
toy after all? His puppet? Was he pulling strings and dancing
me so I didn't even know I danced as he wished, all to hurt
my father, his old friend? My father who would scarcely sit in
a room with his son after this.

"Maybe this is right.

"Maybe you are right.

"A puppet—Arthur Lewis made me dance in fire and I
had no clue." He smiled grimly in amazement and shook his
head.

Blessingame sat silently by him on the front steps of the
house. He was thinking about crossing between worlds and
how easy it was and how impossible it could be. He imagined
a delicate membrane between Marjorie and himself, gossamer

in San Diego but all too leaden once they returned here. Tough with expectation and custom, it lay heavy, suffocating. Never were they able to pierce through to each other, or they hadn't known how.

For several minutes neither man spoke. At last Blessingame rose and fetched a screwdriver and a hammer. Without looking at Hazzan, he chipped at the mezuzah on the doorpost. He was gentle but deliberate, like a sculptor seeking to discover a form secreted in the stone. Flakes of paint dropped away. Slipping, his blade gouged the wood of the door frame. A second time it veered off the surface, gouging a pocket in his fist. "Damn," he muttered.

Another stab and a bright gash of brass lay exposed. Sweating now, frustrated and resentful, thinking of the girl Elsa and the woman Marjorie, Blessingame worked with a savage care to draw the screws without stripping them. He didn't want Marjorie resurrected for him. It had taken years enough—out of all proportion to their days together—to bury the absence of her. Now the fresh memory—so quick, so vivid he could smell her as if she'd just stolen away from his side—only brought home to him that he was older and lonely and alone. Nor did he appreciate this old man, this Jew, catching him up this way in stories and memories that had nothing to do with him. The small cylinder remained fixed to the door frame as if loath to be torn free.

Once more he pried at it with the blade. Abruptly, casually, it dropped into his palm.

All this while Hazzan sat on the steps of the porch without watching what his host was doing. Perhaps he took it for granted. Perhaps he was thinking of something else entirely.

Blessingame studied the cocoon in his palm. Its back was loose, a hinge at one end. Pushing with his nail, he peered inside to inspect the long-abandoned shell, its butterfly already fled. Instead, his eyebrows shrugging high, he discovered a tiny scroll of paper, parchment actually.

Thrown off balance, he turned awkwardly toward his guest, thrusting the cylinder out. Only at the last instant did he snatch it back—still the old man was staring off toward the trees—dig the scroll free with his nail, and tuck it into his shirt pocket.

"Here," he said, pushing the hollow mezuzah at Hazzan.

The old man seemed startled, even terrified to be confronted with the physical reality of the ornament. "No," he said, shaking his head. "You must think me crazy. I must be out of my head after all these years."

He rose from the steps, refusing to touch the mezuzah still extended in the other's hand, and picked up his hat from the wicker settee. "I'm sorry," he said. "I don't know why."

He paused again and took a deep breath, a full breath. "Yes, maybe yes, I do. I buried my wife not long ago, you see." He raised a hand defensively. "It was all right. A blessing really. She had been in great pain. But, well, when it was finished, I had time and I was thinking of many things, and I realized that this, here, was something else I needed to finish at last."

He walked to the bottom of the steps and turned back to his host. "You have been kind to listen. What I needed was to tell someone. That's what I see. It wasn't really a story until now. And only in the telling do I see too what a silly, stupid little story it has been, clutched to my heart like something precious, a secret little prick of pain, all these years. After all these years, I realize better how Arthur Lewis made me dance. And the anger doesn't rise again. It disappears like smoke. *Phff,* what does anger matter anymore? It is too late." He patted his breast pocket. "I think I will keep this blessing after all, for however long. You keep the mezuzah." He fumbled for his wallet. "I am sorry about your paint. Here, I must, allow me."

Blessingame, silent, lips pursed, stood at the top of his steps and allowed the other to reach up to him with a ten-dollar bill. "That cover it?" Hazzan asked.

"You're in the clear," said the judge.

LIFE SENTENCES

The bitter internecine wars of the faculty were long past, consigned to reminiscence and hallway anecdote, and Jeremy Fox missed them. No longer did his colleagues bellow and spume at one another over adding women's studies to the curriculum (and women to the faculty), or while staunchly defending the verities of Plato, Shakespeare, and Keats. (And sometimes threaten too: when begged, Fox would recite the tale of a certain wild old man who, after one such debate thirty years before, had rushed home to fetch an ancient service revolver. He'd waggled the gun in a rival's nose for some little while before firing at last and mortally wounding a commons-room sofa.) Often enough in their youth they'd threatened the dawn as well, with bourbon and cigarettes and argument over things that mattered.

In these latter days of the century, however, Fox could only retreat after a department meeting to his office on the third floor of the humanities building. His gut would be rumbling in outrage and despair, aroused not by some principle worth blood on the floor, but by the petty scurrilousness of younger colleagues.

On a gloomy February afternoon, Fox was doing just that, trudging heavily up three flights of steps. Despite himself, he halted on the second landing, panting for breath. A door burst open somewhere overhead, and a moment later he heard then saw someone descending awkwardly toward him. Naturally, it was Ryan McKnight—it was Ryan McKnight whose future the department's tenured members had just been debating with considerable passion. Because of the diabetes he'd developed as an adult, McKnight's balance was uncertain and his legs stiff. Each step on the staircase was an effort. On level ground he could treat his cane as a jaunty prop. But the stairs demanded he lean heavily on it. Fox hoped he would have the good grace to keep going with a nod.

Instead, the black man paused one step above the landing and flashed a wry grin. "Come from deciding my fate?"

As usual McKnight was wearing a beret, an affectation that Fox had early on expected to despise but found himself rather envying. He pursed his lips. "Can't discuss it—you know that," he said. "Besides, nothing's decided yet."

McKnight laughed a booming laugh that rocketed through the stairwell. "Six years waiting for a secret decoder ring and still not there yet. Well, I guess I can be a good boy a few weeks more." With a salute of the walking stick at his senior colleague, he resumed his labors down toward Ascension Hall's main door.

Fox paused a moment longer to gaze after him. McKnight was cocky, sure of himself—*full* of himself—with a sharp disdain for certain others on the faculty hidden not at all discreetly. Some wanted to kill him for slights real and imagined. Famously, at McKnight's very first public presentation—while visiting the campus on an interview—a member of the search committee had offered a question. It glistened with theoretical fashion. Dialogic this. Discourse analysis that. Lila Wallace was merely preening, of course, a demonstration for the small audience that she remained intellectually hip. Very likely she didn't even expect an answer. Others in the classroom wearily endured her little pretensions—they'd been similarly guilty often enough. Ryan McKnight gazed at Dr. Wallace for a moment with that wry grin of his, sizing her up along with the question. "I can talk that talk," he said at last, stroking a goatee that already showed streaks of gray, "but I won't walk the walk. It's not what I do." Thus dismissed, the woman flushed and laughed shrilly. Intentionally or not, McKnight had made an enemy for life.

But students adored McKnight. He gave himself up to them for conferences and extra study dates and simple bull sessions in a way that few colleagues would imagine any longer. Too much pressure to publish these days. Too long a commute, since new faculty rarely chose to live in the college's remote village. But Ryan McKnight, though junior in rank, didn't fit in among the younger crowd. He was nearly fifty and had no spouse. No, when it came to his teaching and his students, the man seemed something of a throwback, and Jeremy Fox respected him for that.

BY THE time he reached his office, dusk was already gathering beyond the window. He yanked open the bottom drawer of his file cabinet. A wad of old exam books jammed between two bottles kept them from clanking. One was mouthwash; the other, vodka, was the safe bet. As far as anyone knew, he'd been on the wagon for five years, and he had no intention of disabusing them. But he'd only just splashed the bottom of a coffee mug when someone jerked the handle on his door and then bothered to knock.

"Hold on," he cried gruffly, and jammed bottle and mug into a wastebasket behind his desk.

The chairman of the department was hovering in the hall as Fox tugged the door open. "Jeremy?" said Martin Crandall, his head cocked mischievously. He actually put his hand on Fox's shoulder as if they were still intimate friends—as Fox had once been foolish enough to imagine. He'd hired Crandall twelve years earlier, had taken him under his wing, nursed him through the nearly botched conclusion of his dissertation and then a failed marriage, all the way to tenure. Punished for such deeds, Fox had seen their relationship cool in recent years. He wondered what Crandall would be sidling for this time.

The visitor settled himself on a wooden chair. He leaned back, hands behind his head. "I think that went pretty well, don't you? Another session and we should know where the department stands on McKnight."

"Haven't you already made up your mind?" asked Fox.

"Oh, well—I do have my opinions, but I'd rather not force them on our friends. I'd prefer we reach a consensus everyone can live with. Obviously, your own position will be—influential." His mouth twitched. His eyebrows twitched above sleek eyeglasses designed for a younger profile.

Fox didn't respond.

Crandall's usual modus vivendi was to snag people in doorways, to lobby them across the copier, to hammer an agreement that suited him well before any general meeting. This time, however, about McKnight's prospects for tenure, the chairman was being uncharacteristically coy. Of one thing alone was Fox certain—that Crandall would ultimately cloak his own preferences in the garb of duty and selflessness.

"Actually, Jeremy, I didn't drop by to talk business. Last night Meri and I decided it's simply been too long, *ages,* since you've come by. We know how hard it must be, you alone in that big house. We really should have managed something before now. But you of all people understand the chair. Paperwork, petitions. It never stops, does it?" He sighed dramatically. "No rest for the wicked. Anyway. What say you drop by for dinner tomorrow? Just the three of us, just family. Meri's dying to see you."

Fox nodded and pursed his lips. He didn't much care whether his distaste showed. As little as he longed to spend time outside the office with his former protégé Crandall, it was true he'd love to see Meri. And her husband knew it perfectly well.

"That would be grand, Martin, just grand," Fox conceded with a sigh of his own. All he wanted at the moment was to shoo the fellow from his office so he could liberate mug from wastebasket.

SHE WAS shaking her finger at him, eyes alight. "You're nearly an hour early, and I'm not half finished. You wanted time alone with me, didn't you?" she asked, bobbing up on her toes for a quick peck at his cheek. "Ashamed of yourself, Jeremy?"

"Terribly, yes—terribly ashamed," he said, attempting to sound gruff and failing. "You'll have to punish me with vegetable peeling or noodle straining—whatever help I can be."

"There's a pretty picture." She laughed, grasping his hand

and leading him to the kitchen. In a moment he was safely ensconced on a ladder-back chair, no paring knives within reach.

Meri attended to her cooking. Her print dress, its small red-and-white blossoms slightly faded, made her seem more willowy even than she had as a girl—tall and slender and fair, her fine reddish blond hair gathered into a simple fall by a tortoiseshell clip. She might still be the favorite student—Fox half closed his eyes—a young woman of light and fierce wit. Here she was, playing grown-up again, inviting her mentor over for dinner. The first time had been such brilliant fun— a perfect dinner in every meaningful way. (Though the ancient dormitory oven hadn't quite cooked the duck through. Fox and his wife, Barbara, playacted happily, never betraying the secret of the too-pink flesh.) Better than ten years ago that little game, and Barbara long gone, and Meri, her doctorate abandoned for love, married to Martin Crandall. He'd been a mentor too, it turned out, of a different sort.

Fox grimaced at the thought.

Meri sliced spring onions with flashing precision, tip of her knife hinged against the cutting board. "Having you here seems the most natural thing in the world," she was saying, "which only makes me feel worse it's been so long. Why don't you ever come by to see me?"

He resented—suddenly and with a hot flush that flared into his cheeks—her putting him on the spot, her forcing him to lie for the sake of good manners. "Oh, well, I've imagined how frantic you must be—now that you're catering half the dinners in the county. And I'm up to my ears as well with students demanding more and more. They're *consumers,* as the admissions people keep reminding us. I'm merely—what?— another service provider attending to their needs."

Meri darted him a quick smile. Her hands never ceased moving, but she seemed entirely at ease as she prepared the meal. "Yes, and we were such scholarly angels in comparison."

Fox smiled too in sheer fondness. "You and your friends presented other sorts of challenge."

"And anyway," she said, mischief and a stabbing serious-ness playing in her eyes at once, "busy-ness has nothing to do with it. That's just bull. You don't visit me because you can't stand Martin anymore." She smiled again, offhand and devastating.

For a long moment neither of them spoke. Fox's lips re-mained pressed together; he wasn't going to lie again, not to her. At last he shrugged. "But here I am, one way or the other. You've invited me and we'll have a splendid evening."

"I didn't invite you," she said. "He did."

Her fierceness in renouncing the responsibility stung him. Fox sighed, almost asked her for a drink, thought better of it. "Which of you is playing games with me, Meri? I'm an old man and feel it more every day—I'm too slow for this dance."

She came and stood next to him, hands on her waist, and then leaned over and kissed him again on the cheek. The sen-sation was delightful, the whiff of her, the caress of youth, and yet the gesture made him feel more a relic than ever.

"In case you haven't guessed it, Martin and I have reached that stage where it's games we're playing with each other, and you, dear friend, are snared in the middle of it."

"No." He clutched at the edge of the counter and rose. "No. It's none of my business and I don't want any part. Tell him I called—something came up. A root canal. A summons from the provost."

She patted his sleeve. "There's no easy escape for you, Jer-emy. This isn't about just Martin and me. It involves your department and the recommendation you'll be making on Ryan McKnight."

He said nothing—what could he say? The dance was spinning quick and dizzying, and he couldn't even try to keep up.

"Didn't I know how you disapproved of Martin and me after you found out?" she said brightly, twirling the talk off in another direction, baffling him. "Or how furious—how *disdainful*—you were when I gave up on the degree and returned to be with him here?" Meri turned her back on him and fled to the stove as if for protection, seizing a ladle and thrusting it into a pot. "How could I not know? You meant so much to me. And your opinion—I didn't dare ask what you thought outright.

"I couldn't explain it to you then, and I'm not sure I can even now. He, well, Martin was older and so dazzlingly smart, and yet he could be so young and playful and passionate too, more passionate than the fumbling college boys. Maybe that's what's changed."

Fox was shaking his head. Anything not to hear this. "McKnight. What's this got to do with Ryan McKnight?"

She lifted the ladle and seemed not to notice a thin spittle of brown sauce crawling toward her arm. "Let's hope I can face your opinion now," she murmured as if to herself. "Okay. Jeremy. Here goes. Here goes." The ladle plunked heavily again into its pot. "I've been sleeping with him. Seven months now."

"With whom?" he blurted, coming to understand even as he heard his own absurd noise, desperately searching for rhyme or reason, a way out of knowing.

She swiped awkwardly, miserably at a strand of pale reddish hair near her eyes. "I know this must be hard for you. It can't make any sense. But Ryan is who."

A black beret twirled airily in the shadows. He seemed to hear McKnight's booming laugh, to spy his grin.

"You think I'm too old for this sort of thing?—*I* think I'm too old." She snorted. "Wild passion of all things—it's ridiculous, I know. But it's become the breath in my lungs, the blood in my veins, what I feel for him. Still, I'm watching myself and I can't quite believe it. Maybe that's the difference when you're past thirty. But I didn't look for it to happen. I sure didn't ask." Her eyes grew dark and impatient with herself, haunted by her own lack of control.

"Why are you telling me this? Why did I need to know? I *don't* need to know." He stopped, ashamed of his own whining.

"Who am I to tell, if not you?" she asked.

That puzzled him. He didn't know what to make of it. But it vaguely pleased him.

"And besides," she went on, "you *do* need to know, at least I think you do, given the tenure decision."

"Ah," said Fox. "Ah." The dance slowed, and now he could spy the pattern of steps ahead. He was almost disappointed that Meri's design should be so humble.

"Martin knows?" he asked.

She nodded and bit her lip. "I couldn't stand the lie—it was worse than all the rest."

"Well, he's been brilliant, I must say. I'd no clue he was out for McKnight's scalp. Of course, he's not alone in that." He paused and looked at her, but she gave no sign. "And you want me to engineer a way to get the man his tenure." He felt stern and benevolent, revitalized by this position of fresh influence—slightly elevated just now and gazing sagely down at this young woman.

But Meri was shaking her head, lip still caught between her teeth. Her eyes had grown red, though she wouldn't wipe at them, not yet. *"No,"* she cried softly. "Don't you see—I couldn't stand that. Ryan wants to stay, wants me to throw Martin off and live with him here."

She paused, panting lightly. "He deserves his tenure—he knows it and wants it, odd as that may seem. But that'll be the end, for me. I'll go with him somewhere else, anywhere. But not here. No more of this for me."

Fox felt himself reeling once more. "And this part you haven't told Martin."

She shook her head again.

"So. Martin wants to chase McKnight away. And so do you." Fox sat again on the hard chair.

"Some of them in your department hate him—Martin's only too happy to keep me in the loop as far as that goes. Ryan's no diplomat, god knows. Partly it's because he won't play the status game—who's hot, who knows the trendiest theory, who deserves to be someplace more famous. Even the provost does it. The assumption being you aren't *really* good unless some other university is trying to lure you away. As if he couldn't get an offer, a flood of offers, simply picking up the phone."

She put a hand on her hip with a sneer for them all. "They like that he's black, of course. It makes the college seem so hugely progressive. But he should be a good boy and play the game just as if he was white."

"What do you want from me?" Fox demanded impatiently.

"Don't I know you?" she cried. "I know what matters. My guess is you'd decide that Ryan deserves to stay, that it's better for the college if he's here." She shrugged. "And you're Jeremy Fox. Whichever way you come down, your voice matters—you'll carry enough of the others."

"Ah," he said once more, hopelessly. "But that's not what you want. You want me to trust your husband's judgment, rather than my own."

She stood silently before him, her hands ungainly and limp without the knife to focus them, as her friend struggled again to his feet. "Tell Martin I wasn't up to dinner tonight," he said. "I was feeling my age."

AFTER FOUR hours of fitful sleep, Jeremy Fox woke in the night. There'd be no falling away from himself again without resorting to a pill that would leave him groggy through the coming day. Yet neither could he seem to rouse himself. His legs felt heavy, his head and arms leaden, wide awake though he lay in the darkness.

It occurred to him that he hadn't been dreaming of Meri, or at least he didn't think so. It was only lying here awake that he realized he wished he could. He groaned and pushed the thought away, but it pushed back.

Her confiding in him, beseeching his aid, had stirred other demons of loneliness and despair, familiar visitors who'd come occasionally to him in the night all his life. He'd always hoped the prospects of extinction would grow easier to bear with age. Tonight they only seemed more pathetic, casually at hand, grimmer. For the first time in a long time he felt the physical absence of Barbara's warm heaviness, her steady, reassuring breathing, under the covers next to him.

He lay in the darkness, needing to pee. Frustration and fear and longing swept over him. Why shouldn't *he* be the one to catch Meri up in his arms and rush off to another life? He shook his head on the pillow in silent debate or explanation. It wasn't a fantasy of sex—that would be too easy. To some degree it wasn't even Meri who mattered, love her though he did and had all these years. It was the fierceness of her grasp, the way she bit her lip, the life she still wrestled because the wrestling was the living.

Fox switched on a lamp and in the bathroom peed gratefully and with all the fervor he could muster.

"YOU AVAILABLE for a chat?" Ten A.M. and Martin Crandall was already poking his nose inside the office.

Fox was exasperated more than surprised. He wanted to be left alone. "Office hours," he said. "Students will be dropping by to complain about grades on their last essay." He wasn't eager to have this or any conversation with Crandall.

"Fine by me—I'll leave your door on the crack in case they show up."

"What's so confidential?" Fox demanded. Something cavalier about Crandall's attitude bothered him, a risk taking, an exhibitionism. Had he left his own door on the crack in the old days when Meri came to visit?

"Entirely hush-hush for the moment. Can't go any further than us. I'd intended to mention it at dinner—sorry you weren't well, by the way. Better now?"

Fox might have nodded.

"The provost and I were having a drink recently," Crandall said casually, always glad to let drop his entrée with the administration. He tugged at the sleeve of his stylish fawn-colored jacket. "She suggested something rather out of the blue, but I think we—you—had better grab it before she's time to discover other priorities."

"What the devil are you talking about, Martin?" Fox asked impatiently.

"No need to take that tone with me, old friend. Not with the gifts I'm bearing. Listen to me: there's a college trustee who's interested in a smidgen of immortality. He's endowing a chair in his own name—the check's already signed. Got it? The provost is suggesting you be the one to assume it. Yours until you retire." Hands behind his head, pleased with himself, Crandall tilted his ordinary wooden chair back on two legs.

Fox said nothing. He was startled by the sudden swoop of delight that nearly set him trembling. He struggled to remain stern before Crandall. An endowed chair was no small bauble. Less teaching, more time and support for his writing, for travel. Not to mention the honor itself. He wished he didn't care about that, but he did—the college acknowledging his years of service. None too soon, he thought.

He rubbed a hand across his face. "How much does this have to do with the McKnight decision?"

Crandall sat forward and the chair legs banged against the floor. "You're kidding, right?"

"It's something I have to ask," said Fox with a shrug. "Since you're doing the offering."

"No, damn it—it's like I said. The provost asked what I thought. I *thought* it was a pretty good idea. McKnight is totally separate." He sat glaring at the older man. "Naturally, I assume—I hope—we'll find a way to agree on that in any event."

"Will we?"

"You tell me. I've tried to keep my opinion under wraps on this one. But let's face it, Ryan McKnight is a loose cannon." Something restraining Crandall seemed to give way abruptly and he leaned forward. "The man's dangerous. Unreliable. He creates dissension whenever he so much as shows his face at a faculty meeting."

Fox remained calm, dispassionate, as if this were no more than the collegial discussion it might have been. "What about the students?"

"Okay, sure—some of them worship the guy. But not everyone, let me tell you. I've seen the evaluations. He never gets his essays graded on time. He's cavalier about meeting classes and dismisses half of them early. And he's got this edge—you know, that sarcasm of his. Some kids can't handle that stuff." He waved a hand dismissively. "As for his own work? What he's published may be pretty good, but there's precious little to show. He ought to have more in print."

Crandall paused, haughty. "Okay, you want to know where I stand—now you know."

"Does the endowed chair depend on my standing there too?"

"Why are you being such a prick? You don't want it, you don't want it." Crandall's face flushed with anger.

"Of course I do. But I did have this talk with Meri."

Crandall barked an angry laugh. "You think I don't know? Oh no, my Meri tells me *everything,* whether I want or not. Did I want to know Ryan McKnight is fucking my wife?"

Fox lurched quickly to his feet, thrust his head into the hallway to make sure no one was loitering, shut the door firmly. As he turned back, Crandall was glaring up at him, face flushed and twisted, his hair awry.

"This shouldn't matter to me in my professional decisions," said Crandall, "that this old goat is fucking my wife? Or to you? It's your darling Meri we're talking about." He ran both hands through the tangle of his hair. "Don't you get it? Don't you care? Or is this the point for you?—that it's no worse him doing it to her now than me doing it before?"

"Stop it," Fox snapped.

"You like he's humiliating me this way?—coming here, stealing her away, mocking me. Doesn't he deserve tenure as a reward? And I should deliver it. Have it ground in my face the rest of my life."

Crandall's head dropped. "God knows I've tried to keep quiet, let others take the lead. What am I *supposed* to do?" In an instant he'd tumbled from anger and outrage into a raw pleading that was at once painful to witness and pathetic.

"I don't know." Fox pursed his lips. "I honestly don't know."

THERE WERE easier ways both of keeping fit and of providing for his fieldstone fireplace, but in recent years, years alone, Fox's principal exercise had become an hour every day splitting firewood in the yard behind his house. He liked the rhythm and rough precision of the ax, the partnership with gravity and steel. He raised the head easy and slow, only so high. Sliding down the barrel, his right hand met its mate, driving the blade into the heart of the grain. His shirt was already damp under an ancient tweed, and he could feel the reassuring thump of his heart as he breathed deeply into the work.

"Professor Fox!"

Reluctantly, he turned and saw Ryan McKnight picking his way. Why would the man, six years a colleague, make such a point of calling him *professor*, and even out here?

But for once there was nothing playful or mocking in McKnight's eyes. He was breathing hard as well, as if he'd been hurrying much farther than merely from the street. Something was strange in the way he looked too, but Fox couldn't put his finger on it. Only when he realized, a moment later, that McKnight's black beret was missing did he become alarmed. Was this something to do with Meri's confiding in him? Had her lover learned that she'd shared their secret? What if this bareheaded McKnight attacked? Despite his infirmity, he was a big man, powerful in the shoulders. The heavy ax against his leg only made Fox feel helpless. He imagined a ludicrous scene: McKnight cudgeling him to the ground with his cane.

"Tell me—what've I ever done to you?" McKnight cried, his voice surprisingly shrill.

Fox stared at him. "Nothing." He shook his head. "Nothing—what are you talking about?"

"Story's around that you're sabotaging the vote. They say you're out to screw me. What makes you think I don't belong at your damn school anyway?" He halted only an instant. "Is it that I'm black? Are you one of them after all—pretending you're just fine with some of us coloreds around, but only if we're not too loud? I didn't expect it, Fox, not from you."

He was already shaking his head. He held up a hand and shook it *no* as well. The accusation stung. How could McKnight not know his record?—that for years he'd been one of the righteous few, struggling to open the doors of this faculty, battling the Mr. Chipses and the outright bigots who preferred a comfortable country club. Good wars, worthy fights. And here he was being accused. Meri certainly was aware—hadn't she bothered to testify?

Still Fox was wagging his hand *no*. Yet his outrage cooled to a faint nausea as a dirty little doubt seeped into his consciousness—was this perhaps what did bother him after all? Not that Meri betrayed her husband, but that it was with a black man. He didn't want to be haunted by such visions, but he'd imagined them together—yes, he had. White flesh and dark, plunging and twisting, sweating and crying out. Yes, he had, though he fought not to. Was it the color of flesh that haunted him? He wasn't sure. He considered asking McKnight himself here in the chilly afternoon—was this why, was it as simple and nasty as this?

At least he could answer the easier challenge the man had put to him. He tipped the ax against a broad oak stump. "You've been here long enough not to trust those sorts of rumor. As a matter of fact, I haven't tried to persuade anyone of anything. I wish I could tell you—I won't lie—that my own mind's made up, but it's not. You're not an easy man ..." He was going to go on, to qualify that observation, but the words opened out with no easy resolution.

"Damn right," muttered McKnight with an angry laugh. "I'm no easy man. My friends are usually the ones to point that out."

Curiosity nudged Fox to a question of his own. "Why do you want it?" he asked. "Tenure would only tie you down, make it harder to move."

McKnight gave an angry bark of a laugh. "Because I've earned it, damn it. What do I care if some of your friends don't want me? Hell, that'll be true here or anywhere. That only makes it the sweeter."

Fox nodded and remained silent.

McKnight nodded too. Lifting his cane in salute, he turned away, wading gingerly toward the road again through fallen leaves and the last isolated patches of the season's snow.

Fox's damp shirt had grown cold, chilling him. As he reached for the ax, it seemed impossibly heavy. Looking up, he glimpsed a last flicker of McKnight's bare head as he stepped onto the street. And something, maybe the way the man's cane tapped out before him onto the asphalt searching for better purchase, or maybe it was the slant of light through the trees or simply the chill in the air—something made Fox shiver. And he realized then that he'd made up his mind after all. That last glimmer of shadow as McKnight disappeared only sealed it. He grimaced with annoyance. Rather than allowing him to sit down and calmly, sanely, mull the merits of this difficult decision, the answer had ambushed him, an intuition from so deep in the bone that no merely intellectual exercise seemed adequate. It belied the impression he hoped others had of him: a man of care and thoughtful deliberation.

Instead of starting again on a fresh log, he angrily stacked the dozen quarters already on the ground. Had self-doubt, maybe even a splinter of guilt at McKnight's initial assault on his motives, maneuvered him away from what he might otherwise decide? He paused, a shank of red maple in his hand. No, it didn't feel that way. He didn't think so. Nor had the dramatic (and mildly terrifying) appearance of the visitor in his backyard wrought some more profound transformation of his character. Bending one last time, he grunted at the untidy mysteries of the human soul, not least his own. On the whole he preferred dealing with the safely mediated passions of literature, no less and, ultimately, no more than words on a page.

Finally, he, too, retreated from the yard, unhappy with himself and the thoughts he'd discovered. He wondered what price he'd pay for them.

PERHAPS JEREMY Fox had witnessed such transformations before, but no scene came readily to mind, none where he knew the source of secret poisons—and felt partly responsible for their effect. In a little under two hours, Martin Crandall publicly withered with bitterness and rage. His face grew haggard, its creases deeply scored. Despite his quiet diplomacy on a broad front over recent weeks, despite his outright and finally nearly hysterical lobbying during this meeting, after much discussion and on a close vote, the English department decided to recommend tenure for Ryan McKnight.

Meri had been right. Once Fox shared his own thoughts on the matter, laying out the reasons for his hesitation, his ambivalence, his final conversion, four votes from old friends and one even from Lila Wallace had swung with him like sails waiting for a steady blow.

Fox knew the consequences would linger for years, long past his own retirement. Among them now at all future meetings, McKnight would take his place, he and Crandall forced to bear one another to the end of their careers.

The last week had brought no further whispers of an endowed chair from the administration. Perhaps Crandall had only been toying with him. Much as Fox yearned for that distinction, however—a nagging, childish, burning want that embarrassed and harassed him—he decided not to broach it personally with the provost. She could let him know when the time was right.

ABOUT MERI, Fox also waited—all of twelve days. He sensed—he was certain—she would come to him or summon him herself. Not that he actually looked forward to a confrontation. But talk, he believed, they must. Better the initiative should come from her.

From that quarter, however, rang only a deadening silence. The spring semester continued on its course, and in the last week of March, spring actually forced the first shoots of green through muddy soil and gravel paths. Still no word from

Meri. At last, impatient, curious, beaten, late on a Thursday afternoon while Crandall was harnessed with other department heads, Fox walked the half mile from his office through the village.

The neat little clapboard house with dormer windows yielded no sign of telling change. Meri's aging station wagon sat empty in the drive. Before knocking, he peered through a window. As his foot sank into the soft garden for a better angle of spying, Meri tugged the door open, hand impatient on her hip. He jerked back and scraped the mud from his shoe on the flagstone path. She didn't seem surprised, said nothing, merely stepped aside so that he could slide guiltily past.

Inside, nothing seemed amiss either. Far from it: the house shrieked its own tidiness. Not a paper was out of place in the living room, no book astray. Without her invitation, he fled directly toward the kitchen. But it, too, was cold and terrifying, no pots bubbling, no pies in the oven.

"My bags are upstairs," Meri, following, said simply. "You've come just in time."

"This is crazy," he said.

"You don't expect me to stay here," she said. "How could I stay in his house any longer?"

Fox's heart lightened. "Then you're not going away?"

"I *am* going."

"But is that what McKnight wants?"

She glared at him with exasperation. "Ryan hasn't any clue what he wants, certainly not about me."

A surge of panic—of despair and loneliness—startled Fox, stealing away his balance. He grasped the back of a chair, hoping she wouldn't notice. The prospect of Meri disappearing from his life was more terrifying than he'd imagined. "Don't go," he pleaded, his voice betraying him. "Stay with me then. I've plenty of room. Too much. Settle yourself for a while, decide what you need." He was rushing, rushing. "You've still got the catering—why not take over my kitchen?"

Meri laughed in scorn. "My *business* is a joke. It's makework, the kind of thing you give lunatics to distract them, so they won't grow violent." She pressed both hands to her forehead. "This place is hell, Jeremy. You're so deep into it you can't even make out the truth. I've always imagined that's why Barbara left." She darted a quick glance at him, perhaps surprised she'd spoken it aloud. Fox stiffened.

"I used to think it was you, that maybe you'd done something wild and terrible while I was off in grad school," she said. "Barbara was just, well, *gone* when I came back. I wondered—I kind of hoped—maybe you'd fallen for a student or a colleague's wife. Some glorious passion. But you wouldn't do that, would you?"

He stared silently, her words bruising as body blows. He sagged and kept his grasp on the chair. She was far, far off the mark, of course, yet close enough in truth. He was willing to endure. He could endure.

"I suppose she had to save herself. Did she give you any warning? I picture Barbara in her garden, just dropping her spade one day. She'd dust her knees, pull on a jacket, and fly. Was it like that?"

Something had hardened about Meri's mouth and at the corners of her eyes over the last weeks. "This nice village with its nice college and all the nice residents watching your students come and go, generation after generation till the end of time—it's a smug little asylum. But you don't even know your own misery until something wakes you from the nightmare. For me it happened to be love."

"Don't go," he murmured again. "I don't pretend to understand any of it, least of all myself. It's all such confusion; it's all so unknowable."

"Unknowable?" she wailed at him in fury, her arms trembling, the skin across the bridge of her nose stretched white. "*Unknowable?* You made a choice, didn't you? You arranged Ryan's tenure, didn't you? Why, Jeremy? You couldn't do me the one favor? How much have I asked, ever?"

"How can I ignore what he swears he wants, or what I think is best for the school?" Fox spread his hands helplessly, despising all the while the whine in his own voice.

"Screw the school. And him? Screw Ryan too. Like I said, he doesn't know what he should want." Her eyes brimmed, cruel and full of despair. "Have you been here so long, fighting the good fight, serving on your committees, you've forgotten what love is?"

He flailed a hand, lamely protecting himself. The world seemed to be reeling away, the very ground beneath his feet not to be trusted. And yet, the ground didn't give way and neither did he—he held steady in the face of it all. Steadier than he might have expected. Numb and sad and lonely, yes, he remained a still center as the emotional chaos of these people swirled about him, destroying so much.

Meri said nothing more. As if this moment were as good as any—or as if the last exchange with Jeremy Fox, her mentor, a man who'd loved her close on fifteen years, had danced her a final step beyond the precipice—she fled the kitchen to fetch two small bags, pulled on a raincoat too light for early spring, and, still without another word, with no gesture at all, climbed into the battered station wagon in the drive and pulled away.

The silence in the house wasn't empty. It rang with shouts

and accusations that Fox could only imagine, but did not, did not, did not want to imagine. From an antique cabinet in the dining room, he drew a bottle of Martin Crandall's expensive scotch, poured some into a tumbler, took a long pull. But the whisky hit his stomach hard and angry. It threatened to rise again into his throat. Bottle and glass he abandoned in the open, but he did bring himself to shut the door of the house as he left, making his way slowly into the village. At the cross of gravel paths he halted, unable to return to his own house, unwilling to retreat to Ascension Hall, lost.

POETRY OF THE AMISH

Eight A.M. on a Tuesday and I knew there was a problem even before I turned up the long gravel drive. I shouldn't have taken the time to swing by the project, but I wanted to make sure everything was on course, on schedule, before I went in to the office. At this stage, even a few hours could throw us off in a cascade of delay, one day, two days, a week. That would mean disaster for our little company—we don't have the deep pockets to survive for long without income.

The April morning was heavy with dew and smoky swirls of mist, sun streaking through a small patch of woods we'd left standing to keep the country feel later on, like garnish on a restaurant plate. Nearly invisible through the haze on top of the hill, the ragged old house seemed almost gone already, or at least on the threshold of disappearing. Which it was supposed to do. Disappear, that is. I should have been seeing: a bulldozer, my contractor and two workmen with sledge-hammers and picks, a dump truck to haul away what was left, all of it, wood and metal pipes and what-all else. Instead, I was seeing nothing. Just the mist and the small patch of woods, the hill (which would scoop out, down its flank, just perfect for a little pond—houses looking over water fetch half again as much) and the small frame house, paint faded to the sheen of water, standing-seam roof intact maybe a hundred years.

Surprised, worried, I half climbed out of my truck, one foot on the gravel, and that's when I made out the shadow of a flatbed on the crest of the drive. Still not what I was expecting. Leaving the truck on the pavement, I walked up through the mud and gravel. Not what my office shoes needed. And that's when I saw no cab or tractor on the other end of the flatbed, but a pair of horses, *huge,* who'd already been set free to graze in the grass. I guess I was only able to take in one surprise at a time, because I noticed the horses before I took in the men. Must have been a dozen of them, men and boys, all dressed in the same dark blue shirts and pants. The only differences among them were some wore straw hats and those old enough for beards had beards. They saw me coming, but no one spoke, them or me. No birds, no dogs, not a sound— the whole scene was eerie and quiet. Maybe it was the mist lying heavy on everything.

At last I did spy Enis Gingrich, my contractor, near the door of the house, head down, nodding and talking with one old man in blue. I caught the tail end, a smatter of the old Dutch or German or whatever it is they speak by themselves. Enis glanced up, startled to see me.

"What's going on?" I said. I don't think I sounded angry. I don't think I *was* angry—just too surprised by all this.

"Hold on," he said gruffly, but Enis is that kind of guy, thin-skinned. "You wanted the house down. This'll be just as good—won't lose no time at all and won't cost you a buck."

"How's that?"

"They're doing it for the materials. They'll take it down, clean it up, cart everything away too. Best deal you could get."

I didn't like the you's instead of we's. He was my contractor and he was sort of a lapsed member of them too.

Okay, fine. Nothing I could complain about. But I was still shaking my head as I walked up onto the wooden porch. I wanted it done. Fast and clean. Gone. No special deals. Behind me, as I stared out over the valley below that no one, neither me nor the bigger developers, had managed to buy up yet, I heard them getting to work. Bustle exploded into hammer and handsaws.

Location. Location. Location. Right? Well, I'd snared me one mighty fine location. I'd known the family from the time I was a boy in school, their boys riding in on wagons and buses, playing ball with me. Daryl moved into town, Ricky went out of state altogether. Jonathon was the one who stayed on the farm with his folks. But I think he knew from the start. He just loved them and kept it together for them. Worked one, two other jobs to keep it going. His dad went first; his mom not a year later.

When did I start? I was Jonathon's pal. Hell, I was a pallbearer for his dad, since most of his dad's brothers and pals were too old themselves. Me and Jonathon, shoulder to shoulder. So maybe it was right there at the funeral home, night before, and I first say to him, "I want it. I can do something with it."

Jonathon shaking his head, head down. And don't I know him? Since Little League and filching our first cigarettes. Don't I know when his head shaking is the same as his head nodding?

If I don't do it, someone else will. That's for damn sure. One of the bigger boys out from town, knowing that this is the next frontier all right, the burbs spreading out to town first, and then on beyond to Jonathon and his folks' place.

I shouldn't have been watching. I'd already missed a ten o'clock that was probably going to cost me money. But these men and boys in blue. Nail by nail they were what?—they were *disassembling* the old house. No big deal to them. They weren't hushed and solemn. Not anything like that. This was a job. This was work. They'd take each of these planks, each of these nails and tubs and pipes, maybe even the old wiring itself. They'd use it or persuade someone else to buy it.

It wasn't reverence, it was just respect. That's the way they were treating the work and the house. Nail at a time. Two-by-four at a time. I couldn't watch. I couldn't keep myself from watching.

I was so furious with Enis, I kept the house between him and me; otherwise I might have canned him on the spot. Why all this? Why couldn't he hire the damn bulldozer like we'd planned?

We can get maybe thirty houses on this parcel. No one wants land anymore. Who's got time for cutting the grass or planting a real garden? No one, that's who. Back them in against one another. A little angle here, a glimpse of the new pond below there. Enough illusion of privacy. They want new houses, with garages for three or more cars. Most important of all—bathrooms, big ones, walk-in waterworks of bathrooms. One for every bedroom and an extra one downstairs too. No time or money for real plaster. No one wants problems. No one wants old houses. Not like this one where we found *three* different eras of electrical wiring, all plugged into a single board. Can you imagine? I don't know how Jonathon kept it from going up in one big ball of flame.

I confess, there were a couple of Sundays when I sneaked out here alone. Left Margie with Sam and Kimmy for an hour at home. One excuse or another. I'd found a broke chair down in the cellar. It was just fine on the porch.

Who'd swiped that damn chair? The Amish men or Enis? Maybe some boys who'd come through here in the night? Who'd even want a broke chair like that? But it wasn't on the porch this time when I looked for it. Just as well, because they were getting to work on the porch itself, so it was time for me to come down anyway.

Came time for the main timbers and frame, and all I could think of was my own daddy's mother and how she was with a turkey. Grampa would carve of course. Then later, the next day or two in the kitchen, there'd be the pulling off of last scraps for a snack or a sandwich. Gramma guarded the carcass for her stew pot. It came apart in making soup, disassembled by heat and water, bone by bone.

It went faster than you'd think. Surprised me how fast. Though it was the end of the day all of a sudden too. The flatbed was stacked, loaded, tied down, horses straining to get some motion before the downslope. Blue and blue, the men and boys walked away behind. Never a glance back at me. Enis must have left with them.

I was ready to leave too. The house was gone. Swept clean of the earth. Not a nail, not a splinter from what I could tell.

Just the cellar, of course, with its mud-packed floors, big and small stones scrounged from the surrounding fields a hundred years or more back pressed into the foundation. We'd fill it in easy enough. I imagined the rains coming first and beating us to it.

Not enough left even to trouble the dreams of people I'd be building houses for.

BIRNKRANDT AND KAMENSKI

Edna was too weary even to see the house ahead on the small rise with her usual sense of relief. Two other nurses on her ward were down with the flu, or so they claimed. She'd been run ragged by belligerent patients—country people, most of them, succumbing to hospitalization for the first time and acting like guests in a luxury hotel with Edna as their personal, and entirely inadequate, servant—and by doctors who scudded through the county hospital peremptorily. Now that she was well past the age where they'd rouse themselves to flirt or fondle, the doctors, one and all, treated her with impatience and scarcely disguised disdain.

Another doctor would be waiting for her as she pulled up the drive. This one, Dr. Birnkrandt, she'd lived with in this house since he, more peremptory than the small-time local doctors could ever imagine, moved here twelve years earlier in retirement and ill health. Edna had nursed him initially as part of her duties in the metropolitan hospital where he had been chief of staff for decades, then privately at the family home from which all family had fled, before allowing herself to be moved with him to this forsaken place.

Shoving open the door—they never bothered to lock it—she heaved through toward the kitchen with a bag of groceries and wondered what mood awaited her, what mood she'd have to deal with during the evening ahead. The question more than the prospect filled her with dread.

She filled a glass with water and carried it toward the living room. The television blare was so loud she could feel the chat-show nonsense vibrating through the planks and sinews of the house. Which meant the old man hadn't bothered with his hearing aids again. And he'd been smoking too. She smelled the acrid stink. But when she came up behind his chair, she saw no ashtray, no dandruff of ashes on the carpet. The fact that he'd try, even lamely, to disguise his misdeeds made her smile despite herself. It also made her wonder what he was up to. He'd be after something. She knew him that well.

Without warning, he aimed the remote control and snapped the TV off, startling Edna. "What's your excuse for being late this time?" he shouted too loudly, not deigning to turn and find her over his shoulder. He hunched forward and stared at the blank tube.

Half blind and three-quarters deaf, how had he known she was there? The old man could and did surprise her.

"Groceries."

"What?" Now he craned first one way then the other, finding her, waving brusquely to a smaller chair.

"*Groceries.*"

"How'd you pay for them?"

"Paycheck," she shouted, sitting as commanded and taking a sip of water. "God knows, not from anything you've given me lately."

"Damn right," he said, slapping the arm of his chair and glaring at her with something that might have been a smile. "I've had my reasons and I'm going to make it up to you."

She nodded wearily, not wanting to play this out again. Better to make dinner for them both and then get off her feet at last. Some television would be just fine too and maybe a little rye and water.

"No, damn it, don't you not listen to me like that." He was trying to thunder like in the old days, but his lungs wouldn't storm. His voice cracked.

In the old days she'd have shrunk in terror from the thunder and lightning, and she wasn't alone. The vast staff of a world-renowned institution cringed before his fury. Now, before his croaky bluster, she might have been amused or contemptuous but was saddened for him instead.

"Will you eat a chicken-noodle casserole if I fix it?"

Making a face, he waved the question away.

She'd half a mind to throw a bologna sandwich on his plate. His sporadic finickiness exasperated her. Or nothing at all. That's what he deserved. A naked plate.

"I spoke with my attorney today," he said. "I've decided the best thing is to leave you the house."

"Where are you going without me?" she cried, stunned and indignant. She pictured him on a Florida beach. She pictured him being wheeled into a nursing home. As if some other nurse could take better care.

He smacked his lips over his dentures and blinked at her. He shook his head. "How can one woman be so fucking stupid? That's what I get for taking in a fucking Polack." He paused, panting. "Is your hearing worse than mine, or you just too slow to get it? I'm not *going* anywhere. And when I do, you'll be just as happy to stay behind. Your turn'll come soon enough." He blinked at Edna's concerned, confused face again. "He's putting it in the will, you moron. I'm leaving you the fucking house."

Edna nodded. "I don't want the house."

"I don't want the house," he whined. "How the hell else do you think you're getting any of the money I owe? You know the wives scratched every cent they could. Them and my loving offspring."

"Why would I want your house?"

Even as she said it, she realized she *did* want it. It wasn't really his house, after all, not like the big one back home. No matter the money. This was their house. They'd come here together, more or less equal—if he was paying the mortgage, he certainly wasn't paying her, and she was the one taking care of him.

Why now? she wondered. Dr. Birnkrandt never did anything on a whim. Not a single spark of his soul was so casual as that.

"What's going on?" she asked. Her face had gone pale, and she felt weak suddenly, closer to tears than she could have imagined. And she knew how her face blotched when she cried, how it grew doughy and patched with purple pink, how he despised her when that happened. Which only brought the tears closer. "Are you baiting your children again because they haven't been paying enough attention? Well, I don't think you'll get a rise—they're pretty well convinced you hate them by now."

"Did I say anything about those selfish bastards? This's got shit to do with them."

"Then *what*?" she cried. "Are you ill?—did you have another spell without telling me?"

He was shaking his head impatiently, gripping the sides of his ancient green leather chair, the one item he'd claimed from his office, first moving it to the old house and then, again the sole item he seemed to care about, shipping it ahead down here. He was leaning forward slightly, his jaw working without the dentures, him saying nothing, just staring at her as if trying to interpret the symptoms of her malady, as if waiting for a verdict.

Did this really have anything to do with her, or was she only a pretext for goading his family? Why was he pushing this to a crisis so abruptly? All along she'd harbored the sweet, secret notion that she alone of all his women and wives and family really knew him, could read him. Never would she dare breathe the thought aloud, too potent, too dangerous. But suddenly a wall had appeared, a mask behind which he gave nothing away.

Was this all his love for the drama of a moment, something to rouse him and keep him going?—she could well imagine it. She'd seen it before.

Was there someone else? Had yet another new woman wormed her way into his life? The thought was crazy, but he'd had such a history. Who could know?

Or maybe he was the one going crazy for real now. She couldn't imagine Dr. Birnkrandt surviving long without her and her attentions, her little private rubs and strokes, the bits of candy, the bribes he adored.

"*What?*" she said again, beside herself with rage and worry and weariness. She felt helplessly, hopelessly overmatched and resented him for it, for educating her and sharpening her wits over the years, so she was quick enough to see what dolts her local bosses were, and how much swifter, how keen as lightning, no matter ill, reduced, embers of the old flame, was he.

"Are you trying to get rid of me? Is that all this is? Buying me off?"

The inspiration, searing as lightning too, hadn't occurred to her until she spoke it aloud. She didn't dare chase where it led.

Shaking her own head hard from side to side, she wouldn't look at him again. "Keep your damn house," she shouted, not looking at him, not waiting for him, heaving herself up. The water glass—she'd forgotten she was still holding it—knocked against the side table, tumbled at the floor, shattered. Not daring to hesitate or deal with the puddle and shards, Edna stumbled away.

Somehow, suddenly, she was out of the house, into the free and clear. She was driving slowly toward town, not thinking, refusing to think. Her knuckles ached white at ten and two.

Free and clear, she was heading away from her house, the only place she longed to be, for fear of finding out why he intended it for her.

MUGGINGS

Jack Hayes wasn't thinking about Leslie Epstein on the day of his wedding. No, the ceremony itself, staged in a dramatic stone tower in Devon, as well as the events leading up to and trailing away from it, were exciting, memorable, just about perfect because he'd left most of the planning to Margot Hodges. They'd been living together for better than two years—the first woman he'd lived with in nearly twenty years, since the great love of his life in law school. But that's a different story. For one thing, he'd never finished law school, becoming instead a particularly successful insurance broker. A different story.

Some nine months before the wedding, Jack had mentioned to Margot a century bike ride in early July. A hundred miles, up from the sea on the southwest coast of England, across one of the great moors, and a return along the river. "Sure," she said right off, which said a great deal about why they were living together. And sometime later: "You know," Margot mused, as they were walking through Rock Creek

Park with their two dogs (an instance of the consolidation of households), "how 'bout I try the ride too?" In all the time since he'd surprised her with a touring bike for her last birthday, she'd managed only a couple of quick thirty-mile outings with him on the Eastern Shore. Such getaways were tough to schedule. Her most lucrative real estate showings happened on weekends. So the prospect of actually stealing her away to England for a week delighted him. And if she really intended to finish the century across a far more challenging terrain, it would mean the two of them slipping off for some serious training in advance. So much the better.

A week maybe two later, tilting her head with a flip of her short blond hair: "What about, since we'll be someplace special anyway, doing the wedding while we're there? Something small, for family and special friends."

No mammoth production in a Georgetown garden? No wrestling the list down to three hundred of his friends, family, associates, and clients, of her friends, family, associates, and clients? *"Inspiration,"* cried Jack.

Two days before the century ride with its 250 cyclists, rest stops, and medical teams, Jack and Margot were on their bikes, pedaling by themselves along one flank of the river Exe, then across a small floodplain toward a sharp spine of hills. Mamhead, a famously tough climb, wove a long series of switchbacks that Margot attacked and endured without a whimper. As they neared the top, Jack's hand rode in the small of her back, providing that little extra boost she didn't ask for but wasn't too proud to welcome. With that kind of teamwork, with gladness in their hearts, they sped along the top of the ridge toward the tower. It seemed to Jack, not for the first time, a miracle in no way surprising that Margot had managed to find and rent such a wonder from a distance of three thousand miles.

They'd visited the spot twice already. It was Jack who'd discovered—Margot having delegated the actual ceremony to him—that the English still insisted upon certain archaic rules. It turned out that even for the simplest of civil weddings, the couple had to establish residency in Devon for a proper fortnight. Jack joked about publishing their banns on the cathedral door—who knew? Someone might show up to oppose the marriage. But having to make an extra trip in early March was no great hardship. It ratified their creativity and sense of adventure. And they were eager in any event to see the eighteenth-century tower in person and, once satisfied— smitten—also to launch arrangements for hors d'oeuvres and music and flowers. Other than to their business associates, the two-week absence was no burden. It rained most of the time, of course, but they hardly noticed.

Their second visit to the tower had been early in the morning of this same wedding day while ferrying luggage up the Mamhead ridge by car. They'd be staying overnight in the guest suite, reached by spiraling stone staircase above the room where they would be married. From roof or window, Dartmoor stretched vast and dark to the west. Exmoor was a hazy smudge to the north. Below and east, the river carved the county in two, its rolling hills and dark green pasture falling back from the Exe on either side all the way south to the sea.

Arriving now by bike, panting and exhilarated, Jack and Margot were greeted by a woman from Radio Devon in Wellington boots and a waxed jacket, her tape recorder slung over a shoulder. Two Yanks shipping their bikes across an ocean for the Ride for Life (the event was for cancer research) and getting married to boot—well, that was local news and made them celebrities the rest of their stay. Snapping away already was a photographer from the Exeter newspaper, two or three shots as they pushed up the last gravelly hill, two or three more in front of their bikes, hot and sweaty and grinning giddily.

Such responsibilities dispatched, they still had nearly an hour to rush up the spiral stairs, make love quickly while using the handheld shower in the bathtub, and dress for the ceremony. By the time they descended, the local registrar had arrived, her assistant lugging the ornate volume in which Jack and Margot would inscribe their names, along with witnesses from both families. Family and friends, twenty-two all told, had also assembled, gay and noisy, having been fetched to the tower by private coach.

No, it was only two days later that Jack thought of Leslie Epstein again. Or that's not quite right. She'd been present all along as a mote, a fleck of shadow on his attention that drifted all but invisibly in the air. He knew it was there, knew it would flesh once more into sharper focus when the time came.

Jack and Margot were riding somewhere in the middle of a gradually thinning cortege of riders (the serious ones, the time-trialers and other more competitive types, had long since leaped away across the hills) as they climbed a short but sharp rise at mile thirty. Struggling at the crest, Margot pushed up next to him, breathing hard. "Okay," she panted. "You were right," she panted. "Next time I train harder."

He nodded. "You've done great. We can peel off after the next rest stop and finish the fifty. Plenty of others will be doing the same."

"You're a sweet," she said, flashing a smile that betrayed

her exhaustion. "But don't. There's no reason to. I'll be waiting for you on the pier to celebrate."

Jack flushed with joy. She meant it—that's what he knew. She was generous in just this way. Not that he wouldn't stop at fifty if she made the slightest gesture. He'd ridden plenty of centuries. Nothing was hanging on this one. But she'd be just as happy if he went on. She wanted him to finish. And she'd be waiting to greet him at the end. He loved the thought of that.

Thirty miles later Jack was riding well. Since striking off on his own, he'd picked up the pace, pushing himself through pain to an exhilaration of speed and light and the suck and blow of breath that carried him toward a near-meditative bliss. The road hummed, his legs pumped, the moor stretched away with patches of spiny gorse exploding into yellow blossom. Along the way he'd passed other riders, singly or in small packs, and as he soared across Exmoor's harsh, rolling plateau, he was alone, no one to be glimpsed ahead or behind him on this stretch of road. It was only now that the speck on the edge of his vision fleshed itself out. Leslie Epstein. He grunted into the wind with acknowledgment and perhaps some resignation.

"SO, YOU wait for middle age to finally get married and then ride a hundred miles to prove you're still young. Nice." Leslie, sitting at the conference table, saluted Jack with a coffee mug.

"No such thing as middle age anymore," he said, coming through the door, to the group of six other agents about the table. "Our generation, we're young until they check you into the room with ASSISTED LIVING on the door. Or until you roll over first time the company makes a new pronouncement about percentage."

A groan followed the initial laughter welcoming him back. Percentages were why they had gathered here in Jack's office. He was about to make an offer that if they had any sense for survival, Dave Schilling and the others, they wouldn't refuse: to come under Jack's wing, be part of his successful enterprise, and thus provide him greater clout to wield against the corporate bullies. Of course, should he prevail, some thin sliver of any gain would accrue Jack's way. But for security's sake, and to be relieved of the hassle of constant battle, Dave and the others would be well advised.

Why was Leslie Epstein here? In the e-mail message to his personal assistant from London, he'd included Leslie's name on the list of those to be invited. But Leslie already worked for him or with him. She was a consultant, advising his burgeoning staff on marketing and management. Years before, she'd been a successful agent on her own, but she'd tired of the constant selling, the developing of relationships, the cultivation of future clients, and the patient stroking of current ones with problems. The phone calls in the middle of the night became an intrusion on her young family. By chance or foresight, she'd sold her business to Jack before the great sea change in the company. Now she could help with efficiency studies and marketing campaigns on her own terms, not to mention with plenty in the bank and not a little leverage.

Why was she here? She seemed not at all put out. Perhaps she and the others assumed that Jack wanted her, the consultant, to help persuade them. Maybe that's true, thought Jack.

The barb she'd greeted him with was nothing more than playful banter. Yet like an electric ground reestablished, it pricked beneath the skin, invisibly, glancing an echo off his breastbone. The link quivered once more between them. It was a private language that flickered alive and invisible, a charge in the air that the others would never decode. It meant nothing.

"You know, I really appreciate this, Jack. I appreciate all you've done and all you've offered." Dave Schilling was harvesting significant glances from the four other agents who'd been drinking Jack's coffee and bottled water during the course of the conversation. (Dave's blond bouffant was so extravagant that Jack struggled not to ask. A rug? No, it sat too well. Too thick for drugs. Maybe it was that woven stuff they were attaching to the scalp? Jack had already recognized what was coming.) "But truth is, I'm not ready for this," said Dave. "Maybe later I'll have to. But not yet. Thanks." Dave stood and tugged at a powder blue French cuff peeping from his sport jacket. Like his backup chorus, the others rose as well. Jack and Leslie remained behind.

"That went well," she said.

"Yeah."

Was she suggesting that this failure was his fault? That he should have seen it coming or should never have made the offer? Her wit suddenly stung, as if finding a bit of exposed flesh. He tried not to show it, glancing away instead of scowling. "No worse than I expected," he said, hearing the testiness in his own voice. "An opening bid, that's all. They'll be back."

Her lips twitched. She read him too easily. "A little touchy, aren't you, for a first day back?"

Leslie pushed her chair away from the table and rose. She was wearing a blue suit that suited her. It made her neck seem long, her hair dark and full—for someone late in her thirties she showed no hints of gray. The cut was stylish yet professional and made no effort to sculpt her breasts. Yet it was her breasts that Jack was aware of. He remained in his seat as she left with a little wave, her leather notebook tucked under her arm.

Shit, he thought.

The swell and heft of her breasts had appeared to him like a visitation as he crossed the roof of the world on Exmoor. With a vividness that seemed almost eerie, their weight had cupped in his hands, their nipples revealed a secret dark pink, their faint salt and flesh and perfume filled the suck of his mouth.

Christ, he murmured at the conference table in his office.

Whether Leslie was aware of it or not, a dance had already caught them up. These early stages of intimacy and irony, of baiting and teasing, were unpredictable—he could never be sure how they would play out. The dance would develop its own dynamic. It couldn't be stable or frozen in one pose for long. For twenty years and more, it had propelled him and a woman toward something that might be dangerous or passionate or disastrous—or all three. Friendship or collegiality over a long haul, sadly, was never an option. Price of the dance.

It was delicious. The thrill tugged him on despite himself. He was entirely familiar with the arc of its trajectory, and afraid. He felt helpless before it.

Yes, Leslie was married, happily as far as he knew, with two smallish children. But adultery had never much weighed on his conscience. The choice, after all, wasn't ultimately his. If she, whoever she was, wanted to be faithful, she'd be faithful. In that case the dance quickly played itself out. She'd drifted back to her boyfriend in college (one of Jack's dorm buddies by chance) and never breathed a word of what hadn't happened. She'd toyed with it in law school, rolling it around in her mouth (along with Jack's tongue), before retreating somewhat wistfully to the safer precincts of marriage. (This was the one after the one who'd done him wrong—lived with him and left him and changed everything.)

In recent years, however, marriage had gradually disappeared as a hindrance. More typically it was a bookend looming on either end of corporate gatherings in one holiday spa or another. Afterward, Jack would return to his agency, she to hers somewhere across the lower forty-eight, and except for a friendly wave or even a meal at some other conference locale, that would be the comfortable end to it.

Jack turned forty. His family and his closest friends—a couple of guys from high school, one gay, one long married—finally gave up worrying about whether he'd ever find someone for the long haul looming ahead. Jack was just Jack, and pretty damned happy on his own terms.

When who should they start hearing intimations about but this Margot Hodges? Nothing special it seemed early on. Just another of his women, somewhat younger of course, who would put up with him for his charm and his wit and his fun for as long as she was willing to put up with no hope of anything more. But Margot, he confided to one of those old friends, was fun and charming and a little wild too. (One midnight at the Jefferson Memorial, they'd made love standing in the shadows.) Two fully furnished and fully mortgaged houses only a mile apart made no sense, either practically, since he was spending most nights with her anyway, or financially, given the District's real estate market. Her professional opinion. So then they're living together, and that's remarkable enough, the family and old friends agree. When next thing it's two years later and a reunion of family and old friends takes place at a tower in the hills of Devon.

Sitting at his own conference table, staff bustling beyond its large windows and trying not to dart puzzled glances at him just brooding there by himself, Jack sensed the possibility of adultery, no longer such an abstract concept, settle heavily and without any weight at all on his shoulders. His life had been split like a melon into separate halves. Margot was his wife. *Wife.* The sound, the shape of the word, still seemed exotic in his mouth. Yet he had no regrets or second thoughts. He was looking forward to slipping away before six today and meeting her at Café Rembrandt, their favorite little restaurant just up from Dupont Circle, for a first postwedding celebration, just the two of them.

Ah, but Leslie belonged to that separate section of his life, almost to a different life altogether. And his heart was thumping, yes, it really was, as he imagined again this not-so-young Jewish mother with full hips and full breasts and a wry mouth and flashing, caustic wit every bit equal to his own.

Unlike some of his friends, he'd never had trouble waving away the last late-night whisky or even a first glass of wine if he didn't feel like one. But today he sensed what such a struggle, to say no, *enough,* might be like. He longed to step into the dance with lovely Leslie Epstein. The thrill of anticipation cramped his throat and chest. Was it even possible that he could, without warning or explanation, suddenly grow cool and businesslike and collegial? Was that fair to her? He imagined the hurt in her eyes, the perplexity.

"TWO DAYS gone and you're already checking up on me? Not a lot of faith there, Jack."

"Women don't throw their backs out. Middle-aged men, we're the ones supposed to suffer. So I figure you've been partying too wild over the weekend. Now you're paying, aren't you, on company time?"

"Yeah, that's me all right." Leslie laughed and then gasped into the receiver with pain. "*Partying.* A five-year-old tugging my sleeve. Her sister about to push a bowl of cereal off the table. One quick lunge to save it and a Beanie Baby underfoot. Next thing you know I'm flat on the floor and now I'm flat in bed. Boy, Jack, you sure nailed it—we've had some out-of-control fun around here."

"Here's the thing though." Jack tried to keep his jocular tone. "With you not in the office, I'm finding myself thinking about you." This was true. Two days gone in the middle of the week and she was haunting him. Not like on weekends. On weekends he'd be home or cycling with Margot. His life had its regular rhythms, and Leslie had thrown them all off. Two days missing from the office and he couldn't stop thinking of her.

"It's sweet you miss me. Let me guess—Sarah McElroy's screwing up in claims again?"

"No, damn it, she's done fine. We haven't missed a beat with you gone on holiday."

"Holiday."

"*I've* missed you."

"Jack?"

"Yeah, well, there you have it," he snapped angrily.

"Jesus, Jack."

"Jesus yourself." He slammed the receiver down, ashamed and dissatisfied. But at least he'd gotten it off his chest. He felt relieved too. He could get back to work, back to selling insurance, slightly muted perhaps, but back to work.

What would she do now? he wondered even as he strode out to his secretary's desk. Quit? Spread the word around the office? Denounce him to Margot? Would her husband, Harry, confront him in the parking lot? Relieved, yes, but worried too and, yes, excited, he checked the appointment book to see what came next on his schedule.

NOT HONOLULU this time, not Las Vegas, not even the mineral springs resort up in the West Virginia mountains they'd taken over once before. Inexplicably—because it was hardly saving any money in the bargain—the company gathered its most successful representatives together for the annual fall conclave at a hotel complex next to Somerset Mall. After the long cab ride from the airport through a flat prairie of freeways and sprawling suburbs north of Detroit, Jack wandered by himself through the mall's glass and brass, its dazzling fountains and soaring escalators, hands in his pockets, glancing in at expensive watches through the Cartier window. At least he'd have no trouble finding the right memento for Margot, perhaps a scarf from Gucci or Saks, rather than the usual tacky trinket from a beach or air terminal.

He'd actually tried to persuade her to join him on this trip. A weekend getaway—they could skip most of the sessions other than a couple of cocktail parties and the Saturday banquet. But this would be the last big weekend before the holidays for the District's real estate market. Six different open houses were already scheduled. The whirlwind would sweep Margot from start to finish with hardly the chance to change clothes and shower.

"Let's slip away sometime during the week," she whispered in his ear, twisting a lock of his hair. "Maybe an evening at the Hay-Adams?" A quick jab of her tongue, a quick kiss, and they were both off.

Had he really wanted her to come?

He wasn't sure, because Leslie Epstein was flying in as well. She'd been invited separately, so well thought of was she by other executives for whom she also consulted.

In the several weeks since his phone call to her home, neither of them had referred to it—or its message—in so many words. If Leslie acted as if it never happened, she hadn't been avoiding him or punishing him for that intrusion. Far from it. The dance of teasing and abuse had only grown quicker, harsher. Confused, some of their office coworkers seemed now to wonder whether they might actually despise each other. Leslie tried hard not to look him in the eye, but every now and then he'd turn and catch her staring at him. Quickly she'd glance away.

At least some of the time, Jack was excited by the dance. How could he not be? By the standards of most of his adult life, this was glorious. Leslie was smart, attractive, dangerous. She was married to someone else and clearly, perhaps despite herself, attracted to him. It was delicious.

But he also felt, well, not guilty exactly, because nothing much had happened. No, he felt trapped in his own skin, or in habits that rode like tattoos deep under the skin. He liked Leslie, sure, for all those same reasons: she was quick, attractive. He wondered why that couldn't be enough. He found himself standing in front of Tiffany's window, staring but not seeing. He imagined a shrug he might give, but why shrug to himself? What he'd just realized was that he didn't know *how* to simply enjoy her company. He needed the excitement, the momentum toward touch. That was the simple truth. He acknowledged it and seemed helpless to discover another way. The dance swept him along with a life, apparently, of its own.

"YOU SURE gave them plenty to talk about." Leslie looked none too happy.

"Sorry. I may have overdone it a bit."

"You think?"

"Come on—it wasn't so obvious."

"That my newly married boss is acting like a horny teenager? Pretty damn obvious."

"Sorry," he repeated, shoulders slumped.

She exaggerated a sigh. "Well, you were drunk, which they'll always take as an excuse. Most of them were loaded too, so if you behave in the morning, they probably won't even remember."

"I'm not drunk. I don't get drunk." He put his hand on his heart. "I'm only intoxicated with you."

"Oh brother."

It was very late. The banquet's speeches had dragged interminably, followed by mandatory toasts at the bar. Heat and laughter and dense clouds of smoke had swirled about them. Desperate for cool air, the two of them fled at last to the great expanse of parking lot between the mall and their hotel. Out here, silence rang hollow across the acres of empty pavement, marred only by an occasional truck far off on the highway. The November sky was fleshed black behind the great white pockets of light thrown from lampposts. Jack and Leslie, strolling shoulder to shoulder, jostling against each other lightly, kept to the dark spaces. Suburban Detroit, it felt as high and lonely as the Exmoor plateau.

She sighed again. "What now?" She sounded angry, but

Jack sensed—his intuition with her so keen—that the anger wasn't directed at him.

He touched her shoulder and they both stopped. She was looking at him, not closing her eyes even as he leaned forward to kiss her, didn't kiss him back, didn't pull away either.

"You're just married," she said. "What about Margot? I *like* Margot."

This was new. He didn't like it. "That's for me to deal with. Not you."

She shook her head.

Disoriented on this end, he knew he'd stumbled.

Perhaps because he was concentrating on the way her mouth tightened, he didn't notice the car until it was almost upon them. The rough roar seemed to swell out of nowhere. Startled, Jack stumbled as an ancient Camaro jerked up only inches from his hip. It bobbed for an instant like a rusty doll. Out jumped two teenage boys, one brandishing a tire iron.

Jack and Leslie weren't frozen. They'd fallen back a step toward the hotel. And Jack was already reaching for his hip pocket when the shorter white boy with dreadlocks shouted at him. "Your wallet. Give it up."

"Okay," said Jack.

The taller one was only a couple feet away, waving the iron. He couldn't have been more than fifteen. Even in the dim light, his skin flared a full riot of acne. He looked edgy and spooked. "Come on, man, don't shit with us." He waggled the iron.

Jack was trying, he was tugging at the wallet. It held nothing he couldn't afford to surrender. But out of habit he'd buttoned the pocket, and his fumbling fingers couldn't push it open. He twisted at it, he struggled. At last the button popped off, pinging faintly on the pavement. But now the wallet itself resisted. It snagged and twisted in the lining. Leslie wasn't helping. Tucked up close, she was bumping against him. And they were both still edging away as the two boys pressed at them. Their breath was foul with beer.

"Fuck, man," shrieked the smaller boy, "give us the fucking money."

"I'm trying," shouted Jack.

As if this were a final, intolerable defiance, the other boy flailed at him with the iron rod. Jack raised his arm. The rod glanced off, missed his jaw, struck him in the chest. Scared and angry, he wasn't aware of pain. "Police," he shouted.

"Help! *Police*," screamed Leslie, taking the cue.

They were in full retreat now, the two of them, skating longer strides toward the perimeter of light thrown from the hotel. The car had swerved into them from the wrong side to begin, and the boys, foolishly, failed to circle or cut them off. "*Help!* Police," cried Jack.

Instead of charging at him again, the scrawny boy fell back, his eyes wide with surprise and confusion, the iron still hoisted halfheartedly. When Jack and Leslie, together, bellowed for help once more, he fled into the night.

The other mugger darted forward, crouching like a wrestler, his arms spread as if Jack were about to leap at him. "You wanna fight, man?" he cried.

Jack gasped as plumes of pain began to arrive at last. They seared along his arm and into his chest. "Hey, *man*," he panted, "I outweigh you by fifty pounds. Your friend's run off. And the cops are arriving any second. Why on earth would I fight you?"

Ashamed, and all the more furious because of his shame, the boy crouched, imploring like a desperate lover. Jack and Leslie continued to skate toward safe haven.

"You might reconsider your career choices," Jack called. The bravado and wit were for Leslie's sake.

But the boy had already disappeared after his friend into the darkness. The car they abandoned, a hulk listing off-kilter in the parking lot.

"You're nuts," murmured Leslie. She was gripping his left arm, the sound one. He realized she was trembling. "Why couldn't you just give up the damn wallet? They might have killed you." She was trembling, her nose pressed into his shoulder.

"They didn't give me enough chance."

"Jesus, Jack."

"Can you believe no one heard us, with all that racket?"

They'd penetrated the hotel's harsh halo, yet everything remained still. The silence was undisturbed, as if the attack on them were only some shared hallucination from the dark. (The bruises seeping their ache across his chest and arm were reassuring in their way—Jack couldn't doubt *they* were real.) Although their cries had frightened the boys into fleeing, apparently no one inside had been roused. No general alarum had erupted, no sign of security guards racing to their aid.

"I can't go in there," Leslie said, nodding toward the lobby. She was still clutching his arm, her body pressed to him, trembling.

"How come?" In pain, he was also becoming aroused once more by her warmth and scent as his own fear faded like smoke, leaving only a faint but acrid residue deep in his lungs. His head was clear. Adrenaline had burned away the last of the alcohol and left his heart pounding with exhilaration. Desire was driving the fear away and it left him giddy.

"Jesus," she murmured again under her breath. "I had an accident, okay? I peed my pants."

For once he felt no urge to tease her. Instead, he felt sorry and protective. "Here, let's try this." His electronic room card opened a side entrance off the parking lot. Leslie entered first. Instead of heading toward the elevators, however, she pushed open another door into a stairwell. He figured she wanted to climb the three flights to her room. One step up, she startled him by halting, turning to him, eye to eye.

She put her arms about his neck. "Okay," she said, "you can do whatever you want, this once."

This time she closed her eyes. This time she kissed him back.

Slipping his hands up under her light sweater, he cupped her breasts. Their heft and warmth filled him with joy, with elation, just as he'd imagined while riding across the top of the world in Devon. All that remained was to push the sweater clear and bring them to his mouth.

But his right arm was aching. The arm was heavy, hard to keep raised, hard to push. And the blow to his chest had struck a deep bruise. It wasn't aching so much as ringing. Ringing bone deep. Breathing wasn't difficult, but it left him a little breathless.

He was thinking about it and then he was outside, looking at himself as he studied the pain and hoisted this lovely woman's breasts. It was a disconcerting perspective.

"Jack?"

She was looking at him, her gaze switching from one eye to the other.

"You bastard," she said in wonder and dismay.

Neither of them had moved. His hands were still up under her sweater, but he felt he'd fallen far away. He watched himself from far away. Bone deep, oddly hollow, oddly breathless, his chest rang where the iron had struck.

With one great angry shudder, she thrust him off. "What the hell were you doing all these months? Not leaving me alone, wheedling, flirting. Talk about harassment."

He figured she could sue him. He smelled now the odor of the pee that soaked her skirt. It made him sorry for her again. He didn't seem able to say anything, to understand anything, just to watch himself from very far away.

"Jack." She pushed her hands back through her thick, dark hair. "I liked you. You made me like you. What were you after? Just the fun of trying? Or were you aiming at this, at humiliating me?"

He was shaking his head. At least he could shake his head.

She was hugging herself, shivering again. He wanted her to be able to grab his arm, to ground herself against him so that she could stop shaking. He could see the same wish in her eyes. And it was impossible. Without another word, she turned and climbed the stairs as quickly as her heels allowed.

Jack didn't move. His chest rang. He was watching.

BONDAGE

Just as her lips are pulling back from yours, your skin resists, her skin resists, lip clinging to lip, suction and saliva and yearning all causing the little suck that pops at last, the sweetest instant you've ever lived. Lydia's fingers touch your cheek, stroke you akindle, even as she falls away those few inches onto the couch, opening herself to you like a secretly blooming flower. Lydia Khosla is waiting for you. Lydia Khosla is opening herself expectantly, still fully dressed of course, but that hardly matters. Lydia Khosla smiles shy and dangerous. And you realize that she's the one, not you, who's been laying out each step in the dance tonight, from her mother's clutches, to the movie, to the stop-off-just-for-a-minute at your own mother's house, she's been dancing half a step ahead and bringing you along so gently you thought it was your own idea.

But the only thing you can think of this moment is Eric, your fifteen-year-old brother who's lurking, no doubt, somewhere about the house and resenting you claiming the family room and its TV. Mom's safely upstairs. But Eric may storm in at any moment. The doors are French doors, opposing curvy handles, no locks.

Lydia's tugging at you, urgent and hungry, her impatience growing, what with the pressures of curfew a little while off. You know she may curdle if you're not quick about it.

You rear back, unbuckle your belt—her eyes widen at such brazenness, but not with reluctance. It's when you jerk the belt all the way clear of its loops in one ragged flail that her eyes cloud with confusion and a distant fear.

"What're you doing?" she demands.

"Just wait," you say, standing over her.

"Jamie"—and she's breathless now—"you're not going to hurt me?"

Stunned for a second, not catching on, you stare at her. Then you get it with a laugh. There's nothing even to say. You stumble across the room to those French doors and wrap the belt tight around the two handles.

Quick, with a leap and a laugh and a deep hunger you've never felt before, at least not when not alone, you're back with her. But leaving was a mistake. The air's chilled, the flower's started to close. Lydia's eyes have closed partway, are looking somewhere else entirely.

MOVING HOUSE

No surprise to Fanny that her mother is sniffling a good weep into the phone. This is a Sunday burden she's learned to bear. And if it doesn't precisely afford her satisfaction, still she takes some pleasure knowing she's strong enough to provide this service, this comfort. Not that she generally has to pay close attention. So it's some little while before she grasps what her mother is on about this time.

"They're moving what house?"

"*Our* house. Don't you see? Those horrible Dowdys, the ones who bought it from Daddy, they're actually picking it up and moving it cross town to a new lot."

"A new lot."

"Uh-huh. County's putting in a little access road right where we lived. So those Dowdys, they not only get the council to buy them out; it's paying to transplant the house, *our* house, all the way over to Acland Street, like it was a hosta or something."

As she takes the story in, a giddy, almost dizzy triumph

sweeps through Fanny. She wouldn't have expected it. She wouldn't have expected such a full-blown sense of relief. Relief from what? She's puzzled, yet still with this gusting lightness, this soaring. It's as though she's been trapped in a pressure pot twenty-seven years, so long as not to notice, and here the lid's tugged off. *Whoosh.*

Her own nine-year-old daughter sits at the kitchen table working on a take-home math sheet. Her husband pretends to help, but he's yawning, hoping to be rescued.

Standing before the raw wound of basement and broken foundation two days later brings the house back to her. It's gone, of course, already lumbering on a double flatbed through streets blocked off for the move, sheriff's deputies standing with limp red flags in their hands. But the cubby space in the downstairs closet surges back at her, dark and warm and perfumed, where she'd huddle and hide; Daddy's shower stall upstairs, with its confused smells of soaps and mildew; the rough brick scrape to her skin of the small fireplace; the groan of a particular door. Horrible, potent. She shudders. These shards, these bits of memory, haven't afflicted her for years. But this first whiff of them has her reeling. It's no longer relief. That's what tricked her in the first place into venturing back to see. She catches at her mother, who's standing at her side, sniffing into a hankie, not noticing.

And yet nothing so very terrible's come to mind. She's always the strong one for friends and family, with a solid foundation for all to lean on.

It's so *funny,* seeing the basement this way, open to sun and whipping wind with snow flirting at the edges. Metal pipes dangle languorously. Linoleum curls and flaps. A flight of stairs leads toward sky's dead end.

The house's sinews are slack and disjointed, and the lesson sends her careening. All the world's come unstuck. How? Why? She swipes at a loose strand of hair catching in her lips. She's struggling toward something—are there memories lying hidden like the dark matter of the universe, full of absent weight, drawing her?

Her life has been happy, she thinks—as happy as any adult is permitted to wish. Fanny pictures her daughter Emily's sweet face, summons her husband's particular smell, yearns even as they seem snatched forever away by the wind. She wants to cling now to her mother as if she were young again, a child, for whom it had never been permitted to cling, not when it mattered. But then not so very much was at stake.

PASCHAL LAMB

Only when Danny Jacob heard Aunt Madelyn call his mother from the guest room to help fetch the special Passover plates from the basement did he realize he'd never seen those dishes actually stored anywhere. A dozen years, from the time he'd been born, Danny and his parents had driven out from the city to join Aunt Maddie and Uncle Arthur for the seder. (Never could there be reason enough for them to drive in the other direction, deep into the city to Danny's apartment house.) Yet this particular mystery—where the kosher dishes were kept for eleven months and more—had never before occurred to him. A certain suspicion tingled Danny so hard he couldn't sit still. This might be the chance to settle a larger mystery haunting, exciting him, turning daydreams into yearning dreams of dark anguish.

He waited until the two women had ferried the first cardboard boxes up the narrow stairs, and then, as his mother and aunt disappeared into the kitchen, he slipped down the dark staircase toward the single light at the bottom. Once he'd disappeared into the shadows below, he'd be invisible to the adults as they shuttled up and down with more plates and glasses and extra stainless.

He knew every corner of this sprawling basement, its furnace room and storage closets and playroom for a house without children. Each visit he escaped to this realm of privacy and solitude.

At the bottom of the stairs, he spied the massive door of the vault standing open on the green linoleum floor. It was true! He'd guessed it. A first realization: his uncle the wealthy surgeon stored the Passover china in a walk-in safe. Why, Danny couldn't imagine. But it wasn't china he cared about. What else might be secreted away in there? Jewels, golden goblets, green bills beyond count in stacks and suitcases? Or secrets darker still, more alluring, sinister, things he sensed just beyond the horizon of his ability to imagine.

Why would a doctor, a wealthy man, yes, but no Rockefeller, build a vault into the foundation of this house on the farthest fringe of suburbs?

Danny had described the enormous metal door with its black dial and rigid brass handle not once but many times to his small circle of intimates back in the city. Some of them professed not to believe him. But even they joined with the others in imagining the secrets locked safely inside: diamonds, yes, and deeds and maps, and . . .

The door yawned before him. He didn't dare hesitate because he might not ever get another chance, because once he hesitated to weigh risks and penalties, he might not discover the courage to continue. Tugging at the handle, he scraped the heavy door farther across the linoleum and slipped inside. Another cobwebbed bulb was burning in the low ceiling. The chamber smelled of must and dust and damp cardboard.

His eyes were still adjusting to the gloom as he made out a stack of pots waiting on an open shelf. Panting, nervous, he spun to study other secrets. And discovered rows of ketchup, a dozen bottles or more, eight jars of pickle relish, countless cans of vegetables, soups, sauces, more plentiful than the market at the end of their block in the city and just as dusty.

Confused now, baffled, not yet disappointed, he tugged at a heavy box wedged below a shelf. The top flap ripped in his hand, yielding to view no hoard of gold and sapphires, no sinister leather or blood-soaked telltales, but a galaxy of whisky bottles separated by cardboard dividers.

Steps came thudding down the staircase outside. Aunt Madelyn and his mother were approaching for one final trip. Thinking but not thinking, he squatted low behind cartons of canned peaches. The women were brisk and efficient. They wanted to spend no more time on this task than necessary. Each plate, each fork, each pot would still be washed by hand before preparations for the meal could properly begin. Danny peeked out just in time to see a hand flip the light switch and the vault door swing back into the fresh blackness with a slamming thud.

Quickly, while his eyes still burned with the image, he felt his way to the wall and patted for the switch. The light snapped on again, blinding for an instant and eerie. His heart was pounding for real now, but he wasn't scared, not yet. Dragging another carton out from the wall, he sat and studied the evidence before him—he needed to make sense of it. He was disappointed, yes, and perhaps a bit relieved too, and most of all perplexed. Why a treasure trove of ketchup bottles and peaches?

The silence—he wasn't used to an absence so smothering. The harsh light and shadows from the naked bulb. The pulse beating in his throat and ears. Suddenly he was afraid after all, and it was the fear he felt when once or twice a year they were forced beneath their desks in school, huddling, giggling, silent, scared. They were forced to prepare for something—he knew this—for which no preparation could suffice. Forced to apprehend as eight- and ten- and twelve-year-olds the clear and present danger of annihilation. Was that it, then? Was this Uncle Arthur's stash in case he and Aunt Maddie survived the bomb? How long would they hold out on cream of mushroom soup and pickle relish?

Even as he snorted aloud at the bewildering joke, however, another thought, a fragment of memory, came to him. Years ago, his mother reciting for some listener the tale of her younger brother Artie, the gifted one, the chosen one. He was the boy loved by her own mother beyond all measure.

"If she managed to save an egg, somehow, she'd sneak it away just for him. So he shouldn't be hungry. The rest of us, hunger we could deal with. But if anyone dared raise an eyebrow about that egg! *He needs it to study,* she would say. *How will he do for us later if now he is too hungry to think straight?*"

What would his Grandma Bessie do with the egg? Danny wondered. Hard-boil it for easier concealment? Fry or scramble it, better to demonstrate her adoration for the doctor her son would become?

He tugged a whisky bottle out of the ripped box. He fumbled with a wire mesh and a stubborn cork in its throat. He sniffed and sipped at the fiery liquid, concentrating as it crashed to his stomach and rang its heat out to his hands and feet and still burned on his lips.

Bottles and jars and cans, brimful and heavy laden. Replacements for secret eggs Uncle Arthur's mother once smuggled for him? Talismans against a hunger that surely would never come again?

Danny had never been hungry that way.

But, yes, there were plenty of nights of macaroni and cheese, a slice of bread, a suspicion that his own mother only pecked at her portion to save more for him. He knew that Uncle Arthur loved her, his big sister, would do anything for her. For her husband, however, Uncle Arthur had nothing but icily concealed contempt. Danny's father, who'd gone from selling cars to selling women's garments. Always selling but never quite enough, never quite the success he'd pretend to all the world, starting with his son. Who sat here, in Uncle Arthur's vault, wanting to believe his old man beyond anything, beyond all account or blame.

Danny, afraid after all now, tears streaming on his face, and furious, as he pounded his fists into the heavy green door of the safe, pounding and calling, pounding and calling.

TRACKS

I'm not even watching them, waiting for them to leave or nothing. Just hauling a cord of wood to another one of the professors too dumb to know, or maybe not caring, what makes a cord true. No skin off my nose when he pays me for what I'm stacking so neat in his shed.

So I'm not watching so much as swinging past that long drive up the hill. Red van's pulling round the circle, packed tight—clear to any fool the family's heading out of town. First hour of vacation and they can't wait to be gone. Not that they belong here anyways. No matter how many years they lived in that big house, old and new, the way they keep adding to it, like they need more rooms on rooms, for what?

I let them draw past me and I pull over, sitting in my truck. There're these deer tracks and dog tracks, and maybe some coon too, in snow that's still clean and white but not new, maybe four, five days old now. My eyes are just watching these tracks climb the hill, and my truck, it's climbing the drive too, until I'm sitting there, right in front of the house, right in their drive, for all the world to see. And I guess if they don't care, I don't care neither, though someone may remember the truck afterward. But that sort of makes it better, more exciting, more fuck-you, I-got-as-much-right-as-anyone-so-get-out-of-my-face.

You know I know the goddamn door ain't even locked. All of them, they don't lock their doors, like no one's ever broke in. All of them coming from other places where they know better: wouldn't fetch the mail off the porch without locking a door behind them.

It's like the door's open, so they don't care; it's like, they sort of deserve it. Just gets me the madder, like no one like me is brave enough or smart enough or just damn mean enough to pay a visit.

Now my wife, she used to be a cleaning girl here, and she'd tell me things, even though she'd never do nothing, not in a million years, and thinks I won't neither, which is why she can tell me. And of course, I never do do nothing, not while she's working for them. Never even occurs to me. Course, then they fire her and she deserves it, didn't complain to them nor me. And me being here don't got nothing to do with that. It's seeing them drive away, and the tracks neat and pure tracking up the hill almost to their door, and the open door: it's all an invitation and it pisses me off too.

I'm not looking for nothing, though I know where it all is, from my wife. I'm just sort of exploring, checking things off in my mind like, one room to the next. Only one place I can't help myself, just 'cause the professor thinks he's so smart, not knowing my wife would know of course and would tell. It's this big oak desk in his study, made new to look old, solid and heavy. Quick little jimmy, and the lock slips open like butter. Bottom file drawer, under these green hanging files, the watch is tucked nice and neat, like no one's smart enough ever to look there. Well, I ain't smart—I know beforehand.

The watch is old for real and heavy gold. Name on the back probably his own daddy's. Only damn thing in the house I take out with me, something to remember and remind me. I even lock the desk back up. Who knows when he'll think to check?

Then bye-bye. But I got to leave them something too. A telltale, a gift, you know? Back up front there's this little mud porch inside the door, tiles on the floor for boots and crap. So that's what I leave 'em. Pull my jeans down and drop a little load, neat as can be, smack middle of a tile, deliberate.

WOODPECKERS

Like an alarm, the deep quiet of the house woke her. It rang. She sat up on the couch and pushed the hair from her eyes. The television was stuttering images and colors soundlessly. Martin had long since gone to bed, leaving her, not abandoning her, resigned to the rhythms she preferred. For this was Marjorie's favorite time, night or day. The house was hers. Eric and Tabatha asleep in their own beds, Martin snoring reassuringly from far away. The house hers.

She prowled luxuriously, putting the kettle on for tea, stroking the mouse to waken her computer. Tonight she didn't switch on a single light. No need, not with the moon, huge and bright through a scrim of mist, glowing, radiating, lighting the woods and snow, shadowing the house with blaze enough.

Marjorie gazed out through the kitchen window, waiting on the kettle, its blossoming steam breathing toward her face. The cold weather had leached all moisture from the air, all color from the universe. Tonight only black and white and the gauzy mist that rose from snow toward moon, from kettle to Marjorie, and a redness that rang behind everything else, the dryness in her eyes, a dryness from the woods. Red beyond color.

Martin's car gleamed on the gravel drive. She didn't hate the car, didn't hate Martin, had never really noticed the car before. Tonight it gleamed and yawed and rippled, indifferent to her notice.

It was the snap of the second mirror gently webbing that startled her, made her wonder at herself, giggling and guilty. She'd opened the door for the dog, but he lay uninterested. Door wide on the night, Marjorie had fetched a screwdriver from the pantry. The kettle was boiling, she noticed. She was fully dressed after all, even if her slippers slipped on gravel and snow. Driver's mirror first. She couldn't see herself in it. The light was wrong, the angle wrong. Quick peck of the screwdriver, and the surface, like ice, shattered in a web.

It was the snap of the second mirror, the passenger's, gently webbing that startled her, made her wonder at herself, coming to herself in the night on the gravel, giggling and guilty.

Woodpeckers.

STEPS THROUGH SAND, THROUGH FIRE

When the silver headdress slipped again over Gerald Knapper's eyes, causing him finally to lose the balance he'd been struggling to maintain for nearly an hour and plummet from the high white horse—an ill-tempered and ill-treated brute—and into the red Indian dust, the jarring pain in his left shoulder jolted the breath right out of him. He flailed, wrestling against the clenched muscle of his own chest. His eyes widened in despair and fear as he choked. At last, at last, the spasm loosened, allowing him a gasp, a short breath, a flicker of tears. He lay panting, feeling relief and gratitude above all. The worst of the humiliation was surely behind him now.

Even through that first flash of pain and of loose grit slamming into his teeth and nose, he'd heard the ragged cry of merriment from twenty-five boys and men, most of them hired for the occasion. They were his retinue, what had to pass for his family, his friends. Blowing reedy horns, beating cymbals, they accepted his embarrassing tumble as merely another inevitable event in the ceremony. (But certainly also as yet another gaffe by this ludicrous American, a pale, middle-aged man whom they could mock even as they cheered him as hero, the conquering bridegroom.)

"Respected sir," said one old man with an extravagant mustache, gray and coarse as rhino tusks twisting off to either side of his lean jaw. Roughly shoving his large, gnarled hands under Gerald's arms, he hoisted him to his feet. In an instant the others had set upon him as well, patting the dust from his suit, punching at him to demonstrate his own well-being, and shoving the silver helmet back across his brow.

Thus was he planted, sagging but upright, before Ravi Singh, the man about to become his brother-in-law. Ravi wore a casually restrained smile. "Hard luck. No need to worry," said the younger man. His speech was just as perfect though slightly more clipped than his sister's. After college at St. Stephen's in Delhi, Ravi had spent two years in London and Cambridge, whereas Sita had gone to the States. His accent was no more British, however, than hers was American—they spoke the Indian-rooted English of Delhi's new princelings, at home anywhere on the globe.

Gerald sensed not only Ravi's vague amusement but his disdain as well. And for the first time in nearly a month, he realized a truth that had been veiled before—that he was in some sort of struggle with this young man, that they were wrestling in the shadow behind word and deed and even his own conscious intention. But this wasn't what he cared about. It wasn't why he was here. He was too old to waste any emotional force on this younger man, the brother of his bride. Patting at the dust on his linen suit, Gerald was perfectly willing to grin and shrug in disarming acknowledgment of the ludicrous spectacle he presented.

No dust dared soil Ravi Singh's double-breasted blazer, nor his tasseled loafers, nor the polished nails on the hand he flicked at the small mob. Instantly, as if the American were no more than a rather rumpled puppet, they heaved him once more atop the garlanded white horse that had already carried him better than a mile from Ravi's house. Hands bolstered him aloft so that he could clutch the headdress in place. Rampant and in artificial triumph, Gerald rode a last few yards toward the high painted gates of the wedding pavilion. It had been erected in the shadows of a nameless emperor's monument, and Gerald assumed that the staging of a private wedding in these otherwise public gardens in the heart of Delhi was one mark of the family's influence.

All evening he'd struggled against a late arrival. It was the one failure, the one mark of bad grace that he dreaded. Hundreds of elaborate crimson invitations had been launched into the world, clearly announcing 6 P.M. as the start of festivities. But the horse hadn't appeared at Ravi's door until nearly seven, and then the procession scudded so slowly through the streets, what with the cheering and braying of horns and the clapping of hand and drum, not to mention his own precarious mount, that at times they seemed to be drifting in hapless ebb rather than toward his Sita. Now, finally, having survived his fall, Gerald prodded his steed through the twenty-foot papier-mâché arch festooned with auspicious marigolds. To a last ragged cheer from his distracted cohort—they were already peering toward handouts of wedding food and additional gifts of coin—Gerald Knapper, the groom, did arrive.

No one noticed. A spare spatter of guests who'd come early in order to slip away to other affairs were milling about rather vaguely, attentive only to passing trays of food and drink, greeting each other with caws and kisses. No sign anywhere of Sita or her parents. Once again Gerald felt he'd gone wrong, that he should have known better, that even as he was dismounting, he'd stumbled another wrong step in a dance whose proper rhythm eluded him.

Most of his retinue had abandoned him at the scaffolding just inside the ornate movie-set gate. Surprised, alone, he glanced back and saw plastic jugs splashing something clear, no doubt something potent, into their mugs and cupped palms. This, plus handfuls of rupees doled out earlier and hope of more to come, kept a few of these hired friends faithful to their horns and drums, welcoming guests as they appeared. For a long moment, staggering a bit now that he was off the horse, shorn of his make-believe troupe, still balancing Sita and Ravi's great-grandfather's silver helmet, metal tassels and all, on his head, Gerald felt as disoriented as at any moment since arriving in India. He was also struck by his apparent invisibility, given that the elaborate pageant only beginning to gather momentum was in honor of his wedding.

A constellation of enormous tents stretched away to all sides. Carpets large and small were strewn across the dirt and dust and grass, elegant Persian designs next to coir mats and wide strips of green plastic turf.

Not for the first time, Gerald regretted failing to persuade Sita to marry him in Columbus. Larry Tomsich, a friend of many years and local magistrate, would have performed the task simply and tastefully. A few friends in attendance. Perhaps even one of his children might have deigned to come — they'd have thought him merely foolish then, rather than out-and-out crazy. But Sita held fast. She couldn't do such a thing to her parents. Though he sensed even from half a world away that given her age — past eighteen, past twenty-five, even past thirty and fled to America—the family had all but abandoned hope of any proper marriage for her.

Thinking of Sita flooded him with joy like a schoolboy with a first crush. Without warning, it swept over him and rooted him in this moment, this place, glad for the incense in the air, the dust, even the distant waft of burning cow dung in the February night. He loved her with a passion that he'd thought long extinguished. Over nearly a year of dinners and gallery visits and chaste strolls along the Scioto River—and then, finally, when he'd nearly crashed against the limits of what he could endure, the not-so-chaste retreat into her modest TA-funded apartment at the university (never, not yet, not until after this marriage, into the far-from-modest house in Upper Arlington that he'd shared with his wife Caryn)—she'd brought him alive again. For this he was willing to travel anywhere, undergo any ordeal, even a wedding like this.

As Gerald stood gazing into the hazy evening, Sita appeared as if conjured by his thoughts from out of the incense and smoke. Her mother in a plum-colored sari on one arm, father on the other, she came gliding toward him, transformed, and Gerald was frightened. This was his first glimpse of her all day. Her eyes were dark with kohl, their lids the blue of a bird. A single diamond stud pierced her nostril. Her own sari was wound tight about her and yet seemed to be flowing all at once, an infinitely fine fabric of gold embroidery on crimson with a single loop covering the back of her head and neck. Her long dark hair was pulled back tight from her face. Looking up from under at him, she might have been ten years younger. She might have been a stranger.

Perhaps she spied the anxiety in his eyes. She lifted her fingers to her mouth, and that little gesture, covering her lips as if with an alarmed modesty, made all the world right. It was something Sita did—a reflex so delicate and personal to her that for him it seemed an intimate signature. Seeing it this evening, spying it here, almost hurt him with gladness. It certainly aroused him.

Her parents relinquished her with looks of mingled relief and concern. "We must greet our guests," she said, approaching him and touching his arm lightly.

He nodded and the silver helmet nearly tumbled into his hands. "When can I take this damn thing off?" he whispered more fiercely than he'd intended. "It weighs a ton. And I feel like the schoolroom dunce." He smiled to make the plea into a joke.

Lips pressed tight, she shook her head. "Stop, please, Gerald. Haven't we been through this? Come, come—there's no taking it off. Family tradition is family tradition. The bloody thing must be endured."

"Only for you," he murmured.

She cocked her head to the side, acknowledging his tenderness with a little smile. It stabbed him with the pain of his own love for her. And it also forced him to dodge once again the awareness that though she loved him—he dared not doubt it—it was not with an intensity that could match his own.

Touching his arm once more, Sita steered him toward one cluster of guests and then another. Although conversation was almost entirely in English, its sounds had been shaped locally, like the graft of a foreign plant onto sturdy new roots, and Gerald's ear hadn't yet been trained to make sense of them—he missed much of what was said, even when directly to him. On the other hand, no one seemed put off by his awkwardness. They smiled and nodded. They thought it charming that he'd learned to press his palms together and salute them with an earnest *namaste*—charming as a child may be both charming and silly. Like a tolerant, even doting nurse, Sita beamed and steered him proudly about.

Gerald stifled as best he could a swelling resentment. Charming, yes—he'd certainly intended to generate seas of goodwill on behalf of this woman and her family. But not by being a source of amusement, first for Ravi and now these others. In general, he prided himself on his equanimity, his goodwill. It had been hard-won. Caryn's death after five years of battling breast cancer, its remission, its return and blasted triumph, had all but swamped him with despair. To that moment he could trace a chasm spreading between himself and his children, one that had never entirely healed. But his spirits did slowly revive, broadening into an unexpected contentedness in middle age, along with a considerable financial success. Discovering Sita and then persuading her to marry him—these only increased his sense of rare fortune. He was perfectly willing to offer patience and generosity to the world about him. But, but: playing the fool for these wealthy Indians, whatever goodwill it might earn, was wearing his patience thin.

With a sough like a gathering wind, the crowd's attention swerved away from the bridal couple. Gerald, too, turned and spotted a silver Ambassador, still the car of official India, with darkened windows and little flags flickering on its fenders, draw to the painted gates of the wedding pavilion. Like an electric spark, word leaped across the sea of craning faces: Gangaswami had arrived! A celebrity among celebrities, the holy man and political guru alone was permitted to be driven this far. Ravi bestowed this honor on him because of the honor that Gangaswami brought in turn to the family by appearing and even participating in the ceremony.

A young boy, fourteen perhaps, with a shaggy head of hair and dressed in a gray jacket and tight pants, scrambled from a front seat and hurried to open the car's rear door. Heavy curtains blocked any glimpse inside. A massive hand thrust out into the night air wielding a heavy black stick, which it planted in the dust. Another hand grasped at the boy's neck and shoulders, part caress and part throttle, threatening to drag him back into the dark maw of the automobile. But the boy braced himself, one hand against the door frame, legs leveraged into the dirt. Slowly, by stages, an arm, a leg, the gradual shifting of the great bulk of his torso, Gangaswami emerged. Immense in girth, jovial and commanding, he raised a hand in the air and thus allowed the multitude of servants and guests to breathe again. Until that moment they'd been unaware of having ceased in anticipation.

Gerald had first met the god man (as he'd seen him called in the Indian papers, partly in tribute, partly ridicule) shortly after arriving in Delhi. Hurrying to the door of his house, Ravi Singh had grasped the visitor's arm and helped him cross the threshold. As a favor to the rising young political star and scion of one of India's lordliest families, Gangaswami had offered to consult personally on the wedding now being planned. Ravi ushered him through to a salon specially prepared for the audience.

It wasn't until their guest had been settled monumentally onto a vast sofa that the orientation of the room, its deep chairs and other furnishings, came clear to Gerald. He himself had been steered to a solitary hard settee. Sita was perched across the way, impossibly distant. A family crescent seemed to stretch along Gangaswami's arm span—father and mother, several aunts and uncles and who-knew-else—gathered neatly on either side. Ravi remained standing behind the sofa, sometimes leaning casually to whisper in his guest's ear.

For the sake of politeness, Gangaswami picked at the delicacies and sweets set beside him on a platter, sipped at a glass of water. At last he turned his gaze fully on Gerald Knapper. Behind heavy black spectacles, his eyes were small and set too closely together for the amount of flesh about them. Yet they were sharp and full of good humor. He beamed more broadly at the American, and suddenly Gerald was washed by an astonishing flood of warmth. The power of the guru's personality, his sheer presence, was oddly comforting at the same time it was overwhelming. Almost a physical pummeling, it unsettled Gerald in his seat. He felt vulnerable, almost naked before him. Yet he also had to resist an urge to rise and hurry toward the man. This was new—Gerald had dealt with the rich and powerful, but never anyone with such a force. Now he glimpsed how Gangaswami had gathered so much influence, so many protégés among the political elite, from prime ministers to high-tech moguls.

"I do not see that it makes any difference," Gangaswami was saying with a toss of his hand, tilting his head first to one side of the family audience and then to the other without yet taking his eyes off Gerald. His voice was itself a surprise: nasal and reedy, almost childishly high-pitched. "If we want to make a proper wedding, there is no reason not to do so. What do the gods of his parents matter so long as he does not reject ours?"

"Sorry?" said Gerald, looking first at the guru and then to Sita. She was staring into her lap. Her parents, the elder Singh and his wife, looked as startled as Gerald. They didn't seem able to respond.

Ravi understood at once. He glanced at his father and then spoke to Gerald. "We of course originally agreed with the notion of a civil wedding, because a traditional one—a Hindu wedding—seemed out of the question. But now that our eminent friend has opened our eyes to what is possible, the family will be happy to welcome you as one of its sons in the traditional way. No one will dare challenge Shri Gangaswami's ruling."

"Sita?" Gerald said. Still she wouldn't face him but blushed deeply and gave the hint of a shrug. "Sorry," he said again. "But this is a little too quick, a little too, well, crazy. You're not giving me a chance to catch up."

"My friend," said Gangaswami with patience and generous goodwill, "this is a great and unusual honor my friends, Ravi Singh's family, are offering you. We do not say you must give up your gods that you were raised with. Simply that you say welcome to ours, and they will welcome you as well."

Gerald shook his head, but no one seemed to notice. Was this possible? Could he do such a thing? He hadn't been to shul since Caryn's death and never very vigorously before. To what degree did he feel himself bound to have no gods before one who, after all, had been perfectly pleased to keep his own distance? Gerald realized he wasn't much concerned with betraying that God of his youth. Still—he worried whether he might be betraying something of himself in the bargain.

Like moths to a swollen candle, the wedding guests found themselves fluttering toward and about Gangaswami. He was leaning heavily on his cane as he waded through the enveloping crowd. Beaming, his head wagging from side to side, he moved forward, taking notice—making contact, however brief—with apparently everyone. His presence glowed through the throng. The servants, carrying platters of food, circling with beverages, could hardly draw their gaze from the god man.

Gerald's eyes sought out Ravi Singh. Left hand stylishly jabbed in his jacket pocket—who is he, the goddamn Prince of Wales? Gerald wondered—Ravi appeared delighted by the delight and distraction of his guests. He was smiling slightly as he observed the melee. Another move in his complicated choreography was playing out as designed. This time he made no move to welcome his eminent guest personally. He was content—more than content—to stand at a distance and savor ripples of excitement radiating through the crowd of politicians, industrialists, artists in dinner jackets, Italian suits, blue silk *kurtas,* the many beautiful women in golden saris and silver *shalwar kameez.* Such electricity could only brighten Ravi's own star for having arranged it. No doubt the evening was already a grand success for the young man's ambitions. Gerald wondered whether what was to come—a wedding— could be anything more than an afterthought.

For the moment, however, any ceremony seemed far from imminent. And beckoning to Gerald was an entire tent filled with heavily laden tables. He hadn't eaten since midday. As he discovered his hunger, it became overpowering. He spied steaming bowls of shrimp in a pungent green mint and chili sauce; roasted chickens sliced on platters; eggplants and mushrooms and spinach. They perfumed the night with ginger and cumin and spices Gerald couldn't identify. He didn't care. Ravenous beyond reason, all he wanted was to stuff his belly. And also he spied certain gentleman guests who knew how to conjure a magic phrase, sipping tall glasses of whisky and soda rather than the lemonade and other juices in public circulation. Whisky too: he could use a quick dash.

Sita snagged his sleeve as he hesitated. "Come," she said, "come," tugging him away. He resisted, leaning half a step toward the food. But she jerked his arm more sharply. At her touch, the invisibility that had cloaked him since Gangaswami's arrival, and that he'd been enjoying, dissolved like so much mist.

Still the crowd of guests was swelling, hundreds it seemed, surging through tents and across lawns, more and more arriving as the evening grew late. Gerald felt their eyes upon him and Sita as they made their way up toward two high-backed wooden chairs on the terrace of the ancient monument. The grayish hewn stones and few surviving fragments of the emperor's delicate inlay had been incorporated into a high platform overlooking Ravi's party, flowing with explosions of winter flowers—roses, orange and red and peach, purple orchids, strings of marigolds beyond count. Stepping awkwardly, worried about tripping on the uneven stones, feeling that they, he and Sita, were somehow trespassing, Gerald allowed her to lead him along a narrow path that wound toward the thronelike chairs.

"Now what?" he whispered. "Is it time for the ceremony?"

"What a fuss you keep making. One must be patient," she hissed as she turned to sit.

Sita's eyes remained focused on the tips of her toes in their crimson sandals. Faithfully, obstinately, she gripped fast to her role as young bride: joyful, innocent, a tiny bit frightened, she might only have met the man who was to be her husband once or twice during the matchmaking interviews and was certainly still a virgin. Gerald didn't know whether to laugh or cry aloud with rage. He was too old for such pretense. *She* was too old.

"What about dinner? I'm starving." Immediately he hated his own voice—whining and petulant.

Sita chose not to answer, but her stiffness and displeasure at his performance thus far were plain enough.

Bravely, as bravely as he could muster, he righted the headdress and prepared himself for what was to come.

What came was slow to the point of madness. While guests plundered food and drink, greeted each other with kisses, slipped off together for urgent consultations or covert assignations—the view from the monument stripped away the feints of ordinary pretense—the wedding couple received tribute. Among the first to rush up toward them, unseemly in their haste and eager enthusiasm, were women who had been Sita's colleagues in the English department at Lady Shri Ram College before she went to America to finish her Ph.D. Gerald was delighted to meet them at last, Kasturi and Meenakshi and Gopa, so much had he heard about them, though he couldn't begin to match name to face.

Kasturi—it *was* Kasturi?—abruptly grabbed his hand, shook it powerfully in both her own, and looked him straight in the eye in a way that no one, certainly no woman, had done in better than a month. "You are certainly a lucky man, Mr. Knapper. I hope you will be a good one as well. In that case we shall be friends."

Ravi had materialized somehow onto the platform. Sita's friends sensed his presence behind them, and when he leaned ever so slightly in their direction, smiling, they startled into flight with little cries and waves and promises to call on her.

Now the central ceremony of the evening elaborated itself. An old man, perhaps five feet tall, with a heavily pocked face and bulbous nose, slowly climbed the stone steps. He wore an elegantly tailored black Indian jacket. At his hip floated a willowy young woman, perhaps twenty-five and a foot taller than her escort, in a peacock blue sari. The old man bowed toward Gerald but said nothing and kissed Sita on both cheeks. He flicked a wrist into the cool night air, and into it a trailing servant placed a thick silken packet. The old man tugged the knot and drew out a single crisp ten-thousand rupee note, one of a thick company. He leaned forward and tucked the bill like a bright kerchief into Gerald's breast pocket. The packet he laid in Sita's lap with another short bow and then turned away. Gerald wondered whether he would go so far as to brush Ravi's shoes with his fingers as he passed.

"Don't touch that," snapped Sita under her breath.

Gerald's own fingers froze. "I can't leave this thing sticking out of my pocket—it's humiliating. I'm not some boy desperate for a buck."

"It isn't about you. They don't know anything about you. Such things are a matter of form."

"It's all a matter of making a fuss over Ravi's sister is what it is. And of shaming me, or putting me in my place, though I haven't figured out why or what he's after."

"Oh, Gerald." She sighed. She glanced at him despite herself. "He's my brother. He's not after anything except my happiness."

Before he could respond, the next pair of guests was already upon them. Two by two, they continued to appear, all greeting the couple and bearing gifts. It was hard to tell—and there was no opportunity to ask—but Gerald guessed that most were strangers to Sita as well. Some touched their gifts only at the last instant, receiving the wrapped boxes or stuffed envelopes from a servant and handing them in turn to Sita. Nearly all dropped a few golden coins in their laps or stuck notes of large denomination in pockets and creases and even in the silver headdress. Gerald battled grimly not to blush or shout or stalk off the stage entirely. Sita passed the gifts to a family servant who was constructing a small castle of unopened treasures behind the wooden thrones. And two by two, the guests made their way to greet Ravi and be acknowledged for their loyalty and largesse.

Gerald couldn't help but snatch glimpses of Sita's brother as the queue jerked spasmodically along. A prince indeed, it seemed, so at ease was Ravi, so coolly warm in his greetings and deflections. Here was no politician of an American stripe. He received the tributes of these people as his due, for which he was pleased but not indebted.

Well past midnight the last of the visitors paid homage, turning like all the others from wedding couple to host, and then quickly descending into the floodlit darkness below. Gerald rose stiffly. Peering from the lip of the monument, he saw that the tents and tables and buffets of food had grown largely deserted. A general detritus of fallen flowers, of napkins and scattered glasses lay strewn about. Members of the family were gathered in tight fists of conversations. Sita's parents slumped wearily on fabric chairs that had been ferried from the main house, with nieces and nephews, cousins and brothers gathered about for support.

With a daring pat on Sita's knee—and no glance to gauge her response—Gerald rose and strode quickly toward Ravi. He was standing by himself, watching something at the other end of the monument or not watching anything at all. Gerald lifted the silver helmet from his head and thrust it forward.

"Your turn now, don't you think?"

Ravi laughed lightly. "I wondered how long you'd put up

with that bloody thing." He made no move to accept this particular gift. "Besides, you haven't finished with it yet. There are still the priests to satisfy."

"Surely your friend Mr. Gangaswami won't fuss if I'm not wearing the family armor." He tossed the headdress toward Ravi, who had little choice but to catch it. His eyes glittered, but the pleasant little smile never wavered.

Out beyond the last of the tents, safely beyond the precincts of the stone tombs of vanished Muslim rulers, flaring tapers kept the night at bay. A larger blaze snapped and smoked in a shallow pit. As Sita and Gerald finally approached the fire, with her family gathered at the threshold of shadows just beyond, Gangaswami lurched up from several large pillows with the help of his young assistant. Plates were scattered on the ground near his cushions. It was unclear how long he'd sought refuge out here in wilderness and exile. Perhaps he'd fled the unceasing homage and pleas for advice or blessing amid the crowd.

"My friends," he cried in a voice that, nasal and reedy, startled Gerald each time he heard it, "this will be a great moment for you and for your family. And for your friends too, yes, and I am only too happy, so happy, to count myself among the latter."

He grabbed Sita's hand and placed it in Gerald's, drawing them toward the holy fire and the path that twined about it. Gangaswami signaled for two Brahmin priests in attendance to approach. And without another word, the god man turned and strolled heavily away into the night. The practicalities of the affair he would leave to others.

As he trudged the prescribed path around the fire for the third—or was it the fourth?—time, Gerald's head was swimming with fatigue and hunger and a faint dizziness, as if a renewed bout of jet lag had swept him up and beyond himself. This woman at his side—who was she?

This disturbing intuition from earlier in the evening, of Sita become someone else, a stranger, had never entirely disappeared. It wasn't merely the kohl around her eyes or the diamond in her nose, nor that he was glimpsing an undiscovered aspect of her character, one he'd never had the chance to encounter in her American exile. No—he'd prepared himself for that possibility before ever boarding the plane for India. No—what unnerved him now in the late blue-black night of these Delhi gardens was the way she carried herself, the different lilt to her voice, an unrecognizable inflection in her eyes. He feared some more profound transformation of her character that he would no longer understand. Yet none of this—not for a moment—lessened his desire for her. And he reminded himself that these doubts and worries might well be simply a measure of his weariness.

Weariness apparently had yet to graze Sita. A gauzy gold-and-crimson *dupatta* was draped over her head and across the lower half of her face. Through most of the months they had all but lived together, she'd worn jeans or longish dresses, yet tonight she seemed released by the very constrictions of the tightly wound sari. She floated, she *danced* the prescribed steps around the fire as if she'd trained for this moment all her life, in all her dreams.

Which she had, which she probably had, Gerald silently conceded.

Stranger or lover, both she might be, but her simple presence at his side on the path called to him, bound him, delighted him, stoked him, crushed muscle in his chest and groin with yearning. A thought of what lay ahead in the night once they were finally, finally set free (for this the smoke and strange chants and confusion of dance and dust could all be endured) turned him hard, brilliantly and unreservedly hard, as if he were an adolescent boy again and not a man into his fifties. He was simultaneously proud and a trifle embarrassed. (Surely no one could spy the truth.)

He hadn't slept with Sita in something more than four weeks. Why this was so he hadn't quite fathomed. Ravi had assigned them separate rooms of course, for the sake of appearances. Beyond this formality her brother paid no attention. And whatever their roots in rural Bihar, the elder Singhs were Delhi wallahs of many decades—more sophisticated, more worldly than Sita had led him to expect. They were under no illusions about the life their daughter had been living, nor were they particularly troubled by it. Yet each night for four long weeks, she'd slipped free of his increasingly urgent good-night kisses—reluctantly, yearningly, but with absolute conviction. He did not understand but was willing to go along with her wishes, her instincts—her playacting, if that's what it was.

In America he'd also been occasionally embarrassed by his passion for this woman. Never in his life (though he wouldn't admit it to his children, or even Larry Tomsich and other pals at the club) had he been so truly intoxicated with love. A glimpse of her, an accidental brush of her elbow or knee smote him to foolishness. And all he could do was grin and shrug and accept the truth of his foolishness and his delight.

Janice Stein, wife of one of his partners and an academic, had drunkenly accused him one evening of being attracted to Sita because she was exotic—an Oriental, full of mystery and potent sexuality. "It's all illusion. It's all in the sick minds of Western men," she'd mocked over dinner.

Not intending to make an enemy, Gerald had done the unpardonable: he laughed. A strong deep laugh of astonishment and pleasure in just how silly Janice's notion was. Because that was just it: with Sita he felt a marrow-deep harmony more intense than with any person he'd ever known, even Caryn. There was no mystery, nothing exotic, beyond the simple, blissful necessity of there being this woman with whom he could find the best part of himself.

Happily, he'd given up all for her—or, really, given up nothing. His partnership provided money beyond his needs, even with generous tokens of affection (and guilt) to three grown and rather demanding offspring. The work itself no longer provided any satisfaction in itself, rarely much beyond a means to fill his days, which had been so important after Caryn died. Better now to let Sita fill his days!

To India then he came.

And came to himself in midstumble, waking on a narrow serpentine path that wound about the Brahmin flames. His forehead was smeared with orange and yellow paste. Wreaths of marigolds were draped around his neck. Was it Sita who had changed or he himself? The uncertainty rocked him.

He glanced up and in the shadows he made out Ravi watching languorously, hardly paying attention. A sudden searing resentment flared. He grasped with fresh clarity just how Ravi had been twisting and spinning him like a baited animal since his arrival. All while making a pretense of treating him as a new brother, a man to be honored for his own sake, not simply because he was marrying Sita, sister and daughter of the household.

Sacrificing home and family—that had only been an initial gesture, though this, too, he hadn't properly realized until this moment. They'd forgone a secular wedding in Columbus; he'd agreed to come to India to accomplish the marriage as part of an extended stay (no particular length had ever been mentioned and hadn't concerned him); his children, all the family that remained for him, felt no need to attend a wedding they neither understood nor approved of.

As he considered this brief history, humiliations large and small seemed to gather themselves into the ludicrous struggle over the silver headdress. Humiliations large and small—most he hadn't even consciously sensed at the moment, though now they returned with a thousand tiny stings. What had been Ravi's point? What purpose? Merely a rich young man's whim, toying with an American too besotted with his sister to realize the easy sport he made?

No, weighing the past month, Gerald didn't feel that he'd merely been pricked and prodded for sport. He might have been able to laugh that off or arrange a playful revenge. Instead, he'd been stripped and scoured by a thousand goads as by grains of a coarse abrasive. Astonished at himself, that it had taken this long to penetrate his smitten attention, he saw now that Ravi on behalf of his family had undertaken a deliberate process: it was a kind of cleansing, and through it Gerald had been transformed into someone else altogether, at least as far as the world of Sita and her family was concerned. Like some young bride leaving hearth and kin behind, he was being prepared to become part of a new family on its own terms. His wealth—and he grimaced as this occurred to him—was dowry enough for the Singhs to overlook so much else that might compromise the choice of a middle-aged American.

Just as he was reaching the limit of endurance, summoning outrage enough to hurl marigolds from his throat, to cry out some mammoth defiance, to stalk away into a night he didn't begin to understand, the wedding ceremony ended. Sita and he were handed earthenware mugs of holy water. They dribbled some into the fire, which sputtered and sparked. One of the priests followed at their heels and casually dumped out a bucket of less precious liquid. The flame hissed, disappearing into a curl of smoke reeking and fetid.

Guests and revelers had long since departed. A few servants were rolling up carpets, offering token gestures with brooms and wicker baskets, but even Gerald could see that they were only waiting on the Singhs to make their way home. Anything of value had already been whisked away. Just beyond the fringe of shadows he spied, here and there, pairs of eager eyes, young and old, waiting. Once the site was abandoned, the local poor would descend and neatly, precisely scavenge anything abandoned. This was their due.

Strings of electric lights suddenly disappeared into blackness. Only a few torches guttered on wobbly stands.

Sita's mother and father were walking slowly toward a car that would carry them back to the main house. Bent and weary, they seemed oblivious to the world about them. All energy was husbanded for the remainder of this journey. Gerald trailed along after them because he did not know what else to do. Sita had once again disappeared. Nor was there any sign of her brother. Tired, wretched, near tears with frustration, Gerald again imagined himself as a bride learning a first lesson even while being brought roughly into the family: stripped of his past, expected to make a place for himself and be useful.

He recognized the absurd self-pity of such an image, but the recognition in no way freed or soothed him.

A sudden clutch at his elbow. He jerked sharply as if bitten. Panting in surprise, he discovered that Sita had magically materialized at his side once more. She slipped her hand through his arm, drawing close. The gauzy *dupatta* had fallen from her head, and she smiled up at him as she hadn't been able to smile for weeks.

"Thank you, thank you," she murmured into his ear. "You were wonderful. I'm so grateful."

For a moment it was as if he couldn't quite understand her—what was she chattering about? All the tensions, all the resentments that had been building in him through the evening—for better than four weeks in truth—blistered at this instant, hot to the touch and threatening to burst. His transformation hadn't taken after all. He was fifty-six years old and too old for such a change. Disoriented and miserable, he was swelling with an anger that wasn't like him at all.

He panted, he panted, he wouldn't, couldn't quite look at her yet, but walked along with her at his side. Finally, calming a bit, he had to speak. "What was all this, really? Some kind of test? Or am I initiated good and properly now, a member of your family?" The bitterness naked here was as much an outburst as he'd allow himself.

But Sita wouldn't let him spoil her own sense of relief and release and satisfaction. "My dearest. I told you before—it wasn't about you. Believe it or not. It was for my family. And yes, it was for me too. It was selfish and I'm sorry—oh, but it was fun and wonderful. Believe me, I promise to find lots of ways to make it up to you." She brought her hand to her mouth, but it didn't hide the wicked little smile she beamed at him.

"It won't be easy," he said. He wondered whether she herself had known what Ravi was up to. Was she in on the conspiracy? But already his misery and dourness had been lanced, not by Sita directly but by the joy sweeping up and over him that this woman should love him, that he should know such a love for her. If scouring his allegiances, even his character clean away had been a necessary price to make a new life with her possible, then he was grateful for it.

"We'll have some fun figuring out just how you'll manage it," he murmured.

Naming the Stones

A sudden upthrust in his gorge caught him by surprise—
a heave of embarrassed laughter—as he stared at the body
lying propped in an open casket. Peter Cohen considered the
impossible fact before him, and another hiccup swelled out of
his belly. He muffled it, strangled it back best he could. But
this wasn't funny—it struck him as funny, as dizzying—but
not funny. The wrong old man lay there indifferent to him.
Bald skull covered with a white yarmulke; nose a bony thrust
at the heavens even as gravity drew slack jowls earthward;
body bundled in an orthodox shroud (would his father have
howled or been smugly pleased at Peter's decision on that de-
tail, an impromptu made while selecting the coffin itself?) and
impossibly small. No—this wasn't him. There'd been some
error, some grotesque misshuffle.

Stein, the funeral director, had discreetly disappeared beyond a heavy curtain, leaving Peter to identify his father—the
law required it for bodies arriving from out of state. According to plans choreographed a decade before, the old man had

been flown in overnight from Florida—last flight landing ahead of the worst blizzard in fifteen years. Peter himself had arrived out of LaGuardia only an hour earlier.

Already shaking his head *no,* he took a quick step toward the curtain in pursuit of Stein. Peter's mouth twisted in apologetic grimace as if it were up to him to break the news and comfort the professional comforter. Maybe, it struck him, maybe the whole story had been fouled from the start—from the moment the phone startled him awake in Manhattan's predawn twilight. He halted, took a breath, forced himself to edge closer. He peered at the dead man's features and, relieved, was able to shake his head once more. Nothing familiar here, nothing he could attach a name or emotion to.

Surer, calmer, only faintly amused now, he leaned forward to study the stranger. And just below the yarmulke spied a long pale scar circling the scalp. From the ancient day when his father had returned from his hospital not, for once, as surgeon triumphant but as shadow of himself, as convalescent, this welt had been a telltale shade of plum, fading over the years but never disappearing entirely. Now it stood out dead white, nearly invisible but still, once noticed, a telltale sure as any tattoo. Yet the body remained a stranger: his angry, canny father was long gone.

"Yeah," he said after a few minutes to Stein in the foyer. "That's him."

Three days later, days distended by the blizzard, a caravan of two cars inched and skidded through half-plowed streets, high banks of snow trenching above them on both sides. From the cemetery gates a single lane forged on. It had been miraculously cleared, as if the grave diggers themselves were horrified by the delay beyond all tradition—one day, two days, three—forced by forty-six inches of blowing snow.

Beneath a shaggy white crown the granite slab read, simply, *Cohen.* Peter assumed the grandparents he'd never known slept around its base. Perhaps other members of the family lay hidden here as well, their headstones, flat against the earth, invisible under the snow. He stomped his feet guiltily. A mound of warm brown dirt steamed next to a fresh grave. The naked pit steamed obscenely too.

A fierce gust of wind snatched away the hired rabbi's brief murmurs above the pine casket and threatened to dislodge his black fur hat. Rabbi Hirsch's eyes were streaming in the cold as he clutched at the hat and signaled to Stein's men. Smoothly, silently, a mechanical winch lowered the casket into its grave. Peter stepped forward brusquely and grasped a shovel. The rasp of gravel and dirt shimmied in his hands. He heaved the load toward the pit and was grateful that no sound survived the fall. He passed the shovel to his sister, Martha, as a trickle of melting snow slid down his ankle.

TEN WEEKS later the midday glare offended him as a cab headed once more toward the cemetery. Flat, harsh even for early spring, the sunlight articulated grass and asphalt with a nakedness that swept nausea along with it. Stray bits of paper scudded along in the March wind. Peter might have been a sick child once more, confined to the backseat of his father's car on some long journey, cigarette smoke blueing the universe beyond. Instead, he leaned against the taxi's window and stared at the crop of stones sweeping over a rolling hill as his driver turned in toward the cemetery's administration building.

"As I explained on the phone—and there was no need to

make this extra trip, no need at all—we simply cannot add your father's name to the family stone. The board's policy as well as custom are quite clear, I'm afraid. Of course, for his own headstone—for that there's no problem." Rabbi Hirsch, it turned out, was also the part-time administrator of the cemetery. Yet he'd agreed only reluctantly to this new appointment with Peter Cohen. He was younger than Peter remembered and than he sounded on the phone. Facing his visitor across a battered steel desk, the rabbi had a porous black beard and fierce, unexpectedly pale blue eyes. The fur hat of winter he'd abandoned for a small kipa pinned to his hair.

"Last time—the weather, the rush and confusion—the whole thing felt—unfinished. So I needed to come back anyway," Peter said. "To get my bearings." He paused for a moment and tried to meet the gaze of this smug man without losing his temper, without—and he hadn't anticipated this even as a possibility—bursting into tears.

The rabbi only nodded.

"And this *policy* of yours—maybe it's time for the board to reconsider. Aren't there more and more families in positions like this, with name changing and all?"

Hirsch didn't answer directly. Instead he tapped a manila folder delicately with his fingertips. "You must explain this to me," he said. "I'm afraid I don't understand." He smiled, confidential and slightly mocking, and leaned forward across the desk, hands spread before him. "You are Cohen, yes? Your father's name was Cobb. But your grandfather was Cohen as well, like you. No, I confess, this we don't see so often. The point, Mr. Cohen, is that your father changed his name according to secular regulations, not within the traditions of our community. The family stone represents the family, not an individual. You must see we can't abandon that obligation."

A searing dislike—the first intense feeling Peter had experienced in some while—flared hot in his cheeks and brow. But before he could respond—and he did not feel like responding, justifying himself to this man—Rabbi Hirsch noticed something else in the file before him. His eyebrows shrugged high in still greater wonder.

"This here—*Peter*—is your father's given name. And you are Peter as well? I didn't notice this before. Middle name Hayden. Yours too, if I may guess? So let me see—your father changes his own name and then, when you are born, names you after himself. This is true, yes? Not very Jewish, such egotism. So you were Peter Cobb as well. And you have changed back again? Am I right? Good for you."

"My father did many things that weren't traditional. He had a funny sense of names, of naming." Peter's jaw was very tight. He wasn't used to apologizing for his father, and the role didn't suit him.

"Funny. Yes." Hirsch leaned back in his chair and folded his hands across his belly as if he were a much older and portlier man.

THE NIGHT was very late. Even Manhattan slept a restless slumber along this stretch of Madison Avenue, only an occasional cab slicing the wet pavement. The mansion, the jewel, lay dark about him once Peter stepped through the foyer and past a guard at the new security desk. He entered the first of the galleries, a rotunda of plaster and rose marble used as public sanctum by the robber baron who built it. Here he'd received various emissaries, functionaries, who-knew-what more common thieves to do his bidding. As Peter's eyes adjusted quickly to the gloom, for he was practiced at this, only the emergency exit signs provided a faint glow.

His gloves he'd shoved into his pockets, but he left the heavy coat hanging open. This wouldn't take long. It was a moment he'd anticipated, a revelation he'd kept to himself and for himself. In a hidden niche, he located the soft green glow of switches and dimmers. He played them nimbly. Like water from a fountain, light gathered and rose, precise, glorious, unobtrusive.

From room to room of the renovated mansion, he strode and soon the full spectacle was ablaze.

This was his doing. He was the architect chosen to design this critical aspect of the new gallery and, especially, to display the first of its exhibitions, a retrospective of abstract expressionists that even this indifferent town had breathlessly awaited. And he was the first to see, to really see. The paintings were fire and rage and black fury, blue despair; they exploded and whirled, coaxed to passion by light, his light, an art so perfect it drew no attention to itself but appeared both inevitable and unanswerable.

Pleased and oddly impatient, Peter stalked through the galleries as if searching for something that eluded him moment by moment. Tomorrow at the official opening, his work would be acknowledged. But suddenly the thought annoyed him—he had no wish to draw attention to himself. To be named in that fashion struck him as false, as beside the point. The prospect was unpleasant.

As in a courtly ritual, a dance, he carefully retraced his steps through the manor, dimming the hidden sources, and retreated into the frost and growing flurry of the dark street.

Janey had been spending night and day in her office at

Columbia, pressed with late-semester grading and shepherd-
ing one of her acolytes through a doctoral defense. Their two
daughters were away, Samantha in college, Rachel at the
boarding school she begged for. He missed the three of them
with a dull ache and a reluctance to retreat alone to their
empty apartment. And a second decision flared unexpectedly—out of nowhere. He stopped short on the pavement
and turned his face to the cold flat sky, astonished with himself. For he was going south—this was his inspiration—to
Fort Lauderdale, a city he loathed, to visit his father, a man he
had often loathed.

"I'D LIKE you to do me a favor," the old man said. He spoke
as if he'd been mulling it for months, waiting for the right moment, as if he'd known that Peter was on his way. He might
have been grinning at his son, he might have been mocking
him—it was hard to tell, what with his teeth soaking in the
bathroom and his jowls slack.

Peter had arrived on the Galt Ocean Mile half an hour
earlier without calling ahead. It had been five years since he'd
seen his father, had spoken to him only as necessary every few
months. Even now some trace of what he knew was an adolescent petulance kept him from providing fair warning. Yet
his father seemed neither surprised nor put out to find him
suitcase in hand at the door. "You'll have to sleep on the
couch" was all he'd offered as greeting with a toss of his hand.
"I'm not putting Miss Bratinsky out of her room"—referring
to the registered nurse who now lived with him in place of
two previous wives and who, Peter assumed, provided some
of the same comforts if and when his father was up to it.

Miss Bratinsky, however, was nowhere to be seen that afternoon—it was her shift at the local clinic. Old Peter Cobb hadn't actually paid her a salary for years, beyond the roof over her head and groceries for the two of them. When at last he was gone, then, then, she'd receive her reward, her due— this he'd hinted often. His son thought her a fool to believe it. What was left that hadn't gone to the wives? But Peter also suspected that Miss Bratinsky—Edna—was in fact no fool. She had her own reasons for remaining faithful.

"A favor." Young Peter Cobb blew on a spoon of the noodle soup his father had split between them. On the kitchen's small black-and-white, Lawrence Welk was pantomiming enthusiasm for the next act. This alone was full testimony to Peter of how far his wild wicked old father had fallen: *Lawrence Welk*—the kind of half-assimilated clown on whom he'd lavished savage contempt when Lawrence Welk still breathed.

"Yeah. A favor. When have I ever asked you anything?" The old man was querulous but trying to keep calm. His son noticed a tremor in his hand as he spooned soup toward his mouth.

"Okay—so ask."

But old Peter pursed his lips, glanced slyly at his son, coy now and flirtatious. "You'll think I'm ridiculous. But it's not so much for a dying man to ask his son a favor."

"Since when've you decided you're dying?"

"Okay, okay. I'm just asking is all." He blew out a cheekful of air and gathered himself. "Okay, here it is. See, what I'd like is for you to change your name. That's all." Again he paused, as if surprised his son hadn't yet broken in. "And anyhow, not to something new, but something old. What I'm saying is maybe you could take your grandfather's name back."

"Uh-huh."

"I'm not kidding." Old Peter's fury leaped alive at his son's disbelief. He slapped a hand at the counter.

Peter couldn't quite mask a grin—a cruel grin, honed to wound. His father's bizarre request only bolstered his suspicion that the redemption of Lawrence Welk was symptom of some more profound derangement.

Yet a knot of sudden panic twisted deep in his own belly. The unexpected plea had shaken him, startling a buried reservoir of dread out of proportion to what was, after all, no more than a crazy whim. How could he take it seriously? Take his grandfather's name? No—casually snagging a new name, a new identity, a new wife, a new life had never seemed so simple to him. Peter Cobb, young Peter, had clung teeth clenched to his own life and wife and daughters. He wouldn't let them slip beyond reach the way his old man had.

SOMETHING WRONG rustled through the house. Something restless. That's what Peter believed as a boy. At night, lying awake in his room, he heard its walls, its joints murmur with discontent. Sucking a finger, his sister, Martha, heard too, eyes wide but saying nothing. When the murmurs grew insistent, she'd slip up into Peter's bed and hold herself tight.

Problem was, no one could put a finger on the problem. His father had been short-tempered with the place since they first moved out here from the city. He'd tried to solve it, over and over again. The original farmhouse gradually swelled to something grander, with fluted columns across a veranda and a new wing of clapboard and fieldstone. But that worked no charm. The house remained restless.

Peter's mother watched all the while. The prospect of fleeing the city had never really enticed her, but she'd gone along with that, as she had her husband's other plans. "He won't be satisfied," she confided to Peter and Martha while assembling sandwiches. Step by step, she was working through the problem for the three of them. "You'll see. They wouldn't let him buy in Bloomfield, so he's trying to make this do. And it won't—it can't."

Rachel Cobb had begun picking at her hands. Behind a kitchen counter that made her seem very small, her gestures futile, she was spooning out mayonnaise while wearing white gloves to stop the picking, to stop the raw flesh from bleeding. Sometimes her gloves showed secret pink.

The twenty-five-mile move from the heart of the city had seemed wrenchingly abrupt to the two kids. Yet Peter later realized his father had been making plans for months, fretting and plotting even as he lay between life and death in his own hospital. Meningitis, swooping out of nowhere, had gripped him by the throat, crept into his brain, nearly killed him. Another surgeon, friend and rival from the university, had worked the desperate magic of peeling back scalp and skull to relieve demonic pressures.

When after three months Peter Cobb returned to their apartment building at last, stumbling and abruptly aged, his wife, Rachel, darted from the driver's seat. She caught her husband, leaning up into him so that he wouldn't have to lean. He wouldn't acknowledge the fact. On the porch the children were watching and waiting, helpless and witness. One step, two step, up toward the foyer of the apartment building, and already he was clutching for breath. Old Peter clasped his wife's arm but wouldn't sit, wouldn't retreat, not until they'd accomplished the journey inside. His skull bristled as its hair grew back in grotesque patches. The long purple welt that circled his scalp terrified the children. His son hung back—and for this felt shame. But Indian Village Apartments was suddenly no longer home—when, how did the boy realize?—and as his father's strength returned over the following weeks, the great search for a new one was launched.

Almost as soon as the rambling house on the border between dairy farms and new suburbs was identified and purchased, its transformation commenced. As the work progressed, each stage of it, all was topsy-turvy, hope beyond hope. Wandering with Martha, Peter loved the startling discoveries of new light: green canvas awnings, peeled from the terrace early that first autumn, laid the fieldstone bare to a white assault that sharpened and flattened the world; new valances in the library purred a soft illumination from nowhere.

And when the labors were accomplished, each stage, a grand party was thrown to mark the occasion. Cadillacs and Lincolns spilled along the driveway. Some made the trek from downtown. Some swung briefly across Long Lake Road from Bloomfield for evenings under Japanese paper lanterns on the terrace, with smoke and wine and great floods of food. Afterward, always, within a few weeks, the work began again. The house wouldn't be finished. Restless murmurs swelled once more, rustling along the walls late at night.

To pay, Peter senior cadged work; he stood duty at the hospital morning and night. At home he grew more restless, worn.

"Dad," his son challenged him, twelve years old. "Why'd you buy this house if you hate it?"

Astonished, Peter senior grinned, but the grin rang sour. "I don't hate it—I'm just not satisfied. Not yet."

The boy shook his head. "Why wouldn't they let us buy a house in Bloomfield?" he demanded.

"Ha!" his father laughed, but it wasn't a laugh, and he tossed a hand. "The pricks. The pricks. So you know about that, do you? They let me cut their wives and daughters. They let me save their fucking lives. But no way do they let a kike live across the street."

"How do they know?"

"How? They find a way of knowing—names only tell you so much." He placed his hand on Peter's head for a moment. His eyes glinted with a sharp brilliance as if he'd been waiting for this, as if he were seeing his boy for the first time in a long time.

And for a little while after this conversation, perhaps it was weeks, perhaps a few months, father and son seemed to lean toward each other. On two separate Sundays, they cycled together far out beyond the last fringe of developments and through the endless alfalfa fields, leaving Martha and Mother behind. And they talked. How they talked. Of baseball and love, of the old Tiger ball clubs and of girls at school. Young Peter's heart nearly burst with pride that his old man could keep up, could even press him hard, side by side, holding the fine cadence of the long flat straights.

For his part, Peter's father seemed released from—from what? Some private pain or reserve or restlessness. The boy sensed but never knew for sure. He was content to bask in his father's eagerness to share his thoughts, to try them out on his son. Naturally, inevitably it seemed, they came to talk of God, and Peter senior confided in the boy that recently a friend had coaxed him into visiting an Evangelical church. He cast it as a lark, a kind of anthropological expedition to a strange world—fascinating in its way, so different, such an experience, so foreign. He laughed until the tears came.

About this time work ceased on the house as well, never to begin again. Young Peter believed the restlessness had fled for good. At night no murmurs hummed in the walls.

And so he felt doubly betrayed when it was his father who fled into the night with the wife of an anesthetist. Of course, her church cast her out for such brazen adultery, but together they joined another and were married, once Peter senior converted.

"PLENTY OF good it did you, changing in the first place," Peter said to his father.

The old man glanced up. He was mashing shrimp between his jaws. It was hard without teeth, and he was being stubborn about the teeth, as if deliberately to embarrass the son who was standing them dinner on the seafront. "How the fuck do you know why I did it in the first place," he demanded with a soft belch, not at all surprised that the subject had returned but betraying no satisfaction either.

"You must've told me. Or Mom did. One of those family legends. Anyhow, seems like I've always known. Back when you were getting started—early forties, right?—how else could you avoid your medical practice being limited to the tribe?" Pleased with himself, Peter gazed at his father. His ancient dress shirt had yellowed and frayed at the collar. Only a dirty gray wisp of hair remained of what had been a pale fire red that Martha alone inherited. The doctor's nose was more beaked yet also somehow weaker than in the old days. He'd always been able to pass. Not so his son: darker, slender, he was his mother's heir in that regard.

"Once you were *Cobb*, you could all play make-believe," Peter went on. "Cobb opened doors that Cohen slammed shut. Even if they knew and you knew. Not that twenty years later they'd let you buy property in Bloomfield."

"Fuck 'em for that," cawed old Peter, furious and delighted with the memory. Other diners, mostly elderly too at this early hour, glared from nearby tables. "I'll bet Bloom-field's crawling with kikes now. Plenty of *schvartz* even? Am I right?" He wagged his head and shoved another shrimp be-tween his gums.

Miss Bratinsky pushed her nurse's smile against a napkin. She placed a hand on his arm. "*Dr. Cobb*—be good now."

His son's jaw was tight. He sliced a shrimp in two. Sipped his wine. "Haven't been there. Not since Mom moved away. No reason to go."

"That's not *why* anyway," old Peter was saying, wagging his fork. "Good as I was, I could've built any practice I wanted. Hell, and I did. When you're rich, you want the best—they were begging for me to cut them. So that was never *why*."

"So, then?"

"My brother too, don't forget. Your uncle Harry. Got him to do it too. Blackmailed him, since I was the one paying his way through school. Got him away from the old man's *shul*. Made him a doctor instead, a dentist anyway. My sister, Gert, didn't matter. She'd be getting married, so the name would disappear on its own. And Gert always sided with me."

"Sided with you?"

"Against *him*, the old bastard. Against *him*." Peter senior banged his fork down hard and glared at his son. And then as suddenly as it had flared, his rage blew clear like a puff of smoke from one of the Benson & Hedges he still sucked to a nub. The old man's face relaxed, its muscles slackening into a beatific grin, as if he'd only just discovered that he'd left some-thing far behind and was amused.

"I wanted to hurt him and what better way? Steal his name, see—rob him of the future. Well, that's what I wanted, wanted him to know how I felt robbed too. Him content all those years working tool-and-die. Keeping us poor, keeping my mother poor." His eyes grew teary and his son feared the old man would embarrass them anew by weeping at the table. "Christ, she was a saint. If she had an egg, a single egg, she'd hide it away for me so I'd be strong to study." He belched deeply and considered.

"Tool-and-die. That was your grandfather. He made lousy money even at that because he wanted to spend all his time in *minion,* praying and being holy, being such a damn good Jew. But I remember"—and again his eyes lit up as this ragged archaeology unearthed his own youth—"you know, he loved the work too: that he earned his keep. He'd march in our front door, caked with dirt and grease up to his elbows and under his nails, proud and grinning and pious, like he'd just slain Goliath himself. My mother kept a bowl and towel by the door and hot water on the stove, ready to pour when she heard him. Washing his hands—it had to be done just so. Plenty of lather and drama and prayer, and hell to pay if one fucking step landed wrong. Sometimes—years and years later—I'd be scrubbing for surgery and the memory of that sight would rise up in front of me. Him, the self-satisfaction on his face as he dug the grease out from his nails—and I'd *laugh.*"

The old man was glaring again, jabbing his fork in the air once more. "You pretty much hated me all these years since I walked out on your mother—didn't you, you little fuck? But how 'bout this: you ever care how I never did what *he* did? Swore it the day you were born and never laid a hand on you, on any of you. Did I? You ever know that about my so holy old man—your grandfather—with all you think you know?

"It was so I'd study Talmud, be his great scholar. Yeah, he'd take his belt to me. Not because I couldn't or didn't—but because I could, I did! It drove him crazy, the gift came so easy to me. A little game was all it was—and his rabbis were *hot* for me. And he knew I was mocking them, that I didn't care. The better I did and the more the rabbis loved me and the more I mocked and let him know—he'd whip me with that belt. And I'd let him, even when I was as big and bigger than him. I'd let him and I'd jeer him.

"And when I threw it up and went off to Ann Arbor— me fifteen years old and the university opens its arms—I could change my name. Fuck *him*. Ha! That, that was delicious!" He was wheezing now, mouth hanging open, scraps of shrimp still visible. Disgusted, his son was afraid the old man might choke on the mess. Edna Bratinsky sat patting his hand.

Peter was battling an anger that surged up and threatened to sweep him away in its dangerous undertow. "So now you decide maybe I should change mine too. Just like that. Just on your whim. Jesus, Pop—I'm *Cobb* for better or worse. You can't erase my life, everything I've created for myself, just to make up for your own mistake."

"Mistake?" The old man's eyes flared. "Who ever said mistake? I'd do it again a thousand times."

"Then what's this all about?" Peter demanded. "Why now—why out of the blue? Something happened I should know about?"

The old man shook his head and seemed to retreat, lips pressed thin, protecting himself.

Peter shrugged without shrugging. "Why not change it back yourself?" he said. "Who'll that hurt? No one anymore."

"Exactly. That's it exactly." Old Peter stared directly at his son, fiery and sly once more. "What I do is irrelevant. There's no undoing that matters. But why not you? As a favor?"

"Hell of a favor." He set his jaw. "Look, I'm sorry—but this is nuts. Why are you asking me this?"

"I should explain myself to *you*? It's enough that I'm asking. What, you're going to show how tough you are and defy me like I defied my father? And you're making what point?"

Early next morning, a Sunday, Peter sat drinking instant coffee. Neither his father nor Miss Bratinsky had yet emerged, and he'd pointed his chair carefully toward the broad sweep of the ocean so he wouldn't notice whether they came from two bedrooms or one. He'd long ago accepted his own squeamishness on that count.

The night had been long. Despite the wine with dinner and a couple of late whiskies, sleep had come reluctantly. Instead, the alcohol sent him rolling, awake, alert, miserable.

He had no clue what his father was after. Did he intend now to disown his son as he had his father? Did he yearn to be sole and self-created and defiant? Was the point to cut himself off from all ties? Or was he seeking to mend a tear in some delicate fabric? Now that his own father was long dead, did he mean to extend the trajectory of the family name across the very chasm he'd opened?

Peter's resentment had bled away into the darkness, and these questions filled him with dread and sadness and a yearning to reach toward his father as he hadn't done since those long bike rides thirty years before.

But what unnerved him still more was that he hadn't been able to dismiss the old man's bizarre notion. It niggled in his ear; it set his heart pounding; it formed a grit between his grinding teeth. Peter Cobb he'd been for forty-three years (Jr. abandoned at college), but the sound of it—*Cobb*—the sheath of it, had never felt right. *Cobb* reminded him of maple and birch and willow trees struggling in Michigan's sandy soil, shallow rooted all and fragile, easily toppled. Much of the night, except for three or four hours before a harsh dawn woke him, sun blistering an oily light off the surface of the ocean, he'd been repeating the other name, *Peter Cohen*—his father's name but not his father's name. He'd chanted it a whisper, he'd rolled it on his tongue.

"I've got a flight home this afternoon."

Late in the morning Peter senior had finally emerged to make toast and weak coffee for himself. He kept his back to his son and seemed not even to hear the announcement. Edna Bratinsky had already hurried away for her shift at the clinic with a hug and quick kiss for their visitor.

"Can't stand the couch, huh? Well, I'm not surprised," said the old man at last, still not turning.

"WHY SHOULD I like the idea? It makes no more sense for you than it did for me when we married—less—and remember, I refused." Janey scowled, bristling at the notion.

Peter shrugged.

"Not that it makes any difference to me," she said, playfully swinging a plastic sack of bagels against his arm as they strolled along Riverside Drive. Both were wearing light jackets in honor of this rare day: a gift of mild December weather—nearly fifty degrees—a chance to steal a few hours back from the long winter still ahead.

"What a fool I'd feel now if I'd taken yours twenty years ago, Peter. And what about the girls? Have you thought about them yet—or told them what you're considering? You can't really expect they'll go along with this, this—" She sighed and turned to him on the brink of a corner.

"Maybe I should have insisted they take my name too. But I was so happy and *sweet* after they were born." She flashed him a naughty smile, dark eyes alight, her narrow face pink with cold, mild or not mild. "They were my gift to you. But how can they possibly choose *Cohen* now, for heaven's sake? They've never even met their grandfather. And for that matter, it isn't his name anymore either. It'll be bad enough if the retro fashion lasts long enough for them to take their husband's. And probably just to spite me."

"I don't think we're in imminent danger on that," laughed Peter. He wanted to defuse this struggle with Janey. This wasn't a battle between them. Or shouldn't have been. And he'd never any notion that Samantha and Rachel would follow his lead. The battle was with his father alone, unspoken now and on terrain he didn't know. He sensed the sly old man a step ahead of him, circling, setting his snares.

He'd been back from Florida nearly a week. Yet the seed sown there had already struck deep root. Even as he was gathering up the reins of three lighting projects in various stages of disarray, not to mention fielding phone calls and interviews and fresh solicitations only briefly balked when he failed to show for the gallery opening, the favor his father was begging—more nearly demanding—nagged him morning to night. And he wasn't even sure why.

He hardly yearned for some sublime reconciliation with the old man. No, he felt more like wrestling him to the ground, pinning him hard to the dust once and for all. The image—preposterous, preposterous—left him grinning. His father would be spitting up at his son like some barely restrained cobra (where would he stash his false teeth while they grappled?), some old man of the sea startled and writhing, grasped and never quite vanquished.

By the time they'd reached the front step of their apartment building, Janey tossing him the bagels and leaning forward for a quick kiss before flagging a cab for the run up to

Columbia, Peter Cobb had decided that he would be no longer. He waved her off, shrugged, smiled at Mario the doorman.

THE LABYRINTH had twisted and turned Peter Cohen, spun him and confused him, stumped him thoroughly. It wasn't that he couldn't find his way out of the cemetery—that was the easy alternative. He could see the cab waiting across by the administration building. But he'd lost all bearings he'd taken from the map on Rabbi Hirsch's wall for the internal layout of the grounds. And what memories he possessed from ten weeks earlier—of drifting snow and blankness—did him precious little good. Wandering along the lanes and alleys of the graveyard, he was disoriented and unwilling to retreat to the rabbi's office for help. He was also fighting the urge simply to give up the search, bushwhack toward the cab, and flee to Martha's house in Royal Oak.

There were plenty of Cohens, of course, of Kahns, of Kuhns, theme and variations sprinkled among the Levis and Roths and Rosenbergs. He'd hoped to recognize the family stone or its orientation to the road. Nothing seemed familiar. On he soldiered, hands in his pockets, wrestling his own impatience and a gnawing frustration that had swooped out of nowhere. He did not want to be here, didn't feel he belonged, name or no name. There'd be no place for him in this family grove anyway—he and Janey had already made provision for cremation, for wine and good cheer among friends, for seemly scattering later on. His shoes kicked at the gravel. Angry, he sent a small stone skittering along the path.

Angry, he stumbled on the plot. It was the unmarked grave that tipped him off. At a glance he saw that its sod had been carefully knit back in place, but the early spring hadn't yet healed the scars. It was also too early, of course, for a headstone to identify the Peter Cobb who lay there. According to the prescribed rhythms of tradition, that marker would only appear next year when he returned for its unveiling, perhaps bringing the girls along too. And so he recognized the spot and only then glanced for confirmation to the central stone, *Cohen.*

"WE'RE LOSING him," Miss Bratinsky moaned into the phone, trying to sound calm and professional but undone by her own grief. It wasn't 6 A.M. yet and he wasn't awake, and then he was sharply, nakedly awake, up on an elbow in the gray light.

"Is he gone?" he asked.

"We're losing him, I'm losing him," she said again.

"Damn it," he whispered. "Damn it."

"What?" she wept, unable to make him out. "Don't you worry, Peter. All the plans are made. You just get yourself on a flight home."

"Damn him," Peter murmured, though he'd already returned the phone to its hook. Janey was staring up at him, waiting, patient, the love of his life. How could he tell her that the old man had tricked him again? Had managed to win the final round, one quick fall, without his son suspecting it had even begun. Had slipped away free and clear without Peter ever finding a way to say he'd done him his favor.

ACKNOWLEDGMENTS

The following stories have appeared previously in the following publications: "Steps Through Sand, Through Fire" in *TriQuarterly*; "Mt. Pleasant" and "Bondage" in *Michigan Quarterly Review*; "Dean of Women" in *Ontario Review*; "Muggings" in *TriQuarterly*; "Balked Eclogue" in *StoryQuarterly*; "Woodpeckers" in *Salt*; "Poetry of the Amish" in *The Journal*; "Mistaken Identity" in *TriQuarterly*; "Children of God" in *Glimmer Train*; "Birnkrandt and Kamenski" (as "Hirsch and Bratinsky") in *New England Review*; "Life Sentences" in *Virginia Quarterly Review*; "Naming the Stones" in *Salmagundi*; "Chrysalis" in *TriQuarterly*; and "Deserts and Dowries" in *Ontario Review*.